WAR OF THE LAND

DANA CLAIRE

CHAMBERLAIN PUBLISHING HOUSE

Note from Author

War of the Land takes place eight years after the epilogue in the *War of the Sea*. However, this is a complete stand-alone novel with new characters, plot, and action. The other books in the series do not need to be read in order, but you will see glimpses of future characters in each book.

To Jennifer Armentrout who stole my heart with the Covenant Series over a decade ago and inspired me to become an author.

CHAPTER ONE

SAVINA

This voyage marked my last taste of freedom.

In just a fortnight, my life would no longer be my own. My divine father, Apollo, and grandfather, Zeus, had chosen a man I had never met, the Duke of Eloqua, as my husband. We were to be wed, and I was to bear the weighty title Queen of the Isle of Cava—an existence I neither desired nor embraced. But the law was the law and Cava's stated I be married before my eighteenth birthday when I take my rightful place on the throne.

I puffed out a long breath and dug my feet in the sands of Anthemusa. Maybe I'd be more willing to lead the country if I had a partner I actually loved, or even knew. But a complete stranger had been thrust upon me without my say.

A nervous flutter beat in my chest. I'd never even been courted by a man before, and now I was to marry one. The thought might have been comical, had it not come along in a sequence of sorrowful stories.

The sun beat upon my face, gathering perspiration at my neck. I gripped a fistful of sand, squeezing the grains until they slipped through my fingers like the remains of my fading autonomy. In that quiet solitude, I started to sing, a secret pleasure I indulged in during my private moments. My eyes closed to best relish the effortless melody. The song felt like cold water splashed upon the skin after being in the hot sun all day. Refreshing. Cooling. Invigorating.

I belted out the chorus of a ballad, one my brother had once taught me, recounting the tragic tales of the sea's victims before the reign of the passive siren ruler, Queen Yemma. Each note reverberated within my chest, tangling into a knot at the base of my throat—a physical manifestation of my vanishing control over my own destiny.

Lost in the rhythm of my song, I didn't notice the onslaught of birds until their piercing trills cut through the quiet. My eyes cracked open just as a wing walloped me across the face. Birds the size of small children landed on my body, pecking at my clothes. Sherrons, native to this land, looked like a cross between a hawk and a heron, sleek and streamlined but with crooked, webbed feet that now kicked at my torso.

I screamed, horrified. Nearly a dozen birds came at me in every direction, ripping the ribbon tie from the collar of my blouse, pulling threads from my trousers, and pinching my skin.

"Shoo. Shoo!" I flailed my arms, beating them back as I fought to stand. "Stop it! You wretched creatures. Get off me!"

"Oh, my gods!" a deep voice cried in the distance. "I'm coming."

A second set of hands swatted away the descension of winged beasts. I tried to sneak a peek at my rescuer, but white feathers obstructed my vision. Squalls rattled my ears, spewed from beaks diving overhead, trying to grab my hair. They acted as though I'd attacked their nests.

An arm curled around my waist, pulling me back against a very hard, very male body that stole a gasp from my lips. "I've got you," the sultry voice breathed against my ear. "Where did these wild animals come from? My gods, it is as if they thought to eat you."

Caught off guard by another's hold, I thrashed like a trapped rabbit, having no idea what the worse threat was: imprisonment in the arms of a strange man or death by birds.

"Easy there." The arm around me tightened. His hand settled on my hip, trying to steady us, but it was too late. Our limbs tangled, and together the stranger and I crashed into the sand. His large body pressed against my chest, sinking my back into the shore. Red hair—my own—covered my face. But the bird's squawking receded, so all I could hear was the beating of my heart.

Fingertips swept the strands of hair away from my eyes and I froze, utter shock rippling through me. A man, a beautiful one at that, with a sharply angled face, high cheekbones, plump lips, and strong jaw covered in a week's worth of dark stubble stared down at me. My gaze connected with his eyes—amber orbs composed of mesmerizing trails of liquid fire in rich reds and vibrant yellows. I'd never seen a man so striking. My breath caught in my throat.

His fingers twirled a lock of my hair, causing a strange curling sensation to hit my lower stomach. I wasn't even sure he knew he was doing it. His gaze roamed my face as if memorizing my features. The warmth of his breath touched my lips. A tremor of anticipation coiled its way down my spine. I'd never been this close to a man before, to the possibility of a kiss. If I lifted my head up one inch, our mouths would touch. The curious part of me wanted to be daring. But the scared princess—the one who was never allowed to have any relationships outside of her own family—kept still.

The man's tentative smile showed no teeth and didn't quite erase the worry creasing his eyes. "I've never seen a flock of sherron attack a siren before." His voice was husky, unlike anything I have heard. Perhaps an accent from another land. "Are you okay?"

I opened my mouth and then clamped it shut, realizing he'd mistaken me for a sea creature. I blinked. We did share the same color hair and pure white skin, but our eyes were different. Theirs were famously colorless.

He stared at me, gaze assessing the half of my body not covered by his own. His eyes reminded me of flames dripping in honey, a striking color, unique to him alone. The way they roved over me made me feel stripped bare, as if the sherrons had stolen more than a few strings of my clothes.

With a gentle touch, he gripped my chin, moving it back and forth as if he were searching for injury. "What in the underworld made them attack you?"

My face caught on fire. "They...umm." I swallowed. "They don't like my singing."

One side of his lips kicked up. "Has this happened to you before, my little songbird?"

"No!" I lied on impulse.

"You're a terrible liar." He leaned to the side and propped himself on his forearm, barely putting distance between us. Black charcoal locks hung from his forehead. "How would you know they dislike your voice unless you've fought off their rather rude criticism previously?"

My face inflamed as I recalled the first encounter I had with these feather fiends. Not that I'd admit the truth to this arrogant man. His smirk already slithered under my skin in ways no one else had.

"Should I even ask who won the prior battle?" His head tilted, his eyes latched onto mine, then widened. "You aren't a siren, are you? Your beauty may rival them, but your eyes are the color of the Caviar Sea, crystal blue." His finger traced my clavicle until he flicked the collar of my shirt, the dipped neckline now gaping open farther than I would've liked without its ribbon. "I have never seen a siren dressed like a sailor." His lips peeled into a wide grin. "And if your voice angers the animals of this island, I dare say you do not possess a siren's musical lilt."

Embarrassment chilled my manner like an ice bath. I pushed at his chest. "Could you please get off?"

The man laughed, a deep, beautiful sound that rumbled through my body. Yet he made no attempt to stand or roll to the side. His gaze dropped down to my mouth, and my chest felt inexplicably tight.

I cleared my throat, but it didn't steady my voice. "I'm serious. Get up."

The bright sun at his back shadowed his features, but his devilish smile shone through. "You haven't even thanked me yet."

"Thanked you?" My tone elevated. "For almost crushing me?"

His laughter increased. "You believe I am the one who harmed you now?"

The birds in the nearest tree cawed, and my cheeks heated. Why did he still have to be so close?

Through gritted teeth, I asked, "If I thank you, will you stand?"

"Then it wouldn't be sincere." His lips twitched, stifling a smile. "How about a deal? You tell me your name, and we will consider us even. After all, to learn the name of someone as beautiful as you would be thanks enough."

My lips twisted. "What a gilded tongue you have." My words tasted sour.

"In the presence of beauty like yourself, compliments come with ease." His voice, as smooth as syrup, spoke sentiments no one had ever uttered to me. Were all men like this? Or just the daft handsome ones?

"Do we have a deal? Tell me your name and I'll let you up."

"My name is none of your concern." The last time I divulged my true identity to a stranger, they lost their life. I'd made not only a promise to my family but to myself, I'd never be responsible for such a tragedy again. Even if this inquisitor irked me in more ways than the sherrons themselves.

He tsked softly under his breath. "Let me be the one to start introductions. Maybe that will ease your mind. My name is Conleth."

My eyes narrowed. Who did this man think he was? His name could be Poseidon himself, and I would not utter mine in return.

He was quiet for so long doubt crept into my mind. Maybe he'd never stand up. Then what would I do? My brother would find me and lose his mind if he saw a man hovering over me.

"Fine, my little songbird. Keep your secrets. We all have them." He leaned down and kissed the top of my forehead.

Panic flared in the pit of my stomach, but so did something far more powerful, a pleasure unlike any I had ever experienced. Only family members had ever planted kisses on my skin before. I didn't dare allow anyone else so close, nor did I have the opportunity to do so even had I'd desired to risk Zeus's wrath. And now, this annoying yet gorgeous man touched me with such a tenderness, I nearly cried.

Conleth pushed himself up and then extended his hand to me.

I rose without his help, brushing the sand off my hands onto my trousers. My gaze dropped to his body, finally getting a good look at him. He carried no weapons nor satchel. Spots like splashes darkened his boot leather. His chest and shoulders tautened with muscle that pressed against the cloth in a bid for freedom. He had a streak of blood on his hand from a recent injury. But given to him by whom? The cut was clean and precise, not one of battle. Maybe self-inflicted? Then there was the grey mud stuck to his clothes, the way a sculptors' pants held remnants of the hours they worked in their shoppes. And finally, the most puzzling piece, he appeared to be alone on an island inhabited only by women. Curiosity tugged against my pride. Who dared venture to the sirens' island by themselves with the confidence of Zeus?

I frowned. "Why are *you* on this island?"

The right side of his lips upturned. "Have you taken an interest in me now?" The left side of his mouth joined in the grin. "I'm flattered."

I bit my bottom lip, as I often did when trying to hold my own tongue. I wanted to deny his boast, but I *had* taken interest, and he knew it. I'd rather allow silence to answer his question than confirm or deny it aloud.

He retucked his shirt into his trousers, shifting his weight ever so slightly. Sculptor's clay fell off his thighs onto the sand.

"Not that it's any of your concern, little songbird, but I gave Queen Yemma a gift and she returned the favor. And now my business lies in another kingdom. I must be on my way. It's been..." He peered up at the line of birds watching from the nearest trees. "... quite interesting to say the very least. I do hope our paths cross again someday."

I ground my teeth. If he knew he spoke to a future queen, he'd be bowing instead of ridiculing.

"Good day, sir." I turned, giving him my back side.

Several moments later, a hand tapped my shoulder. I spun, ready to fire back at Conleth, but my brother, the former Captain Rylander Bordeaux of *The Sea Singer* and current King of Cava, stood in his place.

"What's wrong?" He pointed to my face. "You have that squinty look like you're mad." Rylander twisted, inspecting the perimeter. His pale irises landed on a flock of sherrons sitting on the obsidian rocks pummeled by crashing waves. He threw his head back and laughed, indenting the dimple in his cheek that we shared. "Were you singing again?"

If he only knew that wasn't my sole tangle. My overprotective brother barely let his own men speak to me. What would he do if he realized a stranger had? I touched my fingertips to my forehead, remembering Conleth's lips on my skin. For some reason, I didn't want my brother to know about our meeting. A secret for me to keep on my last adventure.

"Did they hurt you?" My brother stepped closer, examining that place where my fingers traced the ghost of a kiss. "You know better than to antagonize them with your song."

"I don't sing to ruffle the bird's feathers, and I'm fine. It wasn't nearly as bad as last time." I'd been tinier then. Thankfully, Rylander had been there to protect me. Had he not, they might have carted me off to their nests.

My brother's eyes glittered as if he too remembered the battle between me and my plumy enemies.

"It's not funny." I crossed my arms over my chest and glared. I played the lute, theorbo, and harpsichord, and loved to sing along as I strummed. It wasn't my fault my throat didn't make a fitting instrument to the quartet.

"How with our father's powers of the arts did you end up being so tone deaf?"

I huffed. "My plucking would weaken men's knees. And might I remind you, Apollo is the God of music, not song, like your muse of a mother, Calliope." I nodded to the ivory castle nestled within the inlet behind the trees that Rylander had appeared from. "Nor your sisters, the sirens."

To say my brother and I inherited the good traits of our shared father put it mildly. Both of us wielded a bow and arrow like a third arm, our musical talents knew no bounds, and on many occasions, we'd healed not only ourselves, but others. Sadly, my mother, a human—rest her soul—had no worthy attributes, and a voice so sharp it could slice a steel trap.

My brother wrapped his arm over my shoulder and pulled me into his warmth. "Not everyone's windpipes can be so inclined to heavenly song like mine." He pulled on a strand of my hair and I softened. "Come on, Little Rose. Let's get you back home before my wife has my head or some other body part for being away so long."

I smiled. Rylander was sure to catch fire from my sister-in-law, Lou, over our prolonged trip. His wife had become more and more restless over the years living in the castle on Cava and not on a ship at sea where she'd grown up. Lou, a former pirate captain of *The Freedom*, an all-women's ship—well, except for my brother and a couple of his loyal followers—had been known for their brigand ways and long journeys at sea. So, when Rylander announced at a family dinner he'd be leaving to see Queen Yemma on official royal business, Lou begged to come along and command her ship. When my brother had said no, the whole room went silent, and Lou's blood vessels bulged, darkening her face to maroon. But then she suggested I go with him, wishing me to sulk about my upcoming wedding somewhere other than in her presence. I ran and hugged her. She always knew what I needed, making the hole from the loss of my parents a little smaller.

Back on *The Freedom*, I stood atop the forecastle, watching the crew tie off the lines as the wind filled the sails. The cream canvas billowed in bulbous arcs, thrumming with the impact of the salty air. I closed my eyes and drew in a breath, expanding my rib cage like the sails, thinking that I never wanted to leave this moment or this ship.

"Enjoying the afternoon sunshine?" Uncle Hermes asked. The messenger of the gods had been visiting in his human form as Smitter, my brother's former first mate from his days captaining *The Sea Singer*. Rylander had invited him to join our excursion for old times' sake, but I wondered if it had not been a direct order from my grandfather, Zeus. He didn't condone my expeditions, even disguised as a crew member as I was now. In fact, he commanded my concealed identity from the moment I turned eleven. The first time I didn't take him seriously had also been the last as he showed his fury by murdering an innocent and blaming me for their death.

My uncle extended his arms wide and I threw myself into them. His chin rested on my head. "How was your visit with Queen Yemma? Is she well?"

"It went favorably. She'll be attending the wedding." I pulled a couple inches away and gazed up into his brown, almond-shaped eyes. "Rye petitioned Zeus to extend her human form for two days off the island." I blew out a breath. "Sometimes I think Yemma wishes for her and her people to have legs in other lands. It wouldn't be such a bad idea now that the siren clan is no longer a threat to the humans."

Sirens could only change into human form on their island, Anthemusa. Zeus had extended Yemma the privilege of legs for my wedding on Cava as a favor to my brother and me.

"There are reasons the gods place limitations on abilities of lesser beings. With great abilities comes great liabilities. Having sirens walking amongst us could create future problems for humankind. They can still use their song against mere mortals if they feel threatened. It's easier to keep them to the seas." My uncle kissed my forehead, inciting the memory of Conleth's touch. How his lips felt against my skin… How my stomach pooled with a new sensation I'd never felt before. I placed my hand over my belly button. How could a recollection so brief spread warmth through me?

"Wasn't that thoughtful of Zeus. My father seems to grow a heart when matters concern his beautiful granddaughter." Uncle's words brought me back to the present. He brushed away my red curls and tucked them behind my ear. "I'd venture to say you are his favorite."

I glowered at him. "We both know that's not true. If that were, then why force me to marry?" I wanted to add, "If he's so eager to give me a husband and have me lead Cava, what changed from my youth?" But it wasn't as if my uncle knew about Galen, the first and only friend I had ever told my real name to. No one knew of her death. Zeus made sure of that.

After all my grandfather had done to keep me isolated, stealing away any too bright lights that wandered into my life, now I was to be handed over freely, like a pretty parcel to a man neither my father nor my grandfather knew? What sort of game was Zeus playing this time? What role had he assigned me in it? And which of my loved ones might he sacrifice to win next?

CHAPTER TWO

SAVINA

My uncle has never taken a cross word against my grandfather well. The skin between his eyes tightened, twisting the fake human scar that cut through his brow. "You know what happened to Aphrodite. Zeus believes that because of your beauty and power"—he tapped my nose—"and your intellect, if you don't marry soon, it could start a war."

I pushed out of his embrace. "That is ridiculous. He not only acts based on an unknown enemy, but now he's attributed this anticipated threat to my beauty, power, and intellect?" I rolled my eyes. "I don't believe it. In the seven years he's been preparing for conflict, I've barely been allowed out of the castle and when I am, it's been in disguise. Who would even know of my beauty, power, or intellect?" I gulped a breath, my chest rising and falling. "And is Aphrodite in love with Hephaestus, the man she was forced to marry? Is she happy?" The wind whipped red strands across my face. "I doubt it. Who finds happiness in forced circumstances?" I tucked the flailing tendrils behind my ear.

Uncle Hermes rubbed the back of his neck. "You know I adore Hephaestus. He made me my winged sandals. I wish not to speak ill of any of my brethren."

I drew my palms down my face and groaned. "Why I venture into these sorts of conversations with you, I'll never know." One of the crew rounded the corner, stuffing two tarts into his mouth and my own watered. "My mistake. I'm going below deck to help in the galley. I'll drown my sorrow in sweets."

"Don't overindulge. You have a wedding to prepare for." His chuckle grated against my nerves. I loved him, but he knew better than anyone how to irritate me.

I waved him off and continued to the starboard side, grumbling under my breath.

Krinny looked up from tying a knot, smirking at me as I passed. "Who's angered you today, princess?"

She had been Lou's first mate on *The Freedom* until Rylander and Lou moved into the castle. After that, she was entrusted as my personal guard and had accompanied me whenever I traveled by order of the king. King of Olympus, more like. The arrangement had the sharp stink of Zeus's thunderbolt-wielding hand all over it. I had overheard Grandfather and Rye arguing after we returned from a trip to the isle of Jacar when I was eleven years old. From that day on, I had the kingdom's best cutthroat shadowing me at all times. Poor Krinny lost her freedom to play guard, another casualty of Zeus's inexplicable interest in me.

"Well, was it Hermes or Rye or another bloke?" Krinny's brow lifted.

"Try all of them," I groused.

She leaned in so only I could hear. "Would you like me to slaughter them? Smitter might be a god, but I wager I could find a way." She drew back wearing an ornery grin. Of course she jested, but part of me believed a little action wouldn't bother her either. I imagined protecting a princess who went nowhere and did nothing might prove rather boring for a former weapons specialist, assassin, and pirate.

"What about getting them to give up on this silly be-trothal?" I threw my head back and stared at the sun, silently praying to the gods to hear my plea. The wind—as if an-swering no—tugged hard at my shirt.

"What if I hate the man I am to marry? What if he's boring? What if he's sickly or old?" I spun and grabbed Krinny by the shoulders, fingers digging deeper with each frantic thought. "What if he expects me to bed him our first night of marriage?" My breath quickened. My head dizzied.

Krinny caught my wrists and pried my hands off her shoulders, pinning them by my sides. "Okay, just breathe. In and out. We know he's nineteen, so I do not believe he is sickly and old. He's barely two years senior to you. And I am sure he has the same concerns that you have about compatibility."

She took several deep breaths and released them bit by bit. I matched my pace to hers. My pulse simmered down with each exhale.

She nodded. "That's better. You're getting ahead of your-self. This isn't—"

"Who's getting ahead of themselves?" My brother's eyes narrowed on me as he passed us. "What's wrong? Why's your face green?" He pushed Krinny out of the way. She stumbled backward. "Are you ill? Do you need to lie down?"

"King Rylander." Krinny stamped her foot.

My brother twisted.

"You are not helping."

Rylander's Prometheus's apple bobbed. "Are you saying I can't tend to my sister?"

Krinny tilted her head. "That depends. Would you like to talk to her about consummating her marriage?"

Rylander scratched his head, backpedaling. "No, um, well, I do believe you are best suited for this conversation." He paused. "And by the by, I'd like to meet with the Duke of Eloqua when he arrives at the castle in a fortnight. The second he arrives. Please make sure of it."

Krinny responded, but the words sounded distant and hollow, drowned out by the blood that roared in my ears.

Heat inflamed my cheeks. "He arrives in a fortnight?"

Rylander's forehead wrinkled. "Yes. Smitter got word the duke left his last port stop today."

My pulse raced beneath my skin. "But *we're* only a fort-night away from Cava."

Rylander dipped his chin.

The duke was arriving a month earlier than planned. "Anything else I should know? Is my wedding moved up? Shall I be taking two men as my husband?" I flailed my arms like a brawling wildcat. "Maybe I'll be able to give twice as many children to Zeus. Would that please everyone?"

My brother's face faltered, his cheeks flushing. "I think it's best if Krinny has that conversation with you about your wedding night, as it sounds like you may not necessarily know how—"

"It was a joke, Rye."

Rylander swallowed. "Yes, well, you're not as funny as you think." He placed his hand on my shoulder and squeezed. His calloused fingers scratched and caught the cloth. "Look at this as good news. The duke felt it best to get to know you before your wedding day. I think that's very—"

I held up my hand and continued down the stairs to the kitchen. Nothing he could say would ease my plight.

Rylander had been the light of my life since I wore dia-pers. My sun rose and fell with him. But as I grew, I'd come to realize he was just as much a puppet of Zeus and this kingdom as I had been. Neither of us had much choice. And all the fairy tales he used to tell me before bed faded into a blur, a distant memory, a false sense of hope.

At least some small, reliable comforts remained. Hannah's strawberry tartlets waited in the bolted pantry under a draping of cheesecloth. I reached down and plucked one out of the bunch, staring at it until a tear dropped onto the baked puree center. I broke the treat in half, and in my mind's eye, it became a Jacarian braided dough dessert dipped in warm syrup, passed from my hand into Galen's. I could feel the heat of Jacar's arid grasslands on my face, hear the fading bustle of the market where we'd bought the delicacy.

She was strolling beside me in men's breeches, tall and gangly, her chest compressed by a wide swath of cloth beneath her billowy tunic. Smears of dirt shaded her jawline. A boy to the superstitious sailors who would call her bad luck to their voyage if she didn't dress that way or shear off her coal-black hair above her ears. But to me, she was everything I wanted to be. Mysterious. Adventurous. Lighthearted. And most of all, free.

An orphaned robber turned fabled rescuer of a bored ten-year-old Princess Savina. Galen had bumped into me at the market. Despite my forced anonymity, she'd pegged me for a rich, naïve child. She was right on one count, but I surprised her, catching her wrist when she dipped her hand into my pocket. At first, I'd thought she might shove me down and take the riches anyway—she was several years older and far stronger, after all—but instead, she smiled big enough to touch her ears. "Yer a wee fox of a ting, ain't ye, lass?"

I'd promised I wouldn't turn her in and I'd even hand over the purse she wanted if she'd take me somewhere fun. She'd thrown an arm around my shoulder and, for the next fortnight, had guided me through the sides of Jacar that my overbearing family and escorts hoped to keep me locked away from. Her quick, pickpocket hands had climbed my trellis and freed me from the confinement of my stately rooms almost every afternoon when I was supposed to be studying my books.

"Why ye Princess Savina of Cava, ay? Why ye dressed like that?" Galen pointed to my trousers and blouse as we took a dirt path through the tall grasses.

"Apparently I'm not supposed to tell anyone my real name." I shrugged, never quite understanding my father's and grandfather's orders. Not that I had listened to them. "The outfit helps conceal who I am."

"Well, princess or not, yar love riding down the Jacar river." Galen winked. "So long as ye stay in the rowboat, the crocodiles won't come fer a taste. O' course, if they find out why ye royalty, they might hop right into the dingy to see if princess makes fer finer meat."

A thin string of sticky syrup spread between my parting lips as I laughed from deep in my belly. "I know I taste better than you!" I teased, shoving her hip. She pretended the blow sent her spinning, and she tumbled off the path and into the shoulder-high grass, where she disappeared.

My laugh petered out when she didn't immediately pop up. The pastry dangled from loose fingers, forgotten, as I took a cautious step toward the bent blades that betrayed her path.

"G-Galen?"

Her face popped out to my left, and her breath beat my cheek when she bellowed, "Boo!"

I let out an undignified scream and felt my cheeks heating. "Not funny!"

She emerged fully from the grass, chuckling as she brushed off herself. "That's what ye get fer saying I taste bad."

Her smile blazed bright for a single beat of my heart. Then, with a sound like a fist driven into raw meat, it contorted into a trembling frown. She coughed, and a glob of something wet hit my face. My brain buzzed like swarming mosquitoes, sounding an alarm I couldn't comprehend as I touched my cheek and saw my hand come away red. With a piteous, glottal grunt, Galen's gaze slowly tipped downward, and I followed it to the blade rammed through her chest from behind. A gladius—wide and devastating, an ornate eagle engraving on the steel—caught her blood in its grooves. The creature seemed to shriek at me before it withdrew the sword, pulling it back through my friend.

I only realized the cry I heard was mine when her attacker commanded, "Silence, Savina." He flicked his wrist. "Do not cry for mortals. They are but ants crushed beneath your feet, and you don't mourn for *them,* do you?"

The silken white hair. Those sky-blue eyes. Arms bulging with muscle his toga could not hide. I knew him. I'd sat at his feet and heard his tales. Had smiled at him across my family table.

"Grandfather?"

I shook my head, wishing the memory away. Galen had returned to my mind more and more since the announcement of my betrothal. My last chance for independence crumbled before my eyes. I couldn't have adventures. I couldn't have friends. And now, I'd never find the dream romance Rylander had with Lou. I'd never get to dream again. My life was no longer my own. Then again, maybe it never was.

CHAPTER THREE

CONLETH

As we docked into the port of Cava, I drank in the scenery of my new home from the starboard rail. I'd lived many places over the centuries, each leaving their mark on my soul. But this one breathed fresh life into my vessel. The masts of docked trading ships tipped and swayed in the island's breeze. The shores were lined with schooners, rafts, and fishing boats. Scattered across the rocky coastline, men reeled in their crab and lobster traps, inspecting their catch before handing them off to go to market. Cava's riches appeared to come from the sea, unlike Eloqua, which we had chosen as our fortress while we lay in wait for an opportunity to move against Zeus.

I rubbed my palms together. To protect such beauty was not only an honor but a pleasure. High Priestess Pythia swore Zeus would rain hellfire on all the lands, costing more human life than even my first rebellion. Hard to believe such atrocities as I gazed upon so many smiling, unknowing faces below.

The captain's approach interrupted my thoughts of appraisal. "Your guard offered me coin for your voyage." He gestured to Vanden, who transferred our things down the gangplank to the dock. My trusted friend hauled bag after bag over his shoulder, blond head bent with toil, his golden topknot bowing to Helios. The wind blew wild strands across his visage, in answer to his grunts of effort.

The captain continued, "That will not be necessary. The King of Eloqua insisted on paying for your passage. I've already been granted compensation and will receive a bonus once word reaches him that you've been delivered safely."

I dipped my chin. "Thank you. That is very kind of him and of you."

"My pleasure, Your Grace." He bowed.

I waved over my two uniformed friends. Their black leather vests hugged violet tunics, and their black trousers were tucked formally into their shined black boots. "Let's travel into town and see what the good people of Cava have to offer."

Flick's brow rose as his gaze traced the crystal castle towering over us. "But, milord, shouldn't we head straight to the—"

I held up my palm and let a devious grin spill onto my lips—the one I'd used on the fiery redhead back on Anthemusa. Her plump lips and aquamarine eyes still invaded my dreams. "Not yet. I'd like to gather information on the people of this fine kingdom before we meet the king. And you know where the perfect place to do that is, don't you?"

Flick formed an all-knowing smirk. The bottom row of his teeth slanted so much they seemed to grin in the opposite direction of his mouth. "The local tavern, milord. Where else?"

He dipped low in a mock bow, and my gaze carried back over the water, toward the land I'd left nearly two weeks ago. The peculiar yet breathtaking woman on the beach—the one attacked by a flock of birds—had consumed my mind since we weighed anchor. I'd lost focus, and we'd almost sailed into a storm...a reminder I mustn't allow distractions to get in my way. My enemy closed in each day. Distractions like beautiful feisty women needed to be put in their place, far away from my forethoughts.

Vanden joined us. "Did I hear talks of ale?" He looked behind him. "I know just the man to ask. I'll be right back." He jogged to the helmsman, striking a conversation that forced the much smaller man to strain his neck to answer Vanden's questions.

I rested my hand on Flick's stout shoulder with a firm grip. His toasted skin was wrinkled from far too many days in the sun and his thirst for ale proved unending, but he was also the first man I'd turned to after escaping the clutches of my captor. "Shall we get some grog, old friend?"

Flick licked his lips, his gaze meeting mine. His irises were the dark violet of an impending summer's night storm, yet mischief twinkled in them like constellations. "I'll never turn ye down for that."

Vanden plopped the bags down in front of us. "And some ladies? I could use a healthy dose of both pleasures." He wiped sweat from his forehead and peeled stray blond curls off his neck and flushed cheeks.

I grinned. "I'm sure we can quench both desires in town."

The three of us made our way along the cobblestone street in the late afternoon sun, passing smooth-sided buildings constructed from off-white clay and plaster bearing slatted roofs. The farther we walked into town, the closer and loftier the structures stood, packed in like Flick's teeth.

Sellers from all four kingdoms shouted prices for their goods from every doorway and peddler cart. A strong smell of baker's ammonia and salty cheeses spread out on vintner's tables mixed with the heady aromas of anise and cinnamon, cumin, and black pepper. Sweet figs and raisins roasted alongside unctuous slabs of pork belly that made my mouth water, but nothing rivaled Eloqua's cuisine and entertainment offerings.

The helmsman had provided Vanden with a lay of the city and pointed us in the direction of the Lyre of Hermes Tavern. He implied this place—the largest and most well-known pub in Cava—gathered all the best scuttlebutt. Not to mention...the brothel next door would help satisfy all the needs of my men.

The wooden sign swaying with the summer winds above the door had its engravings gilded with paint. I scoffed at the little shrine to Hermes, imagining only a particularly ardent devotee could have designed it. I shook my head. Hermes was not a god I had any particular fondness for.

My fingers traced the raised scars dotted over the skin and sinew housing my liver like a cluster of stones. For a long time, I carried shame for their hideous image. But now, they served as my strength, a reminder of my survival, and fuel to the future fire I'd use to burn down the man who'd put them there, along with everyone else who idly stood by Zeus's side.

Vanden led our entrance, and we took seats by the unlit fireplace. My hands ached with unspent power, craving to fill it with flames. But since the summer sun provided all the heat the tavern needed, it would go unused until the sun started to set.

I barely heard Flick order from the barmaid as the people of Cava crammed around us, laughing, eating and drinking as merry as men and women should. A smile tugged at the corner of my mouth. My mission to bring the people what they needed hadn't been in vain.

The barmaid placed three filled mugs on the table and a clay plate filled with fresh breads and cheese. Flick, our resident wordsmith, wrapped his long fingers around his tankard and held it high. "A toast to our liege."

After the way my men brought my spirits back from the dead, we were nothing if not equals. "'Friend' is a more than an appropriate way to address me in private. But a cheers to our mission and journey, I would never pass up."

Vanden and I joined him, lifting our drinks.

"To keeping the people safe from those who believe themselves better than us." He tipped his chin up at me, his lilac eyes holding my own. "And even though you ain't want recognition for it"—he turned his body to face me—"to Conleth, for honoring us with your gifts. We will never be able to repay your kindness or mercy. We are forever in your debt."

"Hear! Hear!" Vanden shouted, pounding his free fist twice on the table.

The three of us clanked mugs and threw back our drinks. The ale burned in my chest, a welcome warmth that spread to my toes. My tongue savored the taste, calling forth memories of other shared food and drink with these friends whose loyalty had no bounds. When I escaped my prison eight years ago, they'd nursed my mind back to health and set me on the path to righteousness with many a night ending in grog-soaked strategy talks. It wasn't until Pythia found us that we had laid a solid path to our future.

Vanden extended his cup. His dark eyes, the umber of Jacarian tea, widened with excitement. "I've got my own toast."

"This should be good," Flick muttered, shooting me a conspirator's glance.

"To the women who shall warm our beds, and the rye to warm our stomachs."

Flick punched Vanden in the shoulder. "You've got a one-track mind."

I shook my head. "You mean two."

We laughed, a well-deserved moment of calm before the impending storm. Zeus was close. I could feel it in my bones.

I slathered blackberry jam onto a piece of bread and took a bite. Keys to your enemies' downfall usually lay in the rumors spread amongst the men who served them, so I let my ears pick up the noise of the surrounding tables. Every story held a nugget of truth, and if you could sift through the exaggerations, you'd uncover valuable facts. Weapons weren't always made of metal and stone.

"Royal guards put those invitations in your hand. Why don't you want to attend?" one of the men sitting directly behind me said.

"Because the last time we engaged with royalty, the queen held a sword to our chins, and the king knocked me out cold," the other man answered with a grunt.

I held my finger to my lips, silencing my crew. Their eyes darted to me and then around the room, trying to find my target. Flick's shoulders stiffened. Vanden's throat flexed.

"You're still hanging on to that decade-old grudge?"

"Yes, I've got the scars to remind me daily."

I twisted in my seat. "Sorry to listen in, gentlemen, but am I correct, the queen held a blade to you? Doesn't sound like any royalty I've encountered before. Do they not travel with their own sentinels?"

The stout, burly man laughed, vibrating his whole torso. "Many men would say you're looking for a fight eavesdropping on another's conversation." His forearms pulsed with his clenched paws.

Chairs scraped against the wooden floor. I twisted to find my men on their feet and posturing for a brawl. "Sit down." I waved them back onto the bench.

They huffed and planted themselves.

I pivoted back to my quarry. "My name's Conleth. I'm not looking to cause trouble. I'm simply intrigued. We're new here and learning the land. I understand if you found my question impolite. I'm not known for my subtly. But I *am* curious. If that's not a question you'd deign answer, what can you tell me about the sovereigns of this kingdom?"

The titan of a man extended his hand. "Name's Jebba." We shook. His fingers tightened around mine as if to impose a threat. Using my inhuman strength, I squeezed back. Jebba's eyes widened, but he continued as if nothing happened.

He gestured to his friend. "This here is Leon."

Leon dipped his chin. "This kingdom has no relative. Seven years ago, a naval captain and a pirate wench were crowned king and queen. But they spent many a mighty hostile year roaming the Caviar Sea. One in search of treasure. The other the Siren Queen." He gestured to the front entrance. "One night, we fell into a quarrel outside this very tavern with both of them, a year before they wed."

Jebba interjected, "That was many moons ago. King Rylander is mighty kind and generous. He's provided us with a good living, and we owe him plenty of gratitude." He harpooned his friend with a glare.

Leon rolled his eyes. "Aye. And now he's invited us to the princess's wedding."

In most cases, I would have believed that to be a gracious gesture, but by Leon's expression, I had doubts.

"The princess is getting married. I've heard that." My men chuckled, while I smirked. "And you don't wish to go?" Most lowly townsmen would see a royal wedding invite as an honor and privilege.

Leon, the tall, slender man among them, leaned forward and rested his bony elbows on the table. "Strange happenings around that castle," he confided in low tones. "Some say the gods are to blame." He shook his head. "Since the princess's birth, she's barely left the palace walls. They keep her hidden. No one really knows what she looks like. Just stories passed down to one another."

I strained to search out what lay beneath his words. "No one knows? Does she not frequent the town to see her people?"

Leon glanced over his shoulder, his hands fidgeting on the tabletop. "Rumor has it she's a little peculiar. Those that work in the castle say she spends most of her time within the gardens alone talking to the flowers."

"That *is* peculiar. Does something ail her?"

Jebba elbowed his friend's ribs. "We shouldn't be speaking on things we know nothing of. Most likely she's meek or perhaps lame."

"Doubtful any relation of King Rylander could be meek. Or lame for that matter," Leon muttered.

Jebba slapped him upside the head. "Stop being an ungrateful fop." His green eyes connected with mine. "The king and queen have been mighty generous to us. We've got nothing but kind words for them." He gazed up to the ceiling. "Although the queen can shake a man in his boots. If you meet her, be wary." A weak smile broke across his face. "Best to not bring up the days she were a pirate. Or that you met us, and we told you so."

I tossed my head back and laughed. "You truly fear the Queen of Cava?"

Jebba's lips tipped upward, displaying all his yellowed teeth. "Yes. As should you, stranger. She'll have your head if you anger her." He took a deep drink of his ale and wiped his mouth on his sleeve. "What brings you and your men from Eloqua to our isle?"

"How'd you know where we were from?" Vanden's mug slammed down behind me. His temper flared like oil on a campfire.

Jebba picked up a piece of bread and used it to point at Flick and me. "It's the eyes." Eloqua was known for the violet irises passed down from the island's forefathers. Not all carried the trait, but those who did were a dead giveaway.

Jebba sank his teeth into the loaf's crusted end and ripped it in two. He chewed with an open mouth smile. "Rumor has it the princess has been promised to some sap, a duke from your land. Do you know him?"

I leaned back against the table, trying to cover my smile. "Aye. In fact, I know him well." I tilted my head. "I am the Duke of Eloqua."

Jebba's mouth opened, exposing chewed food. His companion's eyes widened.

"The poor sap betrothed to the princess of Cava, apparently."

Though unbeknownst to her and the rest of the kingdom, we would never wed. But that was a secret carried by me, my men, and the sirens. One that we intended to see through. The fate of the lands at stake.

CHAPTER FOUR

SAVINA

I staggered into my palace bedroom with a grateful sigh that turned into a yawn. I rubbed my eyes, exhausted after several days of sleepless nights onboard the ship. Thoughts of the man on Anthemusa had consumed my dreams and weighed me down; his body pressed against mine, the sweet caress of my hair, his lips when they kissed my forehead, and his smile when he stared into my eyes. No one had ever looked at me that way. Who was he? Where did he come from? And why did he have a meeting with Queen Yemma? His mere presence on the island crawled under my skin and took up residency in my mind.

I eyed my plush comforter and pile of matching pillows, neatly arranged on my four-post chestnut bed. Slumber called to my heavy lids and limbs. If I could snatch a couple hours of shut-eye, I'd be refreshed for dinner and not draw any attention to my restless fiddling that kept happening as I rehashed my encounter with Conleth, a man I needed to forget.

I sank my weary bones onto the bed, pulled off my boots, and tossed them across the room. They landed with a thump and my gaze followed the sound. "What the…" I stopped, my mouth gaping as my eyes honed in. Streaks of blood smudged amid muddy footprints trailing out to my veranda. I stood, eyes darting all around my room.

Someone was here.

A shadow crossed the balcony. Rigid, I inched a hand toward the dagger sheathed on my belt. My fingers curled around the hilt as I marked the silhouette's shape. Waves like ribbons fluttered off a torso outlined along the stone. Long, curly hair blowing in the summer breeze. I expelled half my breath. Only one person with hair like garland dared soil my chambers and wait for me unannounced with no regard to the consequences.

"Calli?" I called out, taking cautious steps. I tore open the plum drapes and pointed my blade at the heart of the figure in the corner. My gaze traveled up her dirt-soiled pants to her ripped blouse and landed on her bruised and battered face. Dried blood dripped under her nose and smudged her chin. The rest of my oxygen expelled in a huff. Sadly, I'd numbed to her wretched dishevelment, it occurred so often.

"What in the underworld are you doing?" I sheathed my weapon, grabbed my niece by the arm, and dragged her back into my bedroom.

She groaned with each step, clearly in pain. "Waiting for you. What do you think I'm doing?" She tore herself out of my hold and hissed, clutching her elbow to her chest. "Why are you so dramatic?"

I frowned back at the balcony. "Why are you so careless?" I dragged my fingers through my hair. "Someone could have seen you. Then what would you have done? It's obvious you're hurt. How would you explain that to Krinny, the guards, or your parents?"

She sat on my lounge chair and kicked her feet up onto my ottoman. "Not likely. I'm like an assassin, completely invisible. Not even the keenest eye could catch me." She pretended to inspect her dirt-covered nails, ignoring my glare.

"Really? Well, if you're such a warrior, what are you doing here? Surely you don't need anything from your feeble aunt."

"I enjoy your charm. What can I say? Everyone needs a sidekick." She lifted her chin and winked, then wiped muddied streaks across her forehead into her hair line.

Even at thirteen years old, folks mistook her for her mother, Lou, from a distance. Long, wheat-colored locks curled down her back in big ringlets, her amber irises glowed like the sun, and she was always dressed in trousers, a billowing blouse, and black boots. Just like her mother, who refused to wear dresses unless forced. Only the dimple on her right cheek, identical to mine and Rylander's, reminded me of our shared bloodline. Other than that, we were nothing alike.

I dug my hands against my hips to keep from strangling her. "Do you want to tell me why you look as though you've been to war and back? Or am I going to have to drag it out of you?" My eyes narrowed. "Why are you really here, Calli?"

Although I'd call us close as sisters, most of the time I felt like her maid, cleaning up the messes she caused outside of the castle without letting the adults know of her transgressions. And that was when it hit me...

"You were sparring with Henrik again, weren't you?"

Calli averted her gaze.

"Cal, your mother is going to kill you." I sighed and removed my belt, placing my scabbard on my end table. "His pirating aside, you know how your mother feels about his father."

Henrik was the son of the captain of *The Black Hollow*, a renowned pirate and Lou's sworn enemy. Calli closed her eyes and tilted up her chin to the ceiling.

"You promised!" I shouted and stomped my foot, gaining her attention. "If you don't stop seeing him, I swear to the gods, I'm going to—"

Calli jumped to her feet, red as Cava's sunset. "You're going to do what? You're not my mother. Stop acting like it."

The muscles in my jaw ticked. "I'm not trying to be your mother. I'm trying to protect you because you're my family and I love you."

Her big eyes softened, then pleaded. "He's my best friend, Sav. He means everything to me. He's strong, smart, funny. I even like his stupid chin. Kinda looks like he put our dimple in the wrong place." Her brow snapped up, lids narrowing. "He's the best partner I've ever sparred with. He's the only one who will actually hit me."

"And that's a good thing? Look at you." I gestured to her blood-caked clothes and growing welts.

Her thick black lashes batted, and a lopsided grin graced her face. "That's why I have you to heal me."

I tapped my fingers along my forearm. "And who's going to heal Henrik?" If Calli looked like this, then he looked worse. Henrik never hit her like she thought. I'd watched them spar once. Every infliction she had, she'd caused. He mostly played defense, but she never noticed. Teenager or not, she fought like her parents, and her godly strength gave her an upper hand in matters of combat. However, she scarred like a human, and Apollo's healing gift hadn't been passed down to her like it had her father, younger brother, and me.

"Calli, how badly hurt is Henrik?"

She bit her lower lip. The fervor she had entered with fled. "I, umm... I left him with Ketner, but I think..." She paused, playing with her thumbs and staring at the ground.

"You think..." I stepped forward, my hands itching to shake her.

She lifted her head. "Don't be mad. But I think I broke his leg or, well, at least sprained it. He can't put much weight on it."

Her words came out so fast it took me a moment to understand. But as I did, as if lava had been poured over me, I screamed, "You what?" My throat clogged like I had swallowed a grapefruit, my chest tightening. If Henrik went back to *The Black Hollow* with an injury, his father would tear this town apart to find the party responsible. Not that Henrik would ever throw Calli under the cart, but he'd have to fault someone for the captain to feel justified. And then some poor soul would take the blame, possibly with their life. Calli and Henrik both knew this.

I grabbed the vase next to me, anger rising like the morning fog. My powers tingled at my fingertips. With demi-god strength, I hurled the glass urn. It smacked into the wall, cracking into tiny pieces that littered my floor with brittle stems. The sun glinted off the drops of water that pooled around the once blue petals that had withered to ashen, a casualty of my powers. When I lost control of my emotions, instead of healing what I touched, I could inflict illness or disease, a power that was increasing in strength as I got older. I had killed many a plant and animal as a child, and even made Edgar, our family's most loyal servant, sick once or twice. Thankfully, I had never fatally harmed anyone, and I wasn't about to start with my niece, so I kept my fists safe at my sides.

Calli squinted, the flames snuffed out of her irises. "You're mad."

"Ares himself would quake before me." I gritted my teeth, advancing on her. "Where is Henrik?" My voice faltered. I pressed my palm to my chest, trying to suppress the acid feeling rising to my throat.

"Ketner's with him at the Lyre of Hermes Tavern."

Ketner, a medicine man from Jacar, has been a part of our family ever since I was born. He served my brother aboard *The Sea Singer*. But ever since Rylander took the throne, Ketner had become a non-official watcher and guardian of Calli and me, and now that extended to Henrik. I sometimes wondered why Ketner put up with us.

Calli wiped at her face with the heel of her palm as if her emotions embarrassed her. "I'm sure he's helping. He's the best healer in all five isles, but if Henrik's leg is broken..." She gulped.

I headed toward my boots, the beat of my heart matching my pace.

"I'll go with you." Calli started to stand.

I held up my hand. "No. You stay put. I'll heal you first, and then I'll go help Henrik, but Calli..."

"Yes?" Hope pitched her voice.

Forced calm swept my body on a heavy breath. "I won't help you two again. Next time, I'll tell your father. And your mother."

Sneaking out of the castle wasn't difficult when most of the inhabitants thought you had never left before. A Princess of Cava sighting was rarer than meeting one of the gods. The rumored reasons why I didn't make public appearances were wide-ranging. The latest suggestions had been that I'd lost my voice and couldn't converse with the public; that a god cast a curse upon me, forcing me to remain on royal grounds; or that an aversion to the sun kept me indoors. All ridiculous. All lies. All helpful in ensuring no one ever noticed me when I traveled into town.

My father had always thought it best to keep me safe behind the palace walls since my powers manifested so strongly at an early age. Then at eleven, Zeus made his own rule for my safety. I was never permitted out of my guard's sight. I had to learn how to escape the castle without being seen. No one bothered me when I went out to ride, assuming I'd fear leaving the property. So, I spent many days creating a path meant for only one horse and one rider.

As Calli got older, I'd shown her where it was, much to my later chagrin. The guilt over her relationship with Henrik ate at me. Their first meeting happened when I'd dragged her out to a dockside Sea Festival. Ever since, whenever *The Black Hollow* came into port, Calli rushed out to train with Henrik. Now they both relied on me to heal their battle wounds.

After Galen, my niece and her pirate were the only two friends I had. But even then, I stayed away from Henrik as much as possible. I never dared attempt at making another acquaintance. Seeing Zeus murder Galen had been enough to hinder my curiosity in relationships. And my fear that one day Henrik would suffer at the hand of my family ate away at the very conscience that tried to keep Calli and he apart.

I bridled my chocolate mare, Winnie. She was a birthday gift from my late mother, and my most trusted companion. "You ready for a quick trip into town, girl?" I patted her side, and she neighed.

We rode out the stable's back entrance, down the dirt trail trampled by my escapes over the last several years, never turning around to look at the diminishing crystal castle. I descended the hill toward town, clenching the reins in trembling hands. Who knew how long Ketner had been with Henrik at the tavern? What if he couldn't tend to him long enough to wait for me? Or worse, what if Captain Fredrick found them? What would become of Henrik or Ketner then?

I kicked my heels against Winnie's side, encouraging a faster pace. The tree line started to thin as we left the royal grounds, and the wealthier houses came into view. Their elaborate spires reached toward the sky, and weighty columns lined their porches. White smoke rose from their chimneys, adding clouds to the backdrop of the setting sun. They were sitting down to dinner inside, I was sure. It made me all too aware that I didn't have much time until our own family supper.

Winnie wound through the last of the vegetation and onto a city street. Clay-roofed homes lined the downward sloping path to the bustling market of shoppes, each stout building butting up against the other. Beyond that lay the coastline. The smell of the sea blew across my face, thick with the scent of summer. Winnie slowed amidst the growing crowd of peddlers and their goods, her hooves clattering against the cobblestone. Voices crowed prices for eggplant, green tomatoes, and squash, while fishermen competed with the cost of lobster, crabs, oysters, and clams. Everything could be bought in the market, from robust Cava wine by the barrel to expertly designed battle armor from Sottom.

In no time, we reached the fountain where the statue of King Delphi sat, a monument built when my father faked his own death. Water flowed from the tip of his aimed arrow into the circular pool below, facing the famous tavern. I clucked to my horse and urged her to the back of the pub where the other mounts stood hitched to a line of posts. I hoped Henrik's wounds weren't as bad as Calli thought. That boy had been through too much already. And although I wished they'd stop seeing each other, there were times I knew their relationship balanced their lives.

After I dismounted and walked Winnie to a trough of hay to keep her busy, I tied her to a column. I rounded back to the heavy front door. This wasn't my first time meeting Ketner here to help Henrik, but I hoped it would be my last. Staring at the swinging wooden tavern sign in honor of my uncle, Hermes, I said a silent prayer: *May the Fates smile upon me.* I pulled the brown hood of my cloak around my head, tugged the iron handle, and walked in.

Five steps from the door, a group of men puffed their chests and screamed profanities at one another. Their drunken shouts stunk of old ale, but since all eyes were focused on them, they provided the cover I needed. I barreled past them, pushing men twice my size out of the way as I headed toward the back. Although no one knew what the crowned princess looked like, I also didn't blend in with women in this pub. The sooner I got in and out, the better.

In the corner, I found Ketner leaned over Henrik, inspecting his leg. It bent in an unfathomable way. Definitely broken. And since only half the contents of a bottle of brown liquor sat in front of a fourteen-year-old boy, I assumed he was in severe pain as well. Ketner used a combination of snake venom and bourbon to numb pain of great magnitude. Although it had healing powers that would help mend the bone and ligaments over time, it wouldn't solve the immediate problem—Henrik's father.

Captain Fredrick's reputation for malice spread across all five isles. No one crossed the seafarer. Not even the kings. The only person ever known to challenge him was Cava's queen, back when she had been known as Captain Lou of the now-retired pirate ship *The Freedom*. They currently operated under an unspoken truce that they'd stay clear of one another until her reign ended, but that armistice only had weeks left. If Captain Fredrick learned Lou's daughter had caused his son's misfortune, I feared what would become of their ceasefire then.

Henrik's tight-lipped smile at my arrival spread into his green eyes. I wanted to smack it off him, but instead I leaned against their table beside Ketner, my palms pressed against the wood.

"Is it broken?" I asked in a low growl.

"Hello, princess," Henrik cooed. "Nice of you to join us." The dimple in his chin danced with his words.

"Shut up." I turned toward Ketner, peeling my eyes off the white markings on his face. "How many injuries am I healing?"

"A fractured leg. A deep gash on his back that goes up and around his right shoulder. His lip needs stitches, and he's missing a tooth." Ketner chuckled when Henrik flashed me a wide, taunting grin. His front incisor dangled from a string of flesh. Blood dripped from his mouth like raindrops onto the floor.

I grabbed his bicep and leaned in. "I'll heal you enough so you can hobble outside and then I'll take care of the rest there." Hidden by my cloak, my hand gripped his thigh. He hissed through his teeth, tears threatened the corners of his lids. "Stay still."

"Because if I could move, I would," he gritted out, then tossed me a devilish grin.

My powers searched for the injury, flooding my veins with a surge of energy. When Henrik's shoulders relaxed, I knew he'd be well enough to stumble out. I wrenched him upright. His smirk vanished, replaced with a grimace and a groan. I glanced over my shoulder to make sure no one was watching and that was when I saw the black and purple garb that signified Eloquan guards. Maybe three or five of them, I couldn't quite tell with such a quick look. But their presence meant that the duke was either here or somewhere nearby.

A slew of curses slipped from my parted lips.

"What's wrong?" Ketner stood, curiosity twisting the white markings on his forehead, cheek, and chin.

"I need you to do me a favor," I whispered. "There should be a group of Cava royal guards along with the Sottom brothers at the local gunsmith two doors down. They're retrieving extra weapons for the wedding, per Rylander's request. Get them and tell them you see sentries from Eloqua at the tavern. They were supposed to report directly to the castle when they arrived, and they haven't. I can't risk them seeing me here. No one from the castle knows of my visits."

Ketner nodded. He knew the risks of me coming to the tavern, and although he'd never tell my brother how I helped the pirate captain's son, I knew he worried about my involvement. He took off in the opposite direction and disappeared into the crowd.

I dragged Henrik to my side, bearing most of his weight. "You are a thorn. A constant blight!"

Henrik rolled his eyes. "It's not like I pummeled *myself* to the underworld and back," he whined as I pushed open the back door. The sun hung low in the sky by the time we exited.

"I know that." I tugged him along after me. With our family's powers came responsibilities, ones Calli was not mature enough or wise enough to grasp.

I drew in a breath, calling forth my abilities. Like needle pricks, it pierced my skin. My palm pressed into his back as I coated him in my magic, never ceasing our trudge to the line of hitched horses. With more force than necessary, I dunked Henrik's head inside their water trough, washing the blood from his face. When I lifted him upright, my hands trailed down his forehead, nose, cheeks, and shoulders, mending the seen and unseen wounds. I lingered at his mouth, restitching his tooth. By the time he blinked those emerald eyes, all the cuts and bruises had vanished.

He wrapped his fingers around my forearm. "You know I care about her as much as she does me. I'd never betray her, Savina. Never." He swallowed. "I love her." He spoke the words with such conviction that a knot formed in my throat. I'd be lying if I didn't admit envy. The two of them loved so hard, they'd be the death of each other. And possibly me.

I placed my hand over his and gently squeezed. "I don't doubt your intentions. I never have. You're a good boy, Henrik. That's not the issue."

His eyes watered as he released his hold and looked away. I could only imagine the horrors he had witnessed having such a cruel father. Calli might have been the first person in his life to show him love, and although I'd never intentionally rob him of that, my foremost duty was to my family and my kingdom. I worried for both their fates and the fates of those around them should word get out.

I knelt and rubbed my hands together before placing them over Henrik's leg. I looked up while my magic worked over the broken bones and torn ligaments. "If you care about her as much as you proclaim, you'll stop seeing her, because if either of you gets caught, it won't be pleasant, and I can't heal death."

"She's worth dying for," he whispered, so low I barely heard him. But the goose pimples on my arms did. I wondered if someday someone would love me with such fierceness. But like cold water dumping over my head, I recalled my upcoming nuptials, and my momentary wish drowned once again.

The back door of the tavern creaked open. "I have to hide," I whispered. A bead of sweat dripped down my back. "If you are questioned, you run."

With that, I moved around the horses and dove behind the hay, praying Henrik would do right by me.

CHAPTER FIVE

CONLETH

An eruption of shouts from a group of men on the far side of the room caught my attention. The din of their fight faded to the roar of ocean wind when a figure hastily walked around them, tightening the hood around her head to conceal herself. But her form and that striking bright red hair curling out of her covering—rich as a painting—had plagued my mind. I knew her immediately. How could I forget my little songbird? For though our meeting was only moments, it had imprinted my heart for what felt like a lifetime.

My mouth dropped open in surprise as she pushed her way to the back of the tavern, barreling through men twice her size, and stopped in front of a wounded boy, sitting in the corner. Blood dotted his lips and trailed down his arm. A tall, muscular man with dark skin like Flick's and a bone through his nose inspected the boy's leg. As if he could hear her footsteps, he drew back, revealing a snake tattoo riding his neck and shoulders and white markings on his cheeks, forehead, and chin that betrayed him as a healer from Jacar—an island north of here. His smile welcomed her as if she'd been expected.

How strange.

My little songbird leaned in, her shoulders tense. She said a couple hushed words to the unlikely pair, then yanked the boy out of his seat, pulling him toward the back door with no regard for his limp. A second later, they both disappeared.

I beckoned for the barmaid. "Flick, pay our tab, then meet us outside." I finished the contents of my cup and slammed it onto the table. With a wave of my hand, I motioned for the rest to do the same. "Vanden, with me."

I stood, nodding farewell to our new friends, and then followed her to the back exit, pushing my way through the throngs of people, Vanden hot on my heels.

My face scrunched as I tried to put the pieces together. How my little songbird had been on the sirens' island a fortnight ago and now graced my presence at a random tavern on another isle weighed heavily on my conscious. I didn't believe in coincidences.

When I opened the door, my jaw dropped. My songbird had flown away, but the boy with the injured leg and cuts along his face and limbs stood attending to a horse. He ran a paddle brush through the animal's mane, combing out knots like he'd been doing it for hours instead of mere seconds. Blood stained his clothes, but the gash along his forehead and arm had vanished. Droplets of water clung to his swept back reddish-brown hair and wet spots dotted his collar. But even more startling, his once limp leg had straightened, bearing his entire weight.

I pointed to the boy. "You there! Come here."

Eyes wide, he tossed the comb onto the street and sprinted like he'd never been injured.

"Follow him," I instructed Vanden.

We gave chase around the corner and into the market square where the statue of King Delphi stood. The boy smirked over his shoulder as he rounded the fountain and took off into the crowd.

"He's taunting us." Vanden's ale breath wafted over me.

"I know." I pointed right. "You go that way." I jumped onto the ledge of the fountain and charged through it, headed left. Water kicked up behind me. The bottom of my pants dragged with soaked weight.

As I leapt off the other side—my boots sopping wet—I skidded to a halt but still managed to crash into the first of five men in red and gold uniforms barreling right at me. The Cava royal guard.

"Duke of Eloqua, I presume." The head guard caught me by the shoulders, righting himself and me from the collision. His arms dropped but he stayed in my personal space while the four men with him took a step backward.

Two of the guards were the spitting image of each other. Black hair, broad shoulders, slim physiques, same nose with a slight bump on the arch. Brothers. Twins, no less. They stood in a practiced line, playing tricks on my eyes.

I shoved my hands into my pocket and rolled back on my heels, flashing an easy smile. Either someone alerted them to our presence, or they were men of impeccable timing. I believed the former.

"Imagine our surprise to learn of your arrival from a local barfly instead of the crier at the castle gate." His fury spilled out like a viper uncoiling from a charmer's basket. "You are the Duke of Eloqua, are you not?"

I wondered who'd run to the guards, but thought better than to ask after the gossiper. Better to let him do all the talking and see what I could learn.

"Did you and your men get lost on your way to the palace?" The guard's forehead wrinkled.

Vanden caught up and moved to shield me. Now the guard stepped back, realizing I wasn't alone. Though it did little to wash away their discontent.

"How dare you speak to our lord with such forked tongues?" Vanden's shoulders pulsed.

I pulled him back in line. "That's quite all right." I bowed my head. "We only wanted to sample your good town before meeting with the king and queen. My apologies."

"The king requests your immediate presence." The guard's eyes narrowed. "We will escort you there ourselves to make certain you don't lose your way this time."

Vanden's lips curled like an animal showing its teeth.

"Very well. We'd appreciate the company. Wouldn't we, Vanden?"

As he nodded, my focus drifted behind the guards. The healer from inside the tavern leaned up against the wood building, arms crossed over his chest, knee bent, boot pressed into the wall. He might have blended beyond reproach had it not been for the white markings along his face. His shadowed gaze cut straight to me. The man tilted his chin up as if to say *it was me who alerted the guards.*

Interesting. Between my little songbird's companion and the magically healed boy, I had more questions than answers after less than a day in Cava.

⟫⟫⟫ ⟪⟪⟪

The soft sounds of the servants tending to their tasks followed us down the palace corridors. Their stares and hushed voices trailed our escort all the way to the throne room.

"You may wait for King Rylander here," the guard, whose name we'd found out was Naven, commanded. He left, shutting the doors behind him.

The grandeur of the narrow room, like an oversized hall, was meant to intimidate those who sought audience with the king, a very Apollo thing to do. I hadn't encountered the god in some time, but his personality surfaced in this room regardless of the "King Delphi" title he'd peddled to his subjects.

Flick, Vanden, and I treaded along the red carpet trailing from the large oak doors, making the gold-cord fringe quiver. We stopped at the golden thrones on the other end of the great hall.

"I think the king means to intimidate us." Flick spun, taking in the room. The twitch of his mouth told me he found humor in such a futile tactic.

"I would have to agree." I chuckled. "Is it working?"

"Not the least bit, milord." Vanden bowed mockingly toward the throne.

My men laughed as we took to the seats in front of the king's chair. The armrests each ended in the head of a lion, the chair legs curled and carved into an abstract sculpture of a lyre. Apollo always leaned toward extravagance.

Arched windows made of stained glass captured soft lamplight filtering the room. Flags bearing Cava's crest—a griffin with a lyre in its beak against a bright, shining sun—hung along the chamber walls. The creature, with its body of a lion and the head and wings of an eagle, transported Apollo between heaven and earth. I wondered if Rylander's name bore homage to Apollo's favorite beast, Rye. I chuckled to myself. The last time I saw Rye, I tried to maim him. I doubted either Apollo or his animal convoy would be thrilled to know I was here.

The door opened, and a man around my stature slipped through. Unlike all the kings I'd met before, he wore brown trousers, a black long-sleeved tunic, and boots. No crown donned his head, no elaborate surcoat draped his shoulders. In fact, nothing about his appearance spoke to his title. But he carried himself like a god. His shoulders back, his chin tilted upward, his walk authoritative. He exuded his father, Apollo's, spirit, save for his colorless, sparkling eyes. They were undoubtedly his mother's, Calliope. I had never had the privilege of meeting her, but I'd heard her beauty exceeded any other muse.

"Your Majesty." I hardened my voice. Contempt dripped off my tongue.

The guards had handled us like cattle on our way here, riding their horses. Not the welcome I'd have assumed we'd receive from the Isle of Cava. Rylander's resemblance to his father only fanned my anger.

"We've had much attention. We are undeserving of such a fuss." I bowed. Though my actions were respectful, my tone could chill the summer temperatures.

Rylander tilted his head. "I express my sincerest regret for my guards. Have they not been accommodating?" A small, unapologetic smile pulled at his lips. "I believe they found your disobedience of a direct order from the king nearly as surprising as I."

Vanden huffed behind me, and I turned to glare. It was one thing for me to be insolent, but I wouldn't allow my subordinates to do so and possibly be met with a blade.

Vanden sensed my warning and nodded.

King Rylander crossed the distance between us. His gaze traveled over me and then my associates. He slipped on a masked face void of emotion, a war tactic. "I appreciate you coming early. I believe it is important for you to get to know the princess. She..." For the first time since he'd walked in, he hesitated. He wavered between studying the ground and the ceiling, avoiding my eye. "How should I say this?" he mumbled as if more to himself than me, scratching his chin. "Might I have your men escorted to their rooms? Dinner will be served shortly, and this matter I wish to discuss is private."

Flick stepped forward. "With all due respect, King Rylander, we go wherever the duke goes." He bowed his head, a formality he gave to all superiors.

Rylander's face inflamed. His lips thinned. I imagined he wasn't used to his commands being met with resistance. "Very well. I will send my wife in for this discussion." He rubbed the arch of his nose. "The gods know you will wish you had dealt with me."

A laugh slipped through my parted lips. "All the more reason for my men to stay. I fear your wife may not be a woman I would want a private conversation with. We've heard she has a reputation for violence."

The lines around Rylander's mouth and eyes softened, finding my words amusing rather than insulting by some god's grace. "Aye, the tavern provided wise warning. Queen Elouise is—"

"Standing right here!" The harsh pitch of a woman's voice sounded behind us.

My men and I twisted around.

Queen Elouise's arms crossed over her white billowy blouse tucked into grey trousers that hugged her hourglass hips. Mirror-shined boots donned her feet. *Does no one in this castle dress like royalty?* Long blonde hair curled over her shoulders in a feint of delicacy, while her eyes burned fiercely enough to melt glass.

"My darling husband, please do go on. I'd love to hear the end to that sentence." Her lips fought a smile that was no kinder than the welcome we'd had thus far.

My men's mouths slackened while mine quirked into a half grin. I liked her spirit, even though her wrath would doubtless land on us next.

Surprisingly, Rylander laughed. "Your reputation proceeds you, my dear. You know that. The duke and I were only speaking repetitive gossip served from the local tavern about your past life aboard *The Freedom*."

Queen Elouise waved off her husband and approached me. She extended her hand. "Please call me Lou. Unless you'd like a blade held to your throat. Elouise is the name my mother called me, and she lies as dust under the earth. Gods only knows if she's joined with Hades or in Elysian Fields."

Flick gasped. His hands clutched his chest. It was unusual to hear someone speak so candidly about the dead, especially a woman. Vanden ogled her openly while I chuckled.

"You, fair lady, are a very surprising delight." I grabbed her fingers and bowed. My lips brushed the top of her hand. She yanked it away, jaw twitching.

"Do not ever do that again," she growled.

This time, Rylander interjected. "Lou eschews royal decorum." He gestured to her outfit and then his own. "In fact, you will see many differences in our kingdom that you'll doubtless wish to change during your rule. By all means, do so." He reached for his wife and drew her into his side. To my surprise, she went willingly. His arm wrapped around her waist. "It is just not our way."

"I do not cast judgment, Your Majesty. I feel that if you rule with your heart while keeping your kingdom's best interest in mind, you are far greater a ruler than a king or queen who dresses the part."

Lou looked up at her husband. "You never know. I may grow to forgive his hand slobbering." She swiveled, facing my stunned men. "Dinner is in an hour. Do not be late. Our cook, Hannah, won't serve you if you are, unless you are a god, and looking at you lot, I do not believe you can claim such a status." She kissed her husband's cheek and then shooed my men toward the exit. "You heard me. Come on. You do not want to get on her bad side. She could as easily poison you as fill your bellies with deliciousness."

Flick stumbled backward, shock blanketing his face. Vanden grabbed his arm and steadied him. Then they both practically ran to the door. For the first time since we served together, they didn't even look for my approval before they left. The queen was quite the intimidator. I'd take note to find her favor along the way.

Lou followed them. She glanced over her shoulder and winked at the king. "Use this time wisely, my dear." Her husband's goal achieved, she slipped through the opening and closed the door behind her.

"She's tricky," I said.

"She is more than I deserve." The king gestured to a chair. "Please sit. This conversation is uncomfortable for me."

The skin between my eyes creased. I had no idea what he was referring to, but his distress radiated throughout the room. I pulled out the chair and sat, crossing my shin over my thigh and relaxing into the red-cushion backing. "Please, Your Majesty, speak freely."

Rylander rubbed his neck. "It's come to my attention that my sister has little experience with men."

My brows furrowed. What in the underworld was the king alluding to? "I've heard she hasn't left the castle often. Is that what you mean?"

The king paced in front of me with hands clasped behind his back. "Yes, that is true, but she's more practiced in both high and low society than the people of this kingdom know. She travels with me to other lands in disguise and is extremely well read, a fan of the arts, and excellent with animals, people, even flowers." He sucked in a deep breath. "She does have some concerns with your upcoming wedding."

"I'd imagined she would. Marrying a stranger would cause unease for anyone. It is why I tried to arrive early to meet her and put her worries to rest."

Rylander's face lit up. "That's exactly what I told her."

I nodded. There wasn't much else I could say, being still unsure of where this conversation was headed.

"I do appreciate your speedy arrival. It's...." He cracked his neck side to side. "It's the wedding night. She is, you know..." He waited as if I would finish his sentence.

Time stood still. Silence fell like a woolen blanket over my head.

Finally, when he offered nothing, I stood. "King Rylander, I hate to be rude, but this conversation has me a bit confused."

"May the Fates smile upon me." Rylander stared at the ceiling as if summoning the gods themselves. "She's nervous about the consummation of the marriage."

The words rolled off his tongue so fast it took me a moment to absorb their meaning. But as I did, laughter bubbled up and soon erupted out of my mouth. "I'm so sorry." I held my stomach as I continued to chortle, rocking my torso with the vibration. "I don't know what to say but..." I swallowed, trying to compose myself.

Rylander's shoulders tightened, lifting toward his reddened ears.

I coughed to choke my amusement. "I am sorry for my mirth. It's just I hadn't really given the matter much thought." Because there would be no marriage, but of course, I couldn't explain that to King Rylander. I placed my hand on the king's arm as I did to steady my men. "I had hoped the princess and I could find friendship first and see where that leads. If that's agreeable to you."

The king rubbed his hands over his face, letting out a long breath. "Gods, thank you."

I squeezed his bicep before letting go. "Well, this has been an..."

"Rye." Footsteps sounded. "Rye, where are you?" A familiar voice—heard only once but carved deep in the channels of my mind—yelled as the doors to the throne room swung open and hit the adjacent wall.

Fiery hair framing a perfect heart-shaped face and a slim frame stormed into the room. Exertion painted her cheeks pink. "Did you know the duke is here, in the kingdom? He failed to..." Her blue eyes widened as they connected to mine. Her mouth dropped open.

I tilted my head. My throat felt thick, my words sticking there. This couldn't be...

"Duke of Eloqua, may I introduce my sister, the Princess of Cava." Rylander waved between us. "Princess, this is—"

"You wretched man!" The princess stormed into the room, practically breaking into a jog. Her gaze traveled my face as my heart plunked into the pit of my stomach. "You.... How are you even..."

Rylander stood aghast, appraising us.

Out of all the fair maidens! The Fates were more humorous than I gave them credit for. I didn't know whether to pummel the old gals or kiss them. But when the princess's cheeks darkened to apple red, I knew my curse would at least be enjoyable. My lips pulled into a lopsided grin. I extended my hand. "The name's Conleth. And yours?"

The princess's hands curled into fists by her sides. "None of your damn concern."

CHAPTER SIX

SAVINA

My earlier troubles—pending marriage, Calli's injuries, sneaking out to heal Henrik, avoiding the Eloquan guards at the tavern—all disappeared. A new plight thrashed my brain like a floundering fish.

Conleth's purple tunic hugged his broad shoulders, tailored to show his strength. His charcoal ringlets of hair were shorter and combed back, unlike the unruly strands tousled by the coastal breeze on Anthemusa. His face, sharp as a diamond's edge, crinkled around his assessing eyes and twisted lips. His mere presence took up more space in the room than I'd ever commanded...

And just as upon our first meeting, I longed to punch him for his daft handsomeness.

I swayed like an apprenticed cabin boy strolling the deck for the first time. I closed my eyes as I sent up a prayer to the gods. Could the stress of the upcoming wedding finally have reached a hysteria so poignant as to conjure this vision? I ground my teeth together, waiting to wake up from this nightmare.

"Savina, open your damn eyes." Rylander clenched my upper arms and shook me. "What in the gods' names is wrong with you?"

I blinked and stared into my brother's pinched face, his irises bright as the spark off a blade striking stone. My gaze trailed over Rye's shoulder. To my dismay, the man from the sirens' island still stood behind him. His lips pulled up into a smirk, but his eyes were wide. At least I wasn't the only one caught off guard. But something about him was different—wrong, in fact.

Rylander twisted his body. "Duke, I...my apologies. She may be ill or..."

I yanked free of my brother's hold. "I'm not ill." I pointed at Conleth. "I..." My lips pressed together. If I said we had met, my brother's temper would flare over my prior omission. But how else could I explain my reaction without looking like I had gone completely mad? I huffed, taking a step back and dropping my arm by my side.

Space. I needed space.

"I'm sorry, brother." I gulped, taking the extra second to look for an excuse, but finding none. I lifted my chin. "I thought he was someone else."

"Savina," Rylander murmured with a hint of disapproval, "this is so unlike you."

Conleth stepped forward. "King Rylander, if I may." His voice weighed me down like my feet were encased in mud. "You mentioned recent travels and preparation. I'm sure the princess is feeling like there's an albatross around her neck with my sudden arrival." Conleth's arched brow dared me.

Well, he wouldn't get a peep out of me, even with his bird analogy insult.

Rylander's face twisted while mine squeezed like I'd sucked on a lemon.

"Yes." The king scratched his head. "We have had some travels as of late. As you have..."

I stepped forward, arms crossed. "I imagine you're in need of rest, Your Grace. After your own voyage and sculpting activities, you must be exhausted." I hadn't forgotten the chucks of clay clinging to his pants on the island. I might not have known what he was doing there, but I knew a sculptor's appearance after a long day of work.

"Sculpting?" The skin between Rylander's eyes crinkled. "How would..." He stroked his chin, turning toward Conleth. "Do you sculpt?"

A smile curved Conleth's lips. The twinkle in his violet eyes lit up like a shooting star, bright enough to be seen but easy to miss. "I do." He turned to me. "Princess Savina, I find it extremely thoughtful of you to learn so much about me prior to our meeting. If only I knew more about you."

I smirked. "Well, with such a lovely subject, learning was my pleasure. I'd love to share more about me. In fact, maybe I should start by singing my favorite song."

Rylander coughed. "I don't think that's necessary, princess. Why don't you play something for the duke instead? Maybe the harp or—"

Conleth lifted his hand in a dismissive wave. "Oh no, I shall love to hear the princess sing. I imagine her voice draws quite the crowd." He covered his mouth with a fake cough, but the hint of a laugh slipped through.

I ground my teeth, my jawbone grating like a war cry. If he thought I'd succumb to an ounce of embarrassment, he was sorely mistaken. "Maybe I could sing for you right—"

Rylander threw his arm around my shoulders and pulled me into his side. "Why don't you get to know the duke a little later? There will be plenty of time down the road for you to dazzle him." My brother squeezed me, none too gently. "Dinner is almost served, and you know Hannah doesn't appreciate tardiness." Rylander looked down at my appearance. "I think you should change." He sniffed. "And bathe."

I pushed out of his embrace, ending up reluctantly closer to Conleth. "Fine."

Conleth stepped just as close as he'd dared on the island. He reached for my hand. Not wanting to cause my brother any more grief than I already had, I allowed it. He bowed and pressed his lips to my skin. It took all my strength not to withdraw, even if the warmth pooled in my stomach in a way I was not used to feeling nor wanted.

Lifting his head, he peered into my eyes, thumb tracing over my knuckles. My breath caught in my throat at the soft, intimate touch. I didn't have much experience with men. Okay, I had none. Attraction had never been at the forefront until now. And I hated my traitorous body for obliging it.

"I am most honored to meet one so full of beauty and grace as you, princess. I do look forward to getting better acquainted."

I curtseyed, matching his stare. "Your tongue waggles compliments with such ease, Your Grace."

Conleth smirked. His voice lowered so only I could hear. "It can do more than just that, Princess Savina."

My cheeks warmed and I stepped backward, jerking my hand away. "Good day." I pivoted on my heels and hurried out of the throne room.

I stomped back to my bedchamber and slammed the door shut. Under my breath, I mumbled curses to the gods about my fate. I pressed my forehead into the wood door, repeatedly banging it until footsteps from the balcony sounded.

Calli squawked, "What happened?" She ran to my side and clutched my arm, spinning me around to face her. "My gods, you look ill. Did you find them? Is Henrik okay?" Her face paled. "Oh no, did Captain Fredrick find out?"

I shook my head. "No, everyone's fine. Henrik is all healed and back to his up-to-no-good self."

Calli's brow lifted. "Okay, then..." Her eyes raked over me, lips twisting. "If that's not it, what's got you looking as though Hades is on his way to whisk you to the under-world?"

I walked past my niece, who had bathed and changed into fresh clothes. Signs of her recent fight had drowned in the flowered oils and soapy water. I threw my body onto my soft bed and sighed with eyes closed. "I met the Duke of Eloqua, my betrothed."

Calli jumped onto my mattress, jostling me. She snuggled into my side like a cat, hysterically laughing. "This is great. Oh gods, this is wonderful news. How poorly did it go? Is he as old as Edgar, or is he portly like Adelphi, or is he more feminine than our dear bloodthirsty Krinny?"

Her delight in my dismal future lightened my mood. Calli took the world by storm. I envied her fearlessness and her ability to find humor in the darkest hour. I pushed her off me and rotated to face her on my side. "The truth?"

She mirrored my pose and nodded feverishly.

"I've met him before." I propped my head in my hand and let a puff of air escape from my mouth that blew back Calli's blonde hair.

"How?" Her honey eyes danced. "You've never even been to Eloqua. Have you?" She sat up and leaned over her folded legs. "Tell me everything. Start from the beginning."

I pushed myself upright and imitated her posture. "You cannot tell a soul what I'm about to admit. You know how our family is. If Zeus found out..."

Calli waved me off. "Oh, shut it. You know I'd never tell a soul. We *all* have secrets." I knew she meant Henrik. If her parents ever knew the truth, they'd ban her from leaving the castle as well.

I held out my pointer finger. She smiled and wrapped her own around mine in a well-used show of secret confidences.

"When we visited Queen Yemma, he was there, on the beach. But he was different then." I squinted, trying to recall what stood out most. "More relaxed maybe. His hair was longer." I tapped my bottom lip. Maybe he recently cut it? But there was more. "He had different color eyes. They were beautiful, a prism of reds, oranges, and yellows, like stained glass filtering light." I shrugged. "I don't know how they changed, but they have. They're violet now. It's not right...It's not him."

"My gods, you're smitten." Calli bounced on the bed.

"I am not!" I ground my teeth.

Calli smirked. "Why else would you go on and on about the color of his eyes?" She impersonated a googly-eyed man trapped under a siren's spell.

I slapped her shoulder. For someone so rough and tough, Calli loved a good romantic story. But unlike me, she hadn't realized that was all they were. Stories...because almost no one got a happy ending fit for a tale.

"Okay, so if you are not smitten, then what *do* you feel?"

I waved off her dopey stare. "Anger for his foulness."

Calli cackled. "It sure doesn't sound like you think he's foul."

I tapped my knuckles against my lips. "How does someone change their eye color with the snap of a finger? Something's not right with him."

"Maybe they simply looked different in the sun. You did meet him on the beach. Were you wearing a hat to shade you from the glare?"

I shook my head.

"See? So maybe it was a trick of the light, or maybe you had a touch of sun madness. He's from Eloqua. I would expect him to have violet eyes."

"I was not suffering from heat. I know what I saw." I crossed my arms over my chest and refocused the memory. Maybe I had seen something different? But regardless, I remembered our conversation. That kind of pompous abrasiveness was hard to forget. "Trust me when I say I do not care for the man. He was most discourteous when we first met. He basically accused me of upsetting the birds with my singing."

Calli flashed me an all-knowing smirk. "Your singing is *only* for the birds."

I pushed her and she faked falling backward, pealing with grunted laughter. Something magical happened when Calli snorted that lit the whole world with sunshine. And it was contagious.

I tried to hide my own smile by biting the inside of my cheek. "I don't know why I tell you anything." I grabbed the pillow behind me and smacked her with it, flooding the room with both our laughter. I hugged the round cushion to my front. "He had business with Queen Yemma. Strange, right?"

Calli righted herself. "What kind of business?"

"I don't know. He didn't tell me. Only that he offered her a gift." I shrugged. "Or something like that. But when I pressed Rylander on our way home, he didn't mention meeting anyone on the island other than the sirens. And today in the throne room, your father didn't even know the duke's first name."

"That is odd. Why don't you ask Yemma at your wedding?" Calli's brow waggled. "You know, when you marry the man of many eye colors."

I huffed. "Do not remind me." I flung myself backward, staring at the ceiling. My voice lowered almost to a whisper. "I know Grandfather is hiding something important about me. I don't know what it is or why, but I can feel it's big."

Calli lay down next to me. Her shoulder grazed mine, and our fingers interlaced at our sides.

"If I didn't fear what Zeus would do to those I love, I'd challenge him for the truth." My chin trembled remembering Galen's gurgled last breath. "But I've seen firsthand what he will do, and I refuse to be the reason for his persecution."

"I'm sorry," Calli whispered.

I twisted my head and stared at her amber eyes filling with water—an abnormal admission of her internal turmoil written all over her face. "Why are you sorry?" A single tear escaped. "Calli, why are you upset?"

Dark lashes cast long shadows over her cheeks as she roved my face. "Because your life isn't your own." More tears fell down her cheeks and onto the bed. She didn't wipe them away like she usually did. In a rare moment, she allowed me to see her vulnerability. The innocence of it stabbed my heart. "I know how that feels. It's like none of us have a choice. We are all playing the roles we are told to, not the ones we choose. There will never be a world where

Henrik and I can be together. We will always be a secret, and he'll never be safe because of who I am."

I opened my arms and motioned for her to curl into them. My throat throbbed as I swallowed my own emotions. "Oh, Calli, it's okay. It'll be okay." I rubbed her back in soothing circles. Her sobs broke like a dam. That tiny hole in my heart ripped open and gushed everything I'd walled away. Why did it always feel like the gods controlled us, like we were puppets on a string? I loved my family, but at times I wondered if beyond that love was something else, something hateful. No matter what Krinny, Rylander, and the others said, I'd never believed my anonymity was to keep me safe. Rather, it felt like the slow build to a volcanic explosion. If a battle marched toward us, where did that leave me?

CHAPTER SEVEN

CONLETH

The gods really did curse man. Directly across the table sat the woman I met on the sirens' island, the woman I'd traveled here to pretend-wed, the woman I'd begrudgingly failed to pluck out of my head since our first encounter, the woman needed for my strategies to thwart Zeus's plan to annihilate humankind. The pure distraction she posed from my mission, my duty, left my skin crawling with unease. I couldn't let unknown feelings disrupt my purpose. I needed to refocus.

"Do people call you duke or Conleth?" Princess Calli asked in between chews of food. She sat wedged between Savina and her younger brother, Adelphi, named after the deceased King Delphi, who I knew better as Apollo.

"Calli," the queen warned from the other end of the table. "Eat your food and mind your manners. I'm sure the duke doesn't want to be battered by your questions." She sent me an apologetic nod as she reached for her goblet of wine.

I stabbed my fork into the rabbit meat laid on a bed of squash and fried potatoes. "I don't mind at all. Please, princess, proceed with your interrogation."

Calli flicked her free hand. "Oh no. Only Savina answers to that title." Calli winked at her aunt. She flung her blonde hair over her shoulder like it stood in her way of eating. "No need to call Adelphi prince, either. He's not the sort."

She elbowed the younger boy, muscular and broad for his age. He had short brown hair like his father's and a dimple shared with Savina, Calli, and Rylander. He wore the family attire of dark trousers and a light, long-sleeved tunic. In fact, the only people dressed in traditional palace garb were the servants and my people. The rest looked like townsfolk. Although strange, I admired the relaxed state of affairs.

"Get off me, Cal," Adelphi groaned, shoving her back. "You are so annoying." He had stayed quiet all evening, as if uninterested in the new company or his family. Instead, he ate like he hadn't in years, already on his third helpings. Definitely a growing boy.

Calli ignored her brother and leaned in. "My mother tried to fight her title, too." Her voice lowered. "You should have heard her and Father fighting over—"

"That's enough." Rylander shot his bold daughter a hard glare.

Calli shrugged like it was no serious matter and continued eating.

The rest of the table adopted Adelphi's silence, including my men.

Lou's manipulation affected their egos more than they'd admit, but regardless, they'd all had their fair share of complaints when I walked with them to the dining hall earlier this evening, accompanied by guards.

Vanden sat between Flick and me. Rylander occupied the head of the table, our elbows within inches of each other, sitting directly across from his wife. All the seats were filled except for one, next to Adelphi. Just as my focus lingered on the unclaimed space, a new voice spoke.

"What did I miss?"

Every head turned to the dining hall entrance, where a blond man strolled toward the table, rolling his sleeves to his elbows. With a scar running through his brow and over his eye, his face didn't quite match his casual appearance. His expression, even the slack way he held his jaw, appeared forced, as if it didn't belong to him. His skin seemed too pure, his hair too perfect, his eyes too punishing. I pushed away from the table to stand.

"Please, Your Grace." The man motioned for me to stay seated. "Do not get up on my account. The name's Smitter." He extended his hand, and when we shook, the sheer force rocked me. My gaze traveled from his grip to his almond eyes. He was not human, nor demi-god.

A shiver ran through me. This was a god. My brow rose. Was this Apollo's human form?

My lips pulled upward. "You look very familiar. Smitter, is it? Have we met before?" I broke our hold and shook my hand to let him believe he'd left a mark. If Smitter was indeed Apollo, the tactic should appeal to his ego.

He eyed my hand for the briefest moment before appraising me. "I doubt we've had the pleasure."

Distrusting. Strong. Intentionally late without worry about the cook's wrath, a scar on a perfect body as if playing games.... My gaze traveled to his tattooed forearm. A caduceus—a winged staff entwined by two snakes. Ice sloshed in my veins. Hermes. My gods, this was Hermes. The very god who'd threatened that I'd be entombed within the rock and taken down from Tartarus if I didn't yield to Zeus's threats. My fist curled around my fork in an attempt to misdirect my fury.

I turned away from him, back to the table. Savina stared, analyzing my reaction. Her eyes trailed down to my clenched hand. I released the utensil as she lifted her brow in a silent question.

I pressed my lips together and said nothing.

"These are Vanden and Flick, the personal guards of the Duke of Eloqua." Rylander extended his goblet toward my companions. "Men, Smitter was my second-in-command when I captained *The Sea Singer*. Now he is royal advisor to the guards." He paused, looking up at the ceiling. "When he's around, that is. We can't quite seem to take the sailor out of him."

My men all nodded in greeting as Smitter said, "It's nice to make your acquaintances."

"Where have you been?" Adelphi motioned with his eyes for Smitter to take the seat next to him. "I'm bored."

"Adelphi," Rylander scolded. He rubbed the arch of his nose with his free hand. "Would it be too much for me to ask that my children behave this evening?"

Calli's mouth twisted. "We are behaving."

"She has a point." Lou picked up a breadstick dribbled with butter and honey. "There's no blood, food throwing, or bickering." She smiled around a bite. "I'd say they are exceeding expectations."

"This is a unique household," Flick blurted.

I poked him with my fork under the table.

"Oof." Flick's glare burned a hole into my cheek.

"We aren't the typical royal home, but that does have its perks." Smitter slid into the seat next to Adelphi. A servant came to his side, serving him a still-steaming dinner. Smitter rubbed his hands together before claiming his fork and knife. "Any good stories told tonight?" He swiveled his gaze to the royals in turn.

"I don't think that's appropriate this evening." Rylander tossed Smitter the same warning he'd used on his daughter. "We have guests."

"What tales do you normally tell?" Vanden reached for the breadbasket. His desire for ale and women extended to food. He could give Adelphi a run for his appetite.

"Accounts of the gods," Calli answered, amber eyes shining.

My men's gazes flicked to me, but I didn't dare return their stares. Neither guilt nor fear ate at my bones. A simple story could never lead our audience to the truth of our mission or the truth to my real, godly name.

"Aye, that sounds like fun. May I tell one to the children?" I smiled, reclining in my seat.

"Oh, please." Adelphi braced his elbows on the table. His chin practically hit his water goblet. "I'd love to hear a new one. Savina, Smitter, and Father repeat their favorites...a lot."

"I can only speak of the ones I *know*, hence why I repeat." Savina prolonged her glare at her nephew before jutting her chin at me. "But I'm sure the duke has a tale worthy of your attention?" With a wave, she prodded me to speak. "Please, Conleth, I'd love to be enlightened. You've been so entertaining thus far." Sarcasm soaked her tone. Any road to friendship with the princess was going to be bumpy. I looked forward to the challenge even though every possible ending would earn me her hatred.

"Anything to entertain the Princess of Cava." I bowed my head. "Have you heard the legend of Prometheus?" I lowered my fork to the plate and placed my hands in my lap. Flick's contempt for my performance stung my shin—in the form of his boot beneath the table—but I ignored him.

The boy's face contorted. "What god is that?"

Vanden snorted. "The best one." He cheered me with his glass. "Do tell, Your Grace." He sipped his wine to hide his smile.

"I don't know about that," Smitter grumbled. "Prometheus is a brigand as far as I'm concerned." He leaned back in his chair. "Although I'd love to hear your accounts of his pursuits. Please, do tell the boy."

I addressed Adelphi. "Prometheus was born to the Titan Lapetus and the nymph Clymene. Although Prometheus was the son of a Titan, he helped Zeus gain victory in the War of the Titans, the celebrated 'Titanomachy.' Do you know who waged that battle?"

I could feel the heat of Savina's eyes on me, but I disregarded her and focused on her little nephew and his enthusiasm.

Adelphi peered up at the ceiling. "Aye, I think that war was between the Titans led by Kronos, the father of Zeus, and the Olympian gods, right?"

"That's correct," I commended. "Your Greek schooling has served you well."

"My grandfather has firsthand knowledge since you know he's one of the—"

Rylander coughed, gaining the attention of the room. "Yes, he has some of the best teachers." The king's pointed glare didn't escape my notice.

I knew the boy's grandfather was Apollo, but I couldn't acknowledge that without showing my hand. "Well, Zeus dethroned his father in that war. It established his reign as the chief god on Mount Olympus."

"Okay, but what does that have to do with Prometheus?" Calli asked before putting a spoonful of roasted squash in her mouth. She swallowed with a loud gulp. "Why do adults always meander about so much when they tell tales?"

My lips peeled upward. "We like to set the scene."

She shrugged one shoulder.

"Prometheus's loyalty in the battle wove strong ties between him and Zeus...at first. But as men multiplied and prospered on the earth, aided by Prometheus, Zeus became concerned about the humans' growing power."

"That's not exactly how I heard the story. I believe that—"

I dismissed Smitter with a flick of my hand. "This is the version I am familiar with."

"Let him tell it. I'm intrigued." Lou leaned forward like her son, interlaced hands under her chin. For the first time tonight, she had abandoned her wine. I had her interest if not suspicion.

"Thank you." I dipped my chin in a show of gratitude. "As I was saying, Zeus was nervous about mankind's rising strength. Prometheus first aroused Zeus's ire by duping him into choosing the worst part of a sacrificial bull. Prometheus wrapped the bones of the slain bull in fat and covered the best part, the flesh, with the animal's intestines. Zeus unknowingly chose the fat-covered heap of bones, while the filling flesh was given to hungry men by their patron Prometheus."

"That's hilarious. I bet Zeus was furious." Calli clapped.

"Calli," Rylander reprimanded, voice laden with exasperation.

Calli shoveled another spoonful in her mouth, not even glancing at her father. "As funny as I find Prometheus, he's sort of a rutting fool."

"Oh, my gods." Savina elbowed her niece in the side. "You should never speak ill of the gods."

Calli rolled her eyes.

"Prometheus was not a fool." The harsh bite in Flick's words echoed. "He loved humans and thought the gods misused their power and privilege." Flick's shoulders strained. "His goal has always been the protection of mankind from beings who believe themselves superior. His duty to those who cannot stand up for themselves is selfless and admirable."

I nudged Flick under the table. I knew he spoke from a place of love and devotion, but we oughtn't illicit concern for where our loyalties lay.

Smitter growled from the opposite end of the table. "I'd imagine Zeus would smite you for such a reckless account."

Lou leaned back in her chair. "Oh, I don't know. I actually find this story refreshing. Please, Conleth, do continue. I'd like to hear how it ends."

"As you wish." I smiled in the queen's direction. "An enraged, vengeful Zeus withheld fire, the most necessary element of civilization, from Earth, condemning humans to untold miseries. Think of all the things we use fire for."

Adelphi sat upright. "To cook, to keep warm, to see, to sterilize, to make steel." He ticked a finger off for each answer.

"Exactly. Prometheus knew that and soon came to the people's aid. He stole fire from the workshop of Hephaestus, the god of fire and patron of artisans and craftsmen, and passed it, hidden in a stalk of fennel, on to humankind."

Savina eyed Smitter at the mention of Hephaestus, and I wondered what that was about.

"And I am sure Zeus loved that." Calli chuckled. "He's not best known for being understa—"

"Knock it off." Savina nudged her niece again. "I mean it. Don't speak ill of the gods, especially Zeus." Real fear crept into her warning tone. If I had to guess, I'd say my little songbird didn't trust her grandfather or like him very much. I'd tuck that nugget of information into the back of my mind. It could work to our advantage down the road. "Their powers, even if they don't mean to inflict pain..." She looked away. "They still exist and are deadly."

I eyed Savina with suspicion. "Is the simple truth 'speaking ill'?" I asked, wanting to support Calli's candor. "Zeus isn't very understanding, but he is calculating and vengeful."

"It is not a god's fault that their breaking points, when pushed, are more powerful or destructive than humans'. Their powers are innate, but so are emotions, and neither are always so easily controlled." Savina sat taller.

For the first time since starting my story, I allowed myself a long look at her. Pythia's warning repeated in my head. There was something about her strong yet controlled posture matched by her beauty, her voluminous red hair, narrowed blue eyes, and slender frame that reminded me of a viper. A deadly animal, quiet in their environment, covered in iridescent scales, waiting to strike. Savina sat similarly, as though every inch and aspect of her might be considered a deadly weapon to be treated with immense care.

I no longer saw the girl I met on the beaches of Anthemusa, the damsel in distress I'd accused her of being. For the first time, I saw why she was so important to Zeus. She possessed the power to bring mankind to their knees. All I needed to know now was how Zeus intended to use her full powers of pestilence and plague on the night of her eighteenth birthday to extinguish mankind. But even if I didn't find out, I'd never let that day happen.

"Prometheus was a thief." Smitter's comment plucked me out of my thoughts.

Lou held up her finger. "I was once a thief. Do you hold disapproval for me as well?"

"That was different." Rylander broke his silence. "And you are now a queen." He winked.

Lou waved off her husband. "I'll always be a pirate." A faint smile crawled across her lips as if recalling a memory dear to her heart.

"His love for humans made him weak." Smitter's chin thrusted outward, still stuck on his hatred for Prometheus.

"Some may say Prometheus's love for humans made him a hero." Vanden dabbed his mouth with his napkin, then placed it beside his empty plate. "He did save mankind, you know, from extinction." If Vanden was looking for a thank you, he wouldn't be getting it from a god. My men knew who Rylander and his family were, but they didn't know who Smitter was. Yet.

Smitter's lips pressed together, his clenched jaw prompted a tic at his temple, but he remained silent.

"Zeus decided to punish Prometheus for making him look foolish to the other gods. He had Prometheus chained onto a rock on Mount Caucasus for eternity, subject to relentless torture. Every morning a vicious eagle fed on his liver, and each night, Prometheus's immortality assured it regrew, ready for the eagle's beak the next day."

"Ew!" Calli's nose twitched.

"Cool," Adelphi added.

"A punishment equal to the crime, if you ask me." Smitter snorted.

"No one did," Lou clucked.

I smiled at Lou's response, one I wish I could have retorted myself.

Savina leaned in. "What happened to him?" The skin around her mouth tightened with concern. "That must have been excruciating."

"It was. His endless pain, the punishment for having helped people, could be heard all the way to Mount Olympus. His screams of agony and despair pleased Zeus, as a testament to the success of his punishment and for the warning it gave his enemies. According to legend, the savage eagle would have feasted on Prometheus's liver until the end of time if the great hero Hercules hadn't wounded the eagle and freed Prometheus from his torture."

"Where is he now?" Savina's worry surprised me.

"No one knows." Smitter swallowed a forkful of potatoes. In between chews, he continued. "There are rumors as to his whereabouts, but many say he's gone mad and lives alone with the eagle who ate his liver." Smitter took a sip from his glass. "My stories are always more jovial, not depressing like this one."

"Yours are always more boastful and egotistical." Lou bared all her teeth in a big smile.

Calli blew her hair out of her eyes. "Isn't anyone worried about Prometheus's escape and what it might mean for humankind?"

Flick stiffened at my side, but all I could do was smile. Calli had brass, just like her mother. "And why do you say that?" I leaned back in my chair.

"Because Zeus isn't just going to accept that Prometheus is free, and what better way to get him out of hiding than go after the humans again?"

Vanden twisted his body, brushing his gaze over me like flames licking coal.

"Tell me, Calli, why do you think Prometheus will care, now knowing the price to pay for aiding mankind?" I leaned forward, my forearms on the table.

"Because if your story is true. He's the God of the People, and humankind is his greatest achievement."

An interesting thought. The only question was...whether or not, this time, I would succeed.

CHAPTER EIGHT

SAVINA

The following day, I vowed to stay away from the duke until I could chart my next steps. His presence not only unnerved me, it enraged me. After last night's dinner, Calli had laid siege to my room, going on and on about his many wonderful qualities: his great story about the god Prometheus; how handsome and strong he looked; how calm, cool, and collected he was with Rylander and Hermes. Even though I reminded her he had no idea of their true godly natures, she waved me off as if *why would that matter*. I had been just about to kick her and her adoration out of the room when her words struck me like lightning.

"I bet if you asked him to step aside, he'd oblige. I don't think he's the kind of power-hungry man who would force a woman into marriage to appease his kingdom and gain a title."

I might have disliked his manners when we met, and my betrothal had blindsided me, but maybe Calli was right. Maybe I could wriggle free of this contract and have a chance at real love, to live out the fairy tale that once existed in my heart. That little thread of hope she provided wove into my mind and stitched a pretty tapestry. I needed a plan before I stated my case to Conleth, though.

The sun climbed the sky on this side of the castle as I set out for the library the next morning. The natural illumination gave the mornings the best reading light. I'd spent many days inside the library, devouring books from all five isles. Unlike other chambers in the palace, the walls in the library boasted not vain portraits but rather rare and valuable novels, reports, artifacts, maps, and other educational materials I loved to peruse. In fact, I was pretty sure this room had remained untouched since the king before my father's rule—a man without extravagant taste in decor.

As I approached the half-opened door, I paused, hearing the undeniable harsh tenor of Zeus within.

"Why call me down to Earth before the wedding, then? I was with Thetis. I do not like being dragged away from the goddess I am trying to pursue, especially when my arse of a brother is also after her." The cold, unforgiving tongue cut through me and sent goose bumps prickling along my skin. I rubbed my forearms. "Too bad I cannot drown Poseidon in his own kingdom."

"I had no idea you were in the middle of wooing Thetis. Regardless, this feeling still vexes me," Hermes answered in a huff. "I assumed my esteemed father could sense what I am missing. Something is different about the duke. I don't like him."

"Don't you think you are overreacting, Uncle?" Rylander sounded miffed, like they had been at this conversation for a while.

"Not the slightest bit." My uncle's distaste for the duke rode his tone. "I'm the god of trickery. I know when something's awry, even if I don't know exactly what."

"Enough! Apollo's visions are consistent. This duke ends up protecting her. I don't care who he is or that he ruffles your pious feathers." The floor trembled, quaking in fright beneath Zeus's irritation. "We cannot let anything happen to her before her eighteenth birthday. She's too important and according to Cava law, she's supposed to be wed. This kills two birds with one stone."

"And why, again, is her eighteenth birthday so significant?" Uncle Hermes asked.

"Should I remind you that you are my son and not my keeper? Would a lightning bolt to your arse like when you were a child do the trick?" My grandfather's voice sent shivers down my spine. His need to protect me never felt like it came from a place of compassion. In fact, just the opposite. But now to discover my uncle had no idea of his intentions gave me greater pause. Why was I so important? He had thousands of grandchildren, yet none save me were locked away in a castle, safeguarded for their future. And what of my eighteenth birthday? What about my upcoming nuptials could be so important to the gods? None of this made sense.

"What if the duke is a threat to us?" My uncle asked.

"A human? A threat?" Zeus laughed without mirth. Every note expelled from his chest was calculating, controlled. "To me, God of the Sky?"

Ice trickled in my veins as I was drawn back to that horrible day in Jacar.

Zeus had stood directly in front of me, flinging blood off his blade in one fluid motion before tucking it back in its sheath. Galen fell to her knees at his feet, shaking hands hovering around the monstrous wound, head tilted in shocked confusion. She looked up at me.

"S-Savina. Help," she choked, blood pouring down her chin with each word. Her breath rattled in a useless lung. "I...I hurt myself." Already her skin was going ashen, her eyes glazing, her mind muddled by the cold hand of death.

I rushed forward, hands outstretched, the power I didn't yet understand warming my fingers. I could fix this.

Zeus's fist bunched in Galen's short hair and the sharp snap of her neck resounded in my head as he tossed her aside like a bit of rubbish. Her body thumped onto the path several feet away and rolled, lifeless limbs flopping at awkward angles.

"Galen!" My scream rent the sky as I ran to her, but I slammed into Zeus's outstretched palm as he stepped into my path.

His voice thundered as he gripped me by the collar. "If people know who you are and what your gift is, you could be taken from me. Your gift is not for them, ungrateful child. It is for me."

My teeth clacked together when he shook me, forcing more ferocious sobs from my throat. Tears fogged my vision as I thought of her lying there, motionless. Gone. "I don't understand. Why, Grandfather, why?"

"You let that urchin tear you from your bed. Let him lead you wherever he wished. You are too important, Savina."

Him? Zeus hadn't even bothered to know Galen before he butchered her. Hadn't bothered to notice she was a girl. My friend. My only friend.

"Do you wish to threaten my plans for your future?" His voice, deep as it was, took on a high, whining buzz when I peered around him to keep my watery eyes on the wavery outline of my dead friend. "You endanger yourself with your frivolous woman's heart. I cannot allow it. You shall never tell anyone outside of the castle who you are and what you can do. And you are not to speak a word of this. Do you understand?"

He shook me again, making my head bobble and my collar cut into my neck. "Do you?"

"Yes," I cried, sounding like a child even to myself.

"No more running around as you please. You cannot be trusted by yourself. You wouldn't wish to aid your grandfather's enemies, would you?" He stroked my hair too hard, unable to mimic true affection as well as he believed. "You want to help the God of the Sky, right?" His fingers knotted at the back of my head, making me whimper. "Answer me!"

"Yes, Grandfather."

"If you so dare to betray me again, I will kill your mortal friends starting with your human sister-in-law and working my way through all who had tended her ship like the bottom-feeders they are to this world."

I hadn't understood then, and I certainly didn't understand now. All the isolation, all the prison bars disguised as pretty rooms, none of it made sense. But Zeus's murderous eyes that day had instilled enough fear that I never wanted to find out.

CHAPTER NINE

SAVINA

I backed away from the door, about to pivot and run as far away as I could get, when the sound of a voice so familiar as if it were my own stopped me.

"Father, we are sorry for pulling you away from the sea goddess, Thetis. But maybe it is for the best. I believe Hermes is only trying to express concern for your granddaughter, knowing how important she is..."

Papa! Warmth flooded me and I didn't even wait to hear the end of the sentence. My heart swelled, my throat constricted.

I pushed open the door, my legs moving of their own accord. "Father!" I shouted as I ran into the room, thankful to be in trousers instead of a dress. My heart and footsteps pounded in sync.

Apollo relaxed in the large armchair opposite my uncle. The legs curved into lion's claws at the bottom, matching the desk Rylander leaned against. When Father spotted me, the tips of his lips pulled into a wide grin that showcased bright teeth as he stood and extended his arms in welcome.

I ran into his embrace as if I were five years old again. "Oh, Father, I've missed you."

Of course, Apollo no longer looked like King Delphi. He'd faked his death eight years ago, but his crystal blue eyes were the same and so were his warm hugs. His now sun-kissed blond hair curled around cheeks both red and youthful, and the laugh lines he'd once carried were smoothed and taut. In fact, he appeared younger than even Rylander.

"My darling Savina, I've missed you, too." He rubbed my back. The warmth of his fingers soothed the chill Zeus had incited. "How are you, my child?"

Hot tears cascaded down my face as I squeezed him. I wished he'd never returned to Mount Olympus and had stayed with me instead. In the last eight years, I had only seen him four times. He took a piece of my heart each instance he left.

"Better now that you're here," I mumbled against his white tunic in between soft sobs.

"No affection for your grandfather?" Zeus's voice rattled me. I froze in my father's arms.

"Savina?" Zeus questioned, as if maybe I didn't hear him.

My father whispered "Go to him" in my ear and pushed me away.

I twisted and forced a smile. Zeus wore his status as the all-mighty ruler of Olympus no matter what visage he chose when roaming Earth. His outline glowed in the morning sun, bathing him in the soft, golden hues. Tall and broad like Rylander and Apollo, Zeus was fit, with hair black as night. Stark white streaks ran through each lock in calculated waves, the strands shorn close to his head. When taking a mortal image, he never wore his hair long like the other men in my family. No, he liked to mirror human soldiers, creating the appearance of an older warrior. A trimmed salt and pepper beard covered his chiseled jaw. But it was the steel blue eyes he shared with Apollo and myself that cut right through me. His gaze held no warmth, as if he saw me as a resource rather than a person.

I swallowed and walked into my grandfather's opened arms. "I'm so glad you're here." I forced the lie from my lips. The taste of acid burned my tongue.

His limbs wrapped around me like a snake coiling around its prey. With one squeeze, he could smite me from the world and send me to Hades's kingdom. I stiffened under his hold, my breaths short but controlled, a trick my father taught me when trying to calm my abilities. Zeus released me, and I slowly stepped backward, mechanically drawing closer to the safety of my father's side.

"I can't believe you are getting married." He tilted his head. His examination of me clung to my skin, itching so badly I wanted to crawl out of it. "It won't be long until you change the course of the world. I couldn't be prouder." His smile didn't reach his eyes. It merely bared his teeth—cold, calculating, ruthless. There was a reason his brethren feared him.

Someone knocked at the door and relief flooded my veins at the interruption.

"Enter," Rylander instructed.

The door opened, and Edgar, Rylander's faithful steward, pushed through. His deep brown eyes scanned the room, ignoring the gods and landing on me. His red-coated lips lifted, accentuating his white-painted face and rouge-tinted cheeks. "Princess Savina." He lowered his head. Tied in a satin knot, his curly silver hair fell over his shoulder.

"Good morning, Edgar." I smiled.

He straightened, eye on his king. "I am so sorry to bother you, Your Majesty." He bowed with right hand over his heart. This time when he rose, his warm demeanor shifted into a palpable uneasiness. He clutched at his gold-trimmed red velour jacket as if beset upon by a sudden winter breeze. "Queen Elouise wanted me to inform you not only is *The Black Hollow* at the port, but *The Serpent's Snare* docked last night. Do you wish to send guards into town to discourage any problems? Your wife has offered her own services, shall you desire to send her as well."

"Of course she has." Rylander rubbed the arch of his nose. "Please let the queen know she is most needed at the castle and not fighting in the streets of Cava. We have soldiers to keep the peace."

Afraid Zeus could hear fear pummeling my heart, I bit my lip, trying to control my pulse. If Calli got wind of this, she'd run out to try to protect Henrik. Two pirate ships never docked here at the same time. It was forbidden for obvious reasons.

I pretended to ignore the conversation and strolled to the wall containing a series of arching alcoves three times my height and an arm's length across. A ladder on both sides of the room rolled from end to end to bring every book within reach. Shelf upon shelf, the tomes were bound in a variety of dark colors from deep reds to forest greens to oceanic blues. My hands grazed the spines as though searching for something specific, but really, it was just a distraction.

"Has *The Serpent's Snare* started to unload?" Rylander pushed off his desk. He might not have known about Calli's involvement with the captain of *The Black Hollow*'s son, but he did know that two swashbucklers strutting around Cava's port was a recipe for disaster, especially two so notorious for trying to slash each other's throats.

I rounded the king's grand desk, a monolith of dark-stained wood carved with vines, and came next to

Rylander's side. Our shoulders brushed. The heat of his apprehension washed over me, mixing with my own trepidation.

"Indeed. It's reported the crewmen are going to the Lyre of Hermes Tavern, which is a frequented place of *The Black Hollow*'s men, especially..."

Oh no, that would mean...

"Captain Fredrick. He'd be there, too." I breathed out loud what I had intended to keep in my head. My voice faltered.

Apollo and Hermes both regarded me with pursed lips. Many a time, I had been reminded to never show emotion—especially vulnerability—in front of Zeus. The inflection in my tone condemned me as surely as did my compressed expression.

"Are you frightened for the lives of the pirates, my dear?" My grandfather's eyes lit up like I'd fed his wrathful cunning a delicious morsel. Zeus used words, body language, and reactions as weapons he'd later utilize against you.

I straightened my spine. "No, not frightened." I didn't dare address him with a title in front of an oblivious Edgar. "It's just that, with the duke here, I wouldn't want our sovereign to look weak or ill-prepared." I stood firm as the lie slid off my tongue. "It would be beneficial to keep the Duke of Eloqua unaware of any exposed enemies like the pirates."

Zeus's speckled white brow curved upward.

Hermes stepped forward. "Princess Savina is right." My uncle turned to Rylander, but I didn't miss the way his eyes sliced over me. He, too, questioned my words. "We need to act. If the soon-to-be crowned king sees turmoil amongst our people, he may change his mind about the upcoming nuptials."

Zeus's face reddened. "That is unacceptable. King Rylander." Zeus spat the superior label, hating to address his demi-god grandson with any form of reverence just to keep up appearances. "We must deploy your best men at once."

"Calli had the same response. The women are fierce in the royal family." Edgar puffed his chest with pride.

Tension bounced off the walls while terror seized my chest and spread like fungus to my esophagus. My body vibrated with the need to dart out of the room and find her. If I didn't catch Calli before she left, she could put us all at risk—the more so with Zeus here. I feared any punishment he might personally serve for interference with my upcoming wedding.

I sucked in a breath, asserting my bravery. "I must go. I will find the duke and distract him while you mind the problem in town. We must keep him away from the potential incident."

Zeus nodded. A proud smile wobbled on his mouth. He thought I was protecting my upcoming marriage rather than my niece. He had no idea his great-granddaughter Calli would stop at nothing to defend those she loved, even if that meant getting between two hostile pirate crews.

No one questioned my request to leave. Once out of the library, I fled through the castle. My boots pounded into the marble floors, echoing in the corridor, when I ran right into Krinny.

"Princess?" She steadied my shoulders, her dark brows pulled together.

I wheezed. "I..."

Krinny wouldn't understand. I had to tell her something, though, or she'd never let me out of her sight.

"What's going on?"

I squeezed my eyes shut, knowing I had no choice but to deceive her.

"Apollo and Zeus are here. You need to get to Lou before she goes into town to confront Captain Fredrick and Captain Niles. The gods will never forgive her if she got involved."

Krinny's eyes bulged. "Two pirate ships are docked, and the gods are here?"

I nodded, biting my lower lip.

Krinny released me. "Stay in your room." She wagged her pointer finger. "I mean it. Do not leave this castle. I'll go to Lou and talk some sense into her. I won't let anything happen to our girl."

I forced a smile while the guilt ate at my stomach like moths to wool. But I had to save my niece. If Zeus found out about her loyalty to humans, especially Henrik, he'd strike against him as his target and possibly ending her life as well.

As Krinny vanished around a bend, I resumed my own pursuit. I busted through the door to Calli's room. My biggest fear slapped me across my face. Her window stood open, the drapes swaying in the breeze. She had escaped, and I knew exactly where she'd gone.

CHAPTER TEN

CONLETH

P lum-red hair cloaked by a floppy-brimmed hat passed our table at the Lyre of Hermes Tavern. I whistled to gain the woman's attention, and she halted. Our eyes met, and she inclined her head—my smile widened. General Ballas navigated her way through the throng of people until she reached our table. Her pale-yellow dress stood out amongst the wenches and rough pirates that frequented the establishment.

"Gentlemen." She slipped her legs over the bench and sat. Vanden slid a tankard her way.

"Thank you." She took a sip, licking her plump lips as she placed the mug back down. Her rosy cheeks puffed in and out. "I'm still getting used to legs—off the homeland, that is. It's oddly exhausting here. So many unnatural hills. Such hard ground. If I am honest, this isn't the form of choice for me." Her smile remained good-natured, never shifting into the sultry leer or vicious snarl the word "siren" evoked.

"Ballas, these are my men, Vanden and Flick." I nodded to each one in turn. "Men, this is Queen Yemma's head guard, General Ballas. She will aid our efforts."

Ballas glanced around and leaned into the table. Her dress pulled taut to her shapely curves. "I have a message from the queen." She swept her hair forward, the ends trailing down her shoulders. Her talons fidgeted through the strands. Although subdued in this form, the nails stretched past a normal human length.

"The queen wonders if it is wise keeping Princess Savina in the dark. She encourages you to tell her the truth. As do I. Savina is a smart woman. Her suspicions will grow, especially considering she saw you on the island, and when we get near, she may even—"

I held up my hand and shook my head. "I understand Yemma's concern, but I can't gamble that Savina will understand or even believe me."

"What if I talk to her? She's known me most of her life. She trusts me," Ballas pleaded.

Flick reached for Ballas's hand and covered it with his own. "She may trust you, and I imagine you care deeply for her. But you'll be asking Savina to believe you over her father and grandfather. We all eat lies when our heart is hungry. Most children yearn for their parents' approval and love." He gave her a soft smile. "I imagine the princess is no different. At dinner last night, she was very quick to defend the gods, especially when her niece spoke ill truths. To compete with her supreme devotion isn't strategic, it's foolish." He squeezed her hand. "Remember, it's not just her life we are fighting for; it is all of mankind's."

Ballas's eyes narrowed. I admired her loyalty to Savina. I knew her people had been freed from the bloodlust of their evil ruler, Queen Lorelei, by Rylander and Lou. They would forever hold that debt, and I understood. Regardless, the bigger picture rivaled their gratitude. I couldn't allow the sirens to lose sight of it.

"Your love for the princess is one of the many reasons I asked Queen Yemma for help." My hand itched where the pink raised scar on my palm still healed. Even as a god, such an unusual cut would take time before its mark thinned and softened. The scar stood as a reminder. "A blood oath cannot be broken." I lifted my finger. "However, if you'd like to wait for us back in the water by the docks, you may."

"No." Ballas's face turned to stone. "We will not leave Princess Savina here on land unprotected. We stay."

"Hey, what do we look like? Mutton stew?" Vanden threw back his ale. "We are pretty competent bodyguards, General Ballas. In fact, no woman has ever complained." His playful smile joined his wiggled brow.

Flick glared, shaking his head at Vanden like a parent.

Ballas's lip curled to accommodate extending fangs. Sirens weren't known for their humor, especially when it came to the laws under the Treaty of Anthemusa. When Apollo crowned Queen Yemma, she had taken a verbal oath to protect mankind at all costs, even from the gods themselves. Part of our blood oath aligned with their accord.

"All right. That's enough." I patted Vanden's forearm. "Have we secured a ship?"

"Not yet. But we should have one within the week, big enough for us all to set sail should the sirens want to join the crew aboard."

"Then it's settled." I raised my glass, and the others' followed. "We kidnap the princess, and we take her to Anthemusa."

CHAPTER ELEVEN

CONLETH

I brooded while my companions talked over the details. This was not a plan I enjoyed. Not one I ever thought I'd utter. Yet the alternative—Pythia's original strategy—wouldn't just clip my songbird's wings but silence her for good.

When the High Priestess had first found me, I still feared the dawn. Though Hercules had snapped my chains like twigs and I'd left the hilltop behind, my liver still panged with remembered agony in the glow of sunrise. When she'd arrived at the roadside inn run by Vanden's family, I'd been holed away in a darkened room, trying to control the shake of my hand enough to pull back the curtain and feel the day's new warmth on my face.

Flick came to fetch me, and I startled at his knock.

"Easy," he said, face poking through the crack.

I swallowed and straightened, still reluctant to show my weakness. A foolish, fruitless grasp at godly pride, since he and Vanden had seen me at my worst those first two mornings, paralyzed in the bed, screaming, waiting for the eagle to break through the glass pane and bury his hooked beak in my flesh.

"My patron, there is a woman here to see you. She claims she is High Priestess of Apollo, come with a dire message. Will you give her audience?"

I latched my consciousness to the words to bring myself out of frightful visions. "Yes." A High Priestess would be better woven into the intentions and actions of Olympus than I at that moment. "And no need for such formalities, Flick. My mere presence endangers your life. A man who faces such peril with me is a friend, not a subject."

He bowed, then thought better of it halfway through, jerking upright with an awkward grin. "Habit," he mumbled.

My responding chuckle loosened the knots in my chest, letting me breathe easier as I followed him down the fragrant cedar stairs, through the common area, into the kitchens where Vanden's mother and sister readied the guest's provided breakfast, and into the family's private office in back.

Vanden hardly noticed my entry, but the woman he ogled from his perch atop his father's desk turned at the sound of the door. Her dense black braids, threaded with yellow and indigo flowers of all shapes, swung around her hips, and she was clad in golden robes. The colors marked her as a servant of Apollo, but her eyes...

"You are an oracle," I said when she fixed me with what were once hazel irises, now glossed over with a milky film.

"I am Pythia, the Oracle of Delphi." She tipped her head and clasped her tawny brown hands. "And you are Prometheus, God of the Humans, which is why I have come. The truth of what I'm about to tell you is shrouded even to my patron—hidden by his father, Zeus. But I have seen through the eyes of Apollo's offspring a future most dire, brought about by your escape."

A hole punched through my heart instead of my liver and I reached out blindly, finding Flick's arm ready to steady me.

"Of course," I rasped, the room fading to foggy shapes for a moment. "Of course he would punish them. He knows it will cut deeper than the eagle's beak."

"Indeed," said Pythia. "It is why I have come to you now. You have the power to stop this senseless slaughter?" She took two steps toward me, ignoring Vanden watching her swaying hips, though I knew—as he probably did not—that she could see him even with her eyes dimmed and her head turned. "Will you hear me out?"

I expelled a trembling breath and drew a stronger one. "Yes." I straightened on my own power and met her eye with jaw tight. "How many shall die?"

She stared steadily back, mouth an unreadable line, her sorrow contained to her voice. "A near annihilation. A fresh slate from which to carve a new image that better serves his pride."

I kept my legs, muscles hardened against the shock by a fury that fanned my inner flame. "But how? Not even his thunderbolts—"

"The very offspring I spoke of," Pythia interjected. "Apollo's daughter, birthed from his human queen on Cava. The people adore him there, though by a different name, King Delphi, for he has reigned with a benevolent hand."

I ground my teeth but didn't interrupt or contradict the lauding of her patron. It would be no use.

"But from his daughter's hands will come destruction. Apollo suspects it, fears it, but Zeus has not revealed the truth, and the girl's powers have not fully manifested. Princess Savina is but a child now, and a gentle soul, but should Zeus put his mighty hand upon her and bend her to his bidding, she will smite the humans with a mightier sword than ever seen before."

I felt Flick and Vanden's eyes searing through me. Their terror fell upon me like Atlas's fated weight. I could not look at them. Instead, I stayed strong on their behalf.

"She has dominion over death, as Hades does?"

Pythia shook her many braids. "Hades rules the dead, and the Fates cut the threads of life one by one, but Savina holds both creation and destruction in her veins. She has her father's power of healing, but hers shall surpass even his. And what she can give, she can take away."

Pythia upturned both palms, raising them in turn as she said, "In one hand, she holds near immortal health, in the other, decimating pestilence. On the eve of her eighteenth birthday, she will come into her full power, and Zeus intends to claim the darker of her gifts." Her voice deepened into a thunderclap that shook the walls. Her head tipped back, her faded irises vanishing entirely in a wash of pure white. "One dip of her fingers into the soil upon which men walk, and they shall fall in droves. One touch of their water, and they will choke on the remnants of their souls as they flee their bodies. The underworld shall be overrun with waves of dead." A wind without a source tugged at my hair as Pythia leveled eyes of solid pearl upon me. "And when the dying cry out to you, Prometheus, you will be powerless but to answer, and Zeus shall make mercy a humiliation. He shall bring you to your knees, only to save a pitiful few who will then revile you, and then return you to your punishment tenfold. No prayers will come to the gods from human lips. All but Zeus shall weaken, and he will craft a new race of feeble minds to pay him fealty."

The wind died down, and Pythia's hazel irises peeked from behind the fog, broken and wet with melancholy. Vanden slipped off the desk, boots striking the floor, a punch-drunk expression blanking his paled face. I fought to catch my breath.

Flick swallowed hard. "Th-That can't be true." He swiveled my way, eyes searching for reassurance. When I offered none, he murmured, "At least say it can be stopped."

"Any future can be shifted," I said with a confidence I didn't feel. But I hated to see them so desperate.

"Then we'll help you change it." Flick dropped into a shaky bow at the waist. "We will swear anything."

"Even our lives," said Vanden, matching Flick's position.

I coaxed them both upright with my hands on their shoulders. "I accept your aid readily, but I do not ask your fealty, friends. You have lifted me up in my time of need, and so shall I you."

I brought my forehead to both of theirs to seal the pledge, then turned to the High Priestess who looked on with subtle approval.

"What must I do to prevent your vision?"

"Kill the girl," she said, voice as stone. "Eliminate her wretched power before it comes to be."

My brows drew together. "You called her a gentle soul."

"Yes. Pure and fiercely steadfast in her compassion. But Savina cannot withstand her grandfather's might. Her power has no effect on him, but the mortal half of her being gives him sway over her. What he will make her do will shatter her mind and her soul. You will do her a mercy with your blade."

Murder a child? A child who was as much a pawn to Zeus as all his demi-god offspring? I tried imagining such a thing—a frightened girl in my grip, a blade in my other hand—and my every sinew revolted. My power flared with indignity and revulsion, heating my fingertips with an ire directed inward. I couldn't. I wouldn't.

"I cannot harm an innocent," I declared to the room. "There must be another way."

Pythia hung her head. "Only her death ensures the land's continuance. Prometheus"—a single tear fell off her jaw and splashed her golden robe—"you do not understand. You have not seen. The heart of this land will cry out. Birds shall fall from the sky. Only the gods, their offspring, and beasts touched by divine power shall maintain dominion. The few humans to remain will bear chains tethered to the gods and their whims and have nothing to sustain them."

My mouth dried, but again that horrendous image of senseless violence against a soul free of wicked intent repulsed me. "To sacrifice one to save many is still a heinous act. You said the girl has the power to heal, beyond Apollo's capabilities. How can I deny mankind one such as she? How can I break her life in my hands and call myself different from Zeus?" I made fists at my sides. "No. I won't. I'll find another way."

Pythia drew herself up as if absorbing the tension spilling off my companions. She studied me long and hard. "You have seven years until the princess's birthright is realized. Seven years to find your different way. I suggest starting by laying a plan to get close to the princess, despite Zeus's watchful eye on the child. She will be wed before her eighteenth birthday, per tradition. You might make yourself a tempting suitor. I can put whispers in the gods' ears that will help support your efforts." She paused on her way to the door, a finger raised. "But heed me now. Should the year come with no other solution, do Savina a mercy and make it quick."

When King Rylander accepted the new, young Duke of Eloqua's proposal, only one piece remained. Finding a way to save the princesses life.

An idea came to me in a dream mere months before our departure to Cava. The sirens had a new queen, sworn to protect man. They were offspring of gods, imbued with mystical powers they imparted to their island. Savina's power could do no harm there, according to what Pythia had revealed. So, a letter was penned, a voyage made, and a deal struck.

Little had I known that my task would bring me to Savina faster than intended. Or that she'd enchant my sensibilities so. How observant she was. To call me a sculptor.

Not an hour before her song assaulted my ears and drew me out, I'd knelt on Anthemusa at a spot where the sand of the shore met the soil of the jungle. With a handful of each, the work began. Each time I used my ability to craft, a sweeter warmth than the blaze brought on by my connection to fire filled my chest—a dance of sparks that flickered in the heart of every person, to a tune of expression only humans could make. There was such a rich array of feelings in mankind. They were beautiful. That beauty, that tune, guided my hands, but I had to cut it short. I wasn't making whole figures that day. Just legs. The legs Zeus would deny the sirens for daring to have power that challenged his brother Poseidon's. That was the gift I presented to Queen Yemma in her throne room, so that her peaceful people could be free to walk on all land.

From her pool, riding atop a shell-shaped wave, she'd extended her hand to me and drew a marked knife across my skin. And I did the same to hers. As we clasped our hands, General Ballas had cut her own hand and placed it atop ours to witness and seal the oath in a spray of fire and saltwater that turned to curls of steam bathing our faces.

The clanking of tankards drew me back to the tavern. So many souls gathered just in this small space. Millions more at risk. Because their ancestors and I had sought freedom from Zeus's tyrannical, crushing hand. My eyes traced over each of my companions, willing to risk their lives for a mission thrust upon them. Yes, we had no choice but to kidnap the princess. But I'd do it a thousand times over if it meant the only blood spilled by Zeus's wrath was mine.

CHAPTER TWELVE

CONLETH

I sat back, my belly full of bread and ale. A familiar streak of brown and red passing the tavern window drew my eye—dark cloak, streaming fiery hair. What was she doing back here? Did she visit the tavern daily? How foolish of a princess to put herself at constant risk. Not a second later, a bald man wearing a dark green tunic cast a glance over his shoulder and then followed her.

My gaze flitted across the room, looking for the small boy and the Jacar healer, thinking perhaps the princess met them here regularly. Could the man following her be with them? After several moments, I found neither them nor her in the pub. My insides rumbled, the same sinking feeling right before a skirmish.

I lifted out my legs from under the table and stood. "I'll be back."

Ballas and my men rose in unison.

"Sit." I waved them back into their seats. "If we all go outside, it'll cause a scene. I won't be in any danger. I'll be only a moment."

Vanden ground his slanted teeth, baring them for me to see, but acquiesced. The other two followed his lead, worry etched in the creases of their faces. Sometimes I believed my comrades forgot I was a god. Even though their concern meant the world to me, I didn't want them to waste it.

Putting them in danger would do more harm than good. I tossed them a convincing smile before turning away.

I slipped out the back door, and as I looked toward the horse troughs where I'd witnessed the boy and Savina yesterday, I froze.

Princess Savina, Calli, and the magically healed boy all stood in defensive positions, facing down three men taunting them with swords and daggers.

I snarled, drawing the men's attention. "What form of intimidation is this?"

"This has nothing to do with you," the one in the front said in a nasally drone, thanks to what looked like a recent break in his nose. Above the purpling bump and watering eyes, his hair was wrapped tightly against his head with a forest green bandana. "Be on your way." He waved me off with this blade, swishing a similar bandana that hung from his weapon's hilt—a pirate's token.

The young women glanced over their shoulders. While Calli perked up at the sight of me, her smile wide, Savina's shoulders slumped, followed by a frown.

"You heard the man, be on your way." Savina straightened and flicked her wrist.

I chuckled. Even when attempting to save me, she didn't hold back her ire. She didn't believe I could defend myself. Meanwhile, her companions were two children.

"As much as I appreciate the lady and her deep concern for my wellbeing, I think I'll stay." I stepped forward, aligning myself next to Savina. Standing in the heat radiating off her body, my chest squeezed as my heightened senses focused on how her quickened breath made her lips puff out into a cute pout. I shook away the thought and leaned into her, my mouth grazing her ear. "We always have such a lovely time together." She shuddered. "I wonder what married life will be like."

"You need to leave. Now." She attempted to step away, but I wrapped my arm around her waist and pulled her to my side.

"What are you doing?" she hissed.

"Let him stay, lass," said the leader, wiping crusted blood off his lip. "It'll be a funeral for four then."

With the pointer finger of my free hand, I counted the men in front of me. "You mean for three."

The boy to my other side laughed. "I like you. Name's Henrik. Pleased to meet you," he said, not taking his eyes off the brigands.

I returned the courtesy. "Conleth. The pleasure is all mine." When the boy flashed a smile my way, I tipped a pretend hat, and Calli laughed.

"Nice of you to join us." Calli waved. "We've been looking for a fourth."

Savina growled. "No, we have not. And we are not turning this into a regular occurrence." This time when she stepped out of my hold, I let her. "We are not a crew." She turned toward me. "You must go. I mean it. This is not a joke. You'll get hurt."

The larger bald man snickered, lust in his panting breath. "Yes, leave. I have plans for the lasses, and I won't share." His tongue darted out of his mouth like a lizard and wiggled fiercely at the women.

"Ew." Calli's lips twisted as her nose scrunched.

"Take a step too close to them, and I'll cut off your member." Henrik flourished his sword.

This friendship wove a thick web. Calli and Savina considered this boy a friend worth fighting for, of that I was certain, but the possessiveness in Henrik's voice suggested Calli might hold a stronger claim on his young heart. It couldn't be Savina. From the interaction yesterday, I'd say she thought of Henrik more as an annoying brother.

The man barked at the boy, snapping his teeth like a savage. My patience thinned, body bristling with the need to teach these men some manners. Protecting humans sometimes meant protecting them from themselves.

"I'll give you one chance to walk away, and we will pretend like this never happened." I crossed my arms over my chest.

"What are you doing?" Savina whispered. "You are *not* helping."

The bald man threw his head back and guffawed. "Or I'll tie you up and give you the chance to watch while they pretend they don't like what I give 'em." A gob of saliva and tobacco spit dribbled from his mouth.

Henrik lunged, but I caught him by his dirty tunic and pulled him back. I whispered in his ear, "All emotion and no strategy will never win a battle. It'll only give your opponent an advantage. Never give them control. Never. It is the most powerful defense you have."

The pirates laughed.

Henrik lifted green eyes backlit with a fire and clenched his teeth. Only a slight dip of his chin told me he understood. The moment was exactly what I needed. The pirates' swords lowered by fractions in loosened grips, believing their largest threat distracted.

Twisting Henrik behind me, I sprinted with godly speed toward my enemies. My fist drove deep into the first man's throat and knocked him onto the ground. He grabbed for his neck, wheezing as red and purple splotches dotted his face. Passing him, I kicked at the tendon of the bald thug's knee with the heel of my boot. He bellowed like the Minotaur, clutching at his leg. I snatched his weapon, tossing it backward to Henrik before catching the arm of the third man whose sword paused inches from my neck. I twisted his limb until I heard a crack. He tumbled to the ground, screaming in agony. All three men rolled on the floor moaning like wounded animals, making the nearby horses snort and stamp.

The girls gasped from somewhere behind me, but my focus remained on the pirates. "Leave. Go back to where you came from and be done with Cava," I ordered, standing over them.

"We can't do that, stranger," a low, gravelly voice said from the darkness of the surrounding alleys.

All four of us looked beyond the hitching posts. Over thirty armed pirates stood in three collective lines of force. The speaker wore a captain's hat that bobbed over the heads of his men as he stepped forward. Dark bushy eyebrows over calculating eyes matched his long, pulled back hair. A deep, silvery scar curled from his forehead, along his cheek, past a sharp chin, and down to his neck, like a snake that slithered up and down his skin. "We just want the boy. I have no use for the women. Take them in peace."

My gaze volleyed to Henrik, then back to the pirate captain, brow furrowing. "Why do you want the boy?"

Henrik crossed his arms with a defiant huff.

"His father is a..." The captain tilted his head, mouth hooked in a foreboding grin. "A friend of ours, and we want the boy present for a little discussion we've been meaning to have."

"No," Calli growled. "Over my dead body."

"That can be arranged, young lady. We have no qualms about killing women." He gestured to me. "But to oblige a worthy foe such as your friend here, we are willing to make a trade."

Calli moved to step forward, but Savina seized her in a stiff, one-armed hug, whispering something into her younger niece's ear. Calli nodded and stood her ground.

I appraised the pirate lord as I walked closer to my three troublemakers...or trouble-finders. "I'm afraid the boy stays with us, Captain...?" I threaded my fingers into Savina's, afraid if I didn't hold on to her, she'd act without thought. To my surprise, the only resistance she gave me was a strong squeeze that cracked a knuckle or two, letting me know she wasn't thrilled with the gesture. In all my time with women, I'd never laid claim to one before, but something about the way these men drank her in frayed my every nerve.

"It's Captain Niles of *The Serpent's Snare*, and I'm afraid you're well surrounded." He chortled, opening his arms to encompass all his men.

My pressed lips curved into a smug smile, eyebrow arching. "Intimidation won't work on me." I motioned for Calli and Henrik to move behind us. "We will be on our way. Do have a lovely day, Captain Niles." I ushered our group toward our only escape between the men nursing their bones on the ground and the dense line of pirates ready to pounce.

"What? Are you mad?" Savina grumbled beside me.

"Have it your way." Captain Niles snarled. "Grab the boy. I don't care what happens to the rest."

A rumble of boots on the gravel thundered behind us. I shoved the girls and Henrik ahead of me and turned, holding up my hands to summon my powers. Flames licked my skin. Fire poured out of my palms and lit up the pebbles at my feet. I motioned with my fingers to raise the blaze into a wall over ten feet high. By the time it burned out, we would be long gone. I turned to the others.

"Run!"

CHAPTER THIRTEEN

SAVINA

S weat trailed down my neck and spine as my arms pumped at my sides. Our boots pounded over the dirt onto the cobblestone road.

"What was that fire?" Henrik wheezed.

That was an interesting question that no doubt wouldn't be answered until we were all safe. Our escape was more important than the earth-shattering truth—Conleth, my betrothed, the Duke of Eloqua, could summon flames, a power no mortal man should hold.

"Ketner's house," Calli called out as she swept away strands that clung to her wet face. She darted ahead of me, her blonde hair swinging from side to side.

I grabbed her arm and pulled her back in line with me. "No, Cal. No one can know where he lives."

Calli ripped her arm out of my grip and made a right down the next alley, ignoring my warning and heading straight to Ketner's sanctuary. I growled, increasing my pace to match hers.

"She can take the memory." Henrik huffed and puffed behind us. I looked over my shoulder at him. His face, void of concern, told me one thing: he trusted Calli. "I let her do it all the time when I see something that's too dangerous for me to know. It doesn't bother me."

I noticed Conleth lifting his brow at the comment, but thankfully he stayed silent and continued to sprint. It would be a conversation we'd have to have at another time. Getting away from an angry mob of pirates who wanted to slice and dice us topped our priority list. But I wouldn't be able to forget what I had just learned. I wondered how many memories Calli had stolen from Henrik.

"We will talk about this later." I pinned my gaze on Calli, but she kept sprinting, her eyes trained on our goal.

If the king and queen ever found out the extent of Ketner's involvement in our dangerous activities, Rye and Lou wouldn't be forgiving or understanding. I couldn't pinpoint the moment Ketner had become our knight in shining armor, but I also couldn't remember a time he wasn't there for us either.

Calli burst through Ketner's door, Henrik right behind her. I fell back and followed through with Conleth. Calli leaned over, her hands resting on her thighs as she breathed heavily. Henrik threw his head back against the wall, staring at the ceiling as he sucked in air. Oxygen wheezed through my nose. Conleth's chest puffed in and out, matching my own.

Ketner sat behind his desk holding a vial of blue liquid sizzling with white steam. His free hand froze over a journal opened in front of him, most likely the ingredients to his concoction. A large vat of water boiled over a fire behind him. The mist rose like a cloud hanging over his head.

"What in gods...?" Ketner's eyes darted from person to person, finally landing on Henrik. His lids narrowed, his jaw rolled. The white markings on his dark face moved like inchworms. "Back room. All of you. Now."

Ketner threw the ampoule and its contents into the fire and stood, heading to the back of his one-bedroom home.

We followed him to what looked like a thin pantry closet. Ketner opened it and pushed us through, one by one. He held on to Conleth's arm. "I will kill you if I must. The safety of these three is my highest concern."

Conleth placed his hand on top of Ketner's and squeezed. "That is fair, but I come as a friend. No harm will come to them. Not from me."

Both men appeared calm, almost too calm. They had similar natures in that they only seemed to fight when they had to and avoided killing when they could. I might not like Conleth, but at least my fear of marrying a brute was laid to rest.

A table and six chairs sat in the middle of the secret room. Calli, Henrik, and I plopped down. Maps hung next to two large cabinets pressed against the back wall with shelves containing what appeared to be potions, toxins, and other tonics Ketner probably used to heal and purge the body. Other than that, the small room stood bare.

"Water?" Ketner asked.

I nodded. "Please."

I was grateful that his first thought was to care for us and not berate our foolish and dangerous behavior barging into this home. In fact, most of the time when we called on him for help, he didn't judge. He'd fix what he could and never mention it again. Maybe the nature of a healer was to do just that. Tend to the broken, mend what could be, and move on to the next assault.

"Something stronger, too." Henrik's fingers drummed against the tabletop while he stared at Conleth, who had taken to leaning against the wall rather than sitting. "What are you?"

"He's like us, right, Savina? A demi-god?" Calli's honey-colored eyes widened with excitement. Only she would find delight in our near-death experience.

"Calli." My head thumped into my hands. "By the gods, is anything sacred to you?" I knew she was an impulsive thirteen-year-old who had never had her heart broken by life's cruelty but her nature to trust anyone who appeared noble scared me. I feared one day she'd entrust her secrets to the wrong person and suffer the consequences.

Conleth didn't answer. He didn't even move. He just stared. At me. Though candlelight bathed half of his face in shadow, there was no mistaking his light violet eyes roaming over my body. Studying me. Maybe he tried to figure out what we were, or at least what *I* was? After all, he was betrothed to me.

"Well, what are you, duke? Clearly you aren't human." Calli huffed when he didn't answer quickly enough for her impatient temperament.

"Is that right?" Ketner's voice stayed even, although a hint of curiosity laced his tone. He opened the cupboard and plucked several mugs from inside. "Does your kingdom know of your identity?"

Conleth still didn't answer. His broad chest and muscular biceps strained against his aubergine tunic as he crossed his arms and continued to glare at me through his thick black lashes. My heart accelerated under his scrutiny, but I didn't dare drop our locked gazes. If he was waiting for me to speak first, he'd be here for a long time.

Ketner balanced bottles and mugs in his hands, holding them to his chest as he closed the door. "Why don't we move on to a different question for now. What in the underworld happened?" Ketner placed the jug of water and bottle of brandy on the table with four pewter tankards surrounding them. He matched Conleth's position and leaned against the adjacent wall.

Henrik grabbed a cup and poured brandy almost to the rim. Then in one large chug, he finished its contents. He went to fill his cup again and Conleth moved in fast, even quicker than I saw him run outside. He placed his hand on top of the empty glass. "Don't. A clear head is too important. Do not drown your emotions in numbing drink. The warrior I saw back at the tavern is better than that."

Henrik's lips thinned but eventually he nodded and released the tankard. *Interesting.* Henrik didn't listen to anyone, and for him to take advice from Conleth? I'd sooner guess the world had been set on fire, not just the space behind the pub.

Ketner seemed to catalog the exchange the way he did everything. "Since no one is offering up an answer, Savina, why don't you start? What happened out there?"

All eyes focused on me.

I inhaled a deep breath and, on my exhalation, started from the beginning. "I was at the castle when the news came that *The Serpent's Snare* docked last night while *The Black Hollow* was still in port. Today, both pirate crews were rumored to be swarming the Lyre of Hermes Tavern. I knew Calli would come to Henrik's aid, so I followed her into town. When I arrived, they were surrounded by two pirates from *The Serpent's Snare*. A third one had followed me onto the scene."

"Did you use your powers?" Ketner's eyes volleyed between Calli and me.

I cringed. Why was everyone trusting the duke to witness our own secrets when we knew so little about him?

"No." I glared at Conleth, gesturing with my chin. "He showed up mere moments after me and took out three of their men." The bitterness of my tone hadn't escaped Conleth. His jaw popped as I spoke.

Ketner's gaze traveled over to Conleth. "You killed them?"

"No. Conleth isn't like that." Calli rubbed away the sweat on her face with her hands, pushing back the strands of blonde hair that clung to her skin. "He's virtuous."

Henrik's mouth twisted. Although he might respect Conleth, he didn't seem pleased by Calli's admiration.

"He left them wounded but still very much breathing." Calli filled her cup and chugged the contents. Water dripped from her mouth, and she wiped it away with her sleeve.

"Good. If you had killed them, this would be worse." Ketner spoke directly to Conleth. "Henrik's father is the captain of *The Black Hollow*. Watching over him is a full-time job when he's in port." Ketner chuckled.

"Thanks," Henrik mumbled. His head thumped into his hand.

"But he is one of ours and we protect our own. Calli and he seem to always get in a bit of trouble. Savina here is normally part of their clean-up crew. In other words, we save their arses on a regular basis."

A slight smirk tugged on Conleth's full lips, and an unwanted thrill shot to my core. I rubbed my stomach, as if disciplining its betrayal. *He is the enemy*, I reminded my traitorous parts.

"What powers would you have used to save them, my little songbird? I hope it's not your singing voice." Arrogance exuded from every one of his pores as he cocked his brow, studying me with an impenetrable gaze.

My cheeks flamed. My nose flared. I pinched my lips together, refusing to indulge his ridicule.

Calli burst out laughing. Ketner and Henrik joined her, but Ketner's amusement stopped when I glared in his direction.

"She can heal anything and control light," Calli said once her fit of laughter ended.

I chose to stay silent. For the life of me, I couldn't understand why my family had decided to divulge our abilities so easily. Was the fact that Conleth saved our lives and had powers himself enough? What would Apollo say? Gods, what would Zeus do?

"How can you control light?" A challenge glinted in Conleth's irises before his gaze trailed to the dimly lit lamps on the wooden table.

I shook off the faint brush of lingering resistance and sighed. I held up my hand and snapped my fingers. The lamps' flames snuffed out. The room went pitch black and I heard Conleth suck in air. I snapped again. The room lit up like the brightest sun on a summer's day. I expanded my fingers and the light shone even brighter.

Conleth's eyes darted to the unlit lamps and a slow smile reached his lips. "Impressive, princess."

I shrugged. Many demi-gods had more exciting tricks than I. Like my brother, Rye. He could sing anyone into walking off the plank. His voice and his eyes held powers of control. He too could heal like myself, only he couldn't inflict disease or illness. I rarely acknowledged that part of my power, not even Calli knew. Only Zeus, my father, Rylander, and Lou were aware. Since it only seemed to affect small animals and organisms, I hadn't worried too much about what I could do to a loved one, but there was this small drop of fear that trickled in like dew on a blade of grass.

"Your turn." I poured brandy into my empty mug and sipped in an effort to calm my crackling nerves. The warm liquor burned my insides. My eyes watered, but I welcomed the small distraction. "What, other than start a forest fire, can you do?"

Conleth snorted. "Well, my little songbird, I have the power of fire, that is true. But I also have foresight."

"Like Grandpa Apollo?" Calli turned her head to me, her nose twisted. The thought of anyone other than Apollo knowing the future soured both our faces. His various visions had already caused so many problems in our lives. We didn't need another god adding to that.

"Apollo is the God of Prophecy. I cannot see what may or may not happen in the future. I can..."

Ketner stepped forward. His seafoam green eyes lit up. "You have intuition and prudence in your decision-making. Am I correct?"

Conleth nodded.

"That's not a bad ability to have, my friend." He rubbed at the ends of his tightly tied beard.

Conleth pushed off the wall. "It is not."

Ketner tapped his bottom lip. "So, who is your father and..."

Shouts sounded from the alley behind us while pounding feet vibrated the wooden floors. I gripped the table as it shook.

Henrik stared at the trembling bottles on the back wall. Worry creased his lips, and with good reason. If his pirate captain father knew Henrik caused this disturbance, there'd be hell to pay. "We are two humans and three demi-gods, up against a mob of angry pirates." He turned back toward us. "What do we do?"

Conleth's unsettled focus remained on me. He tilted his head. His eyes traced over my mouth and a warm thrill shot to my core. I placed a hand over my stomach as if to control its disloyal tendencies. Another full minute passed before a smirk hinted on Conleth's lips. "Princess, you inspire greatness."

The skin between my eyes pinched. "What's that supposed to mean?"

His smirk turned to a full grin. "I'm in the mood for song and I know just the singer I shall seek."

CHAPTER FOURTEEN

CONLETH

Savina's glare pierced me to my core. How bewitched had I become in such a short period of time? And to a woman who clearly thought of me as a prison sentence rather than an ally. But if I had been honest with myself, that was exactly what I would become to her. When she found out what I intended to do, she'd hate me even more than she did now. A small ounce of guilt slipped into my conscience. I'd believed I had been her savior for convincing Pythia to spare her life, but even I knew there were worse condemnations than death.

Pulling a free breath into my lungs, I mustered the energy to push my thoughts deep down inside where they belonged. My duty lay in my oath to save mankind, not one demi-god.

Savina frowned. "What do you mean 'singer'?"

I ignored her. Instead, I pushed off the wall and began doling out orders. "Henrik, you stay here with Calli and Savina. If men get inside, you fight." I eyed the bandolier lined with throwing knives slung over his shoulder and chest.

He tipped his head, his shoulders back and chest proud like a soldier.

I turned to Ketner. "I have an idea, but we need to get back to my men. The pirates haven't seen you, so you'll be more helpful to me out there than here."

Savina jumped from her seat. Her body bristled. She crossed the room in two long strides. The scent of rich florals filled my nose as she raised her chin to look me in the eyes. "But they've seen *you*." She poked me in the chest, hard. "You just being in Ketner's presence could doom him." She jabbed her finger against me for the second time.

I wrapped my hand around hers. The heat of her skin caused me to swallow, but I held my mastered indifference across my face. "As much as I like you touching me, that was not so pleasant."

Her bright blue eyes narrowed in my direction. "Let go of me."

I released her hand, and she stepped back, but the small puffs of breath, the rapid rise and fall of her chest, made me wonder if I affected her as she did me.

She clenched her fists at her side. "I won't let you leave here. I won't risk losing Ketner because of *you*."

I tilted my head. My jaw ticked. "I'm sorry. Did you think this was up for debate? That our new crew was taking a vote?"

Her mouth dropped open, and my gaze fell to her lips, and I sucked in a breath. She didn't even realize how much of a temptress she was. The gods blessed her with unadulterated beauty and seduction, and I'd forever curse them for it.

"A speechless Savina is rare. Well done, Conleth." Calli laughed.

Savina glared at her niece before returning her gaze to me. "You don't get to dish out orders and have us follow them like we are your faithful servants back on Eloqua. You aren't leaving here with Ketner. But if you want to leave and get yourself killed..." She pointed to the hidden entrance, barely big enough for me to fit through. "Be my guest."

I wrapped my hand around her hip and drew her closer. Her body shuddered under my touch as she closed her eyes. A stab of desire flared inside me. This wasn't supposed to be. I hadn't expected such a magnetic reaction between us. Without thought, I pulled her body flush to mine. "But, my darling fiancé, wouldn't you miss your soon-to-be husband if I perished? How would you ever go on without me?" I soaked each syllable with insolence and mockery, a defense I had learned to use in covering up my own inner turmoil.

Calli snorted but I didn't look at her. My eyes stayed glued to Savina's.

My little songbird frowned. She pushed off my chest and my hand dropped away behind her. Her cheeks flushed and from the way her chest heaved, I knew a poisonous retort tickled her tongue.

"Savina." Ketner's authoritative voice broke the mounting tension. "I agree with Conleth. It's safer for Calli and you to stay here. And Henrik, for obvious reasons." Savina started to object, but Ketner held up his hand. "At this point, the royal family is most likely wondering where the both of you ran off to. Knowing Rye, he will send out the Sottom brothers and Krinny to fetch you. When they catch wind that two young females with your descriptions are being pursued by pirates, madness will ensue. You must stay hidden."

Henrik stood from the bench. "We can't go out there, Sav. If Conleth and Ketner are willing to get help, we need to let them go. *The Serpent's Snare* has over one hundred men and *The Black Hollow* has almost double those numbers." His fingers pressed into his palms, his knuckles whitening. "If my father finds out Captain Niles came after me, there will be a war in Cava. He'll kill anyone in his path." Henrik's gaze traveled to Calli. "I can't let anything happen to"—he swallowed and refocused back on Savina—"innocents because of me."

Ketner wrapped his hand around Savina's forearm. "Stay and protect them. If something goes wrong, you'll need to be here to heal them." He released her and turned to me. "Let's go. I fear if you stay any longer, you'll be the one needing to be healed." He gestured to a red-faced Savina.

Without glancing back at my new fascination, I pushed my way through the hidden pantry and into the living room. Ketner strode behind me.

"You've left quite the impression on the princess. I dare say she's not a fan." A dry chuckle escaped his throat.

I glanced over my shoulder. "I made fun of her singing a while back and she hasn't forgiven me."

Ketner's lips twitched as he grabbed four vials from his desk and tucked them into his pockets. "Well then, may the Fates smile upon you."

I grinned. "May they smile upon us all." I proceeded through the front door. Ketner stepped in front of me and I grabbed his arm. "Wait. I need to change."

Ketner's brow rose as I waved my hand from my head down to my feet, changing into my godly visage.

For the most part, I looked the same: black hair, wide muscular build, but my hair grew longer and curled at the ends, my flamed-color eyes returned, and my attire changed from Eloqua colors to a white billowy tunic and grey pants. My form morphed to the one Savina had met on the siren's island.

Ketner's eyes widened. "You're not a demi-god at all," he breathed. "You're a God."

I nodded, but shared nothing else. Only a god could change his form. I knew Ketner would see the truth, but to go undetected, I had no choice.

"Let's go." I tugged on his arm and led him back toward the tavern. Disgruntled pirates passed us along the way, but they gave no mind to our existence. They were looking specifically for a young boy, two females, and a man dressed in Eloqua colors.

My eyes easily picked out the crewmates of *The Serpent's Snare*. Each member wore a green bandana either on their arm, forehead, or leg. Each also held a scowl and weapon. Their long gaits moved with determination as they pushed people out of their ways.

Ketner leaned in and whispered, "I know who you are, and I know why you go by the name Conleth. It means prudent and fire. Only one god represents those words." His brow twitched. "What I do not understand is why you would come knowing that Zeus will be attending your wedding. From my understanding, he has been searching for you for almost a decade, Prometheus."

His emphasis on my godly name only provoked a smile. Ketner was a smart man. Only Queen Yemma had connected the chains to the human name I had taken on. I was impressed. "It's too long of a story for now. But I can promise you, my silence is for good reason."

"I will not lie to Rylander. If there's ever a moment in which he inquires about your—"

I turned, placing my hand on Ketner's chest. "I'd never ask you to lie. I will tell you this. Given my powers of intuition, I'd surmise your loyalty to Rylander means you withhold certain aspects of the princess's actions knowing it would do more harm than good if revealed. You're protective over her. And if I am correct, you *will* help me. Because the real danger is not today, it is down the road, and it all has to do with Savina. I am the only one here who will protect not only her, but mankind. If you believe anything, believe my intentions."

Letting that sink in, I turned and slinked through alleyways toward the last place I'd seen my men. We found Ballas, Vanden, and Flick standing in a circle near the fountain. Many of the vendors hawking food moved with haste, packing up their goods. Despite the mouthwatering smells, the town still reeked of fish and salt water, and now an added sense of foreboding.

I circumvented a child running with a box of apples. "Did I miss anything?"

My three friends spun in my direction. Scowls crossed their faces.

Vanden growled. "You really know how to bring a man close to death, milord." He bared his crooked teeth. "Where have you been? There's an uprising of pirates looking for a man who yields fire?" Vanden tapped his foot on the ground while crossing his arms. His eyes narrowed. "Know anyone like that?"

I patted him on the shoulder. "Thank you for your worry, old friend. But I'm sure they won't recognize me like this." I waved a hand over my appearance. My men might have been used to seeing me like this, but no one else here had yet.

"Who's that?" Vanden pointed to Ketner.

"A new acquaintance, one we don't have time to let earn our trust. It must be given and accepted now."

Ketner stepped up, shoulder to shoulder with me. We were the same height, although my width extended past his. "My loyalty resides with Princess Savina, Calli, and Henrik. As long as their well-beings are at stake, I am worthy of your confidence."

Ballas pushed my men out of the way and approached Ketner. Her red hair had been pulled up and pinned under her hat. Although she wore a human form, her eyes and hair stood out as clear distinctions. "Then we have the same goals. It's nice to see you again, Ketner. It's been a long time."

Ketner's eyes dipped down to her legs then back up. "General Ballas?" His palms pressed into his lids and dragged down his face. "I've seen it all today. You have legs?"

"I do indeed." She dipped her chin. "A tale for another time, perhaps."

Vanden ignored Ballas and Ketner pivoting in my direction. "Word is running rampant that the royal guard is on their way, and they plan to engage." Vanden scratched his chin. "I think we are about to have a battle on our hands. We need a strategy."

Ketner's eyes never left Ballas. "That's what you meant by singing." Ketner put my plan together in his mind. "The sirens."

I nodded. "General, how many of your people do you have in the waters and on Cava right now?"

Ballas leaned in and spoke in a hushed voice. "One hundred, just like you asked for."

"One hundred?" Ketner shouted.

"Shhh, healer, you'll bring us nothing but unwanted attention," Vanden grumbled. He never liked new people, especially ones we didn't have time to vet properly.

"I need you to have them all sing. They must draw the men of *The Serpent's Snare* back to their ship. Can you do that?"

Ballas looked over each shoulder. "It may bring others. It's hard to single out one group of people. We can try to sing to those who feel like they belong to the ship, but it's not foolproof. I can't guarantee the safety of the townspeople."

I tapped my lips while thinking. A mass exodus to the pirate ship wouldn't bode well for the people of Cava but... "What if you sing them all to their homes? This way all the pirates will return to their ships, the guards to their station, and the civilians to the safety of their houses."

"That could work." Ballas nodded, tugging her hat even lower. "I'll do my best." She took off toward the coastal edge in a full sprint. Her legs wobbled like a newborn calf's, but sheer determination appeared to drive her forward.

"Flick, I need you to ride back to the castle and speak to the king. Tell him we are with the princess and his daughter, and they are safe. I worry that they might send out men looking for them and they can't be found with the pirate's son."

Vanden gaped. "You have the young boy? The one *The Serpent's Snare* men are after?"

Flick cursed under his breath.

"Yes. He's apparently friends with the lady royals."

"Lovely." Flick rolled his eyes. "What should I say to the king when he loses his equanimity because you're harboring his daughter and sister?"

I smiled. "You're the wordsmith. That's for you to decide." I squeezed his shoulder. "Now go! We will meet you back at the castle."

Flick shook his head, mumbling as he headed toward the horses we left behind at the tavern.

"I hope he's a well-spoken wordsmith because Rye doesn't take lightly to his kin in trouble, especially his darling daughter," Ketner warned.

"It's the best I can do." I turned to Vanden, but before I could say anything, a troop of royal guardsmen galloped through the square, their horses' hooves clapping against the stone. Pirates, vendors, and townspeople scrambled, trying not to get trampled. Some didn't move in time, while others were jostled into each other. More and more red-and-gold uniformed soldiers approached from all angles, corralling everyone around the fountain, caging them in. "We need to get the innocents out—"

Multiple earsplitting pops penetrated through the rest of my words.

Gods help us...all these people could be dead if General Ballas didn't make it to the water soon, a consequence I could not bear.

CHAPTER FIFTEEN

CONLETH

C haos erupted in the fountain square. Shots fired, filling the air with the acrid scent of gunpowder. Bullets
soared past us. As a group, we ducked into a crouch against
the marble wall of the fountain. My gaze jumped from
civilian to pirate to guard. While the vendors and patrons
poured into alleyways and inside shoppes that lined the
square, the royal guards took to the perimeters and advanced. Pistols fired. Blades clanked. Shopkeepers closed
their doors, barricading them from the inside. Those left
outside shouted and pounded on walls, windows, and doors
trying to find safety. How had this escalated so fast?

I scanned the crowd, calculating our next move. That one
moment of distraction allowed a rogue bullet to puncture
my thigh. Another whizzed past my ear. The flow of power tingled along my skin, sparking under my palms as I
pressed them into the injury. I called to the round lead ball
inside my tendon until it popped out and bounced on the
cobblestone. Not a drop of blood followed.

Vanden threw his arm over my shoulder. "Thank the
gods for your celestial-armored hide." He twisted his head,
looking back at Ketner. "We need to take cover."

The skin around my wound stitched back to its original
form, not a scar left in its place. "Go!" I yelled, pointing to
an abandoned cart from a street seller.

I glanced over my shoulder and noticed several shadowy figures climbing up the side of the tavern. Quivers hung along their backs. I squinted, trying to make out who they were. The sun reflected off gold adornments lining their jackets. It took me a moment and then I realized. "No!"

"What?" Vanden huffed and puffed as he ran next to me.

"The royal archers are going to the rooftops so they can pick the pirates off one by one with their arrows. It's a massacre."

Vanden hissed as his eyes traveled to where I pointed.

We reached the south end of the square and positioned ourselves behind an abandoned vendor's cart. I pushed it on its side, providing a wider girth of coverage. Eroded and worn, I couldn't be sure this oversized wooden box would last long, but it was the best we could do for now.

Vanden poked his head up then crouched back down. "There are four dead in the middle of the street. Two are women, the other two men. All townspeople. Pirates and guards are shooting at everything and everyone. There's too much debris."

The whinnies of royal horses mixed together with the screams and pops of gunfire.

"Should we fire back?" Vanden pulled out his pistol, readying for a fight.

"No." I rubbed my temple. Saltpeter tasted sharp on my tongue. My head turned to Ketner. "Why would the king encourage such a vicious attack on the pirates, especially when his people's lives were caught in the middle? If the sirens don't succeed, he'll have a mutiny on his hands."

"I don't know. It's not like Rye. He'd never orchestrate this." Ketner shook his head. "Something's not right. He wouldn't have given this order."

My mind reeled with possibilities. Could Zeus be here already? Was this the start of his chaos?

An arrow whizzed overhead and nearly missed a pirate adjacent to us. His body jerked as the next arrow impaled his shoulder. Then another pierced his stomach and he pitched forward. A third and final blow caught him right in the eye, sending him backward. He crumbled to the ground. Blood gurgled at all the entrance points. Nothing about these tactics were strategic. Instead, they screamed pure madness.

Ketner pulled out several vials from his pocket. "I have four. Should I try to get to the injured and help ease their pain?"

I grabbed his arm. "No. I'm not letting you die. Put those back in your pockets. We may need them later." Not only would the princess never forgive me, but my intuition told me I needed Ketner in more ways than one.

A thump sounded as a dead body fell from above, landing in front of us. Blood poured out at the seams of the man's slashed throat. His limbs twisted in an unfathomable way. Anger coated my throat like bile. Why would the king command his men to attack? This show of authority had no purpose other than death.

A gunshot zoomed by Vanden's head. I reached for him to pull him under cover, but another came from a different angle and penetrated his shoulder.

"Gods," Vanden hissed through his teeth. His upper body went limp as he hunched over.

"Help him." I tossed Vanden as gently as I could toward Ketner and I stood. I held up my hands and flames licked my skin. I sparked my fingers like the end of a match, igniting everything discarded and turned over. Carts, hay,

barrels, crates. Shouts erupted as the guards' gazes redirect-
ed toward the growing heat. They began yelling for buckets
of water.

Not a moment of satisfaction lingered before a bullet
from higher ground rained down and hit me in the back,
pushing out my front. A jarring ache stung my chest. Sure, I
was a god, but that still had been uncomfortable. I buckled
and went down on one knee. A sharp burst cut through my
torso as I cupped my hand to the exit point. I summoned
my powers. Liquid heat hurried through my tendons, muscles, and tissue, repairing the damage from the bullets.
Another zinged by, grazing the cartilage on top of my ear.
I turned to see the bald pirate from earlier standing on top
of a cobblestone wall set behind the whorehouse. He lifted
his other pistol and aimed directly at my head.

I closed my eyes and cursed. A life—no matter
whose—was precious to me. I hated taking out humans,
but sometimes they gave me no choice. When I reopened
my eyes, the fire from my fingertips shot out like knives
slicing through my target and lighting him up from head
to toe. A scream howled from his lungs. His body spasmed,
his hands clutching his singed face before his body fell off
the wall and collapsed to the ground. It jerked several times
before settling in a roasted heap.

My head swiveled back to Vanden as I moved to the now
bullet-impaled cart we hid behind. "Are you okay?" My gaze
raked over his pale, wrinkled skin. He panted in and out.
Sweat dripped down his face. He struggled to nod. "It's
okay, old friend. Just breathe."

He threw me a weak smile in return.

I sucked in a deep breath. The air, thick with blood, tasted
like wet, hot metal.

Ketner held his hands against Vanden's shoulder. "I gave him my potion to numb the pain. The good news is the bullet went right through. The bad news is we need to get him stitched up. He's losing a lot of blood." Ketner's gaze traveled to the chaos then back to me. "You need to do something drastic. We've got to get him out of here."

Where were the sirens? They should have been singing already.

"Can you light this whole square up with your powers?" Ketner asked, now using a found gun to return fire, pushing the enemy back from the other side. I watched as the pirates shot at anything that moved and the guards followed suit. It was a blimey bloodbath. But if I used my magic, more would die, and I wasn't sure I could bear—

Just then soft, sweet sounds wafted over the crowd. The music weaved through the din, growing in intensity. I stood and examined the arena. The bullets stopped. Swords, pistols, and daggers all clattered to the ground. The song bellowed out like a vine, snaking around the men and teasing them to move on their own accord like puppets on a string. I twisted to tell Vanden and Ketner we must move when I noticed their eyes glazed over in a catatonic state. Like a cloud, they drifted.

I cursed.

My head wagged back and forth, searching for something. A fallen candelabra with three candles laid across the way. I rushed to grab one from an overturned trolley. I held my finger to it, melting the wax and rolling it into small ball shapes. Sweat poured down my neck and spine as I hurried to make four. Vanden lay on the ground unable to move, but his eyes darted from the castle to the port, clearly confused about what home meant to him. But Ketner had already started for his house.

I raced to Ketner, stuffing the wax in his ears. I smacked him across the face. "Wake up, for goodness' sake, man!"

Ketner jumped back. "What the..." He shook his head like a wet dog. His gaze darted around. "Vanden?"

We both ran to my comrade's side. Ketner aided an injured Vanden to sit up as I placed the rolled wax into his ears. Together, we lifted him to stand upright. I propped his arm over my shoulder to steady him so we could move together as one.

"We need to get him back to the house so Savina can mend his wound," Ketner said, speaking loudly due to his earplugs. He pulled out another vial from his pocket and handed it to Vanden, who threw it back in one gulp.

I grabbed Ketner's chin with my free hand and made him focus on my lips. Slowly, I mouthed, "Find Ballas by the docks. Stop the singing. And meet us back at your house."

There were other gods on the isle, and I didn't want to chance them learning about the sirens. Sure, they'd have suspicion on what had transpired, but hopefully no one would tie the seductresses to the disturbance. For now, they'd done their job. The pirates would no longer be in search of the boy. Or, having too many wounded on their hands and the royal guards after them, my hope and guess was that by nightfall, *The Black Hollow* would set sail.

Ketner nodded and took off toward the harbor, pushing through the throngs of entranced men.

I wrinkled my nose. The once succulent smells from the vendors had vanished and were replaced by smoke and burning wood mixed in with the foul scent of fish and open flesh.

As I walked back toward Ketner's home with Vanden in my arms, the sirens' song ended. And by the time we reached Ketner's cottage, he had returned.

"Hold him." I transferred Vanden to Ketner's arms. I waved my hand over my body, summoning the Duke of Eloqua visage. Within a breath, my hair shortened, my eyes blinked flipping hues, the scruff on my chin vanished into smooth skin, and when I looked down, I once again donned the kingdom's colors.

I held my hand out to hold up Vanden while Ketner opened the door, but Vanden's eyes fluttered, and his weight toppled onto me. His chest stilled. His breathing ceased.

"Wake up," I yelled, smacking his face.

Ketner grabbed Vanden's wrist and studied it. The healer sucked in a sharp breath, his eyes lifting to mine. "There's no pulse."

CHAPTER SIXTEEN

SAVINA

My constant pacing sounded against the floorboards. What in the underworld was going on out there?

About twenty minutes ago, Henrik lost complete control over himself. His green eyes glazed over while his body moved like a puppet on strings. Calli and I tried to stop him, but he kept attacking us to get to the hidden door. With no other choice, Calli finally knocked him unconscious with a nearby candlestick.

"I'm sure there's a reasonable explanation." Calli's gaze followed my relentless march. Her tone was even, but I saw the fear in her amber eyes. She kept looking at the hand she clocked him with as if she couldn't believe what she had done.

"Really? Like what? Henrik looked possessed. He didn't even know who we were."

Calli shrugged. "Anything is possible in our world. Maybe someone took control of him?"

"Are you seriously—"

My name sounded in the distance. *Conleth?* The secret door flung open, and Ketner pushed through. His blood-covered clothes reeked of gun powder and burnt wood, and his face dripped with sweat. "Come quick," he said, his voice hoarse.

"My gods. Are you hurt?" My heart pounded in my chest, the bones of my rib cage rattled.

Ketner didn't say anything as he turned and rushed back through the entrance. Calli and I ducked out after him and back into the main room of the small residence.

There, we found Conleth cradling an unconscious man in his arms. His head bobbed from his neck as Conleth moved closer to us. "You need to heal him. He's not breathing."

"Clear this and lay him down," I instructed, pointing to the rectangular desk Ketner had been working at earlier today. Ketner cleaned the area, moving empty cylinder vials, a large jar filled with his signature brown healing liquid, and a pewter bowl containing metal instruments and rags. His knuckles were covered in a mixture of blood and soot.

Conleth placed the man down with care. His eyes stormed with emotion as they stayed fixated on his friend. His cheek twitched as I leaned in to listen for his breath.

Blood dripped from the man's shoulder where he had been shot. "Is the bullet still in there?"

"No. It was a clean hit right through." Ketner placed a small pillow under the man's head.

Calli approached my side with wet towels. She used them to wipe down the man's face and neck. The white cloth stained red as she gently wiped at the injured area.

Without ceremony, I ripped open his tunic and let the threads dangle. My hands hovered over the wound until they pressed into his wet skin. The sticky blood clung to my palms. I called upon my ethereal powers. Tingles spread across my limbs with each sweep of magic. My powers were limited. If he was too close to death, I wouldn't be able to retrieve his life. Perspiration beaded along my brow. My touch trailed around the wound, begging life to find its way back to this man.

"I don't know if I can…" I panted. I attempted to swallow, wet my tongue, but my throat dried. Black seeped into the edges of my vision. I squeezed my lids shut, fighting the dizziness that tried to overpower me.

"Savina, you must. He means too much to me," Conleth pleaded. The nicknames and humorous tone he normally taunted me with had vanished and were replaced by pure desperation and urgency.

Soft hands cupped my cheeks, lifting my head. Thumbs wiped over my damp skin. My head grew heavy in his hold. The power he had over my mind and heart didn't make sense.

"Can you take from me? From my godly powers?"

His words parted the fog in my brain. My lashes fluttered. "I've never tried," I breathed, staring into begging eyes. A flicker of light shone in his irises, a prism of fire shadowed the violet hue and licked the edges of his pupil, a color I would never forget from our first meeting. But with a blink it descended. A purple ring returned.

"Your eyes," I whispered.

Conleth's hand left my face and covered mine on top of the body. "Focus on me. Take what you need. Imagine you are transferring my life into his body."

I nodded and sucked in fresh air.

Heat poured into my veins like molten lava. I clenched my teeth to block the bile threatening to come up my esophagus. Needle-like pricks stabbed my palms as my power grew with more ethereal energy then I'd ever had. Every cell in my body came to life. My arms trembled.

The lamps flickered above us, my control over light and darkness toying with our surroundings.

"That's it, Savina. Pour it all into your healing ability," Conleth encouraged me.

His face paled, yet he forced a smile. Sweat dripped from his forehead onto the floor. His normally pink pouty lips had gone white. I imagined my own mouth looked similar. My chin quivered. It took my entire focus to stay upright.

My gaze traveled to the hand I held. Conleth's veins swelled, and the skin turned purplish grey, the color I always saw before... I gasped as I withdrew my hand and held it to my chest.

Sweat dripped off Conleth's brows. "No." He grabbed my wrist and threaded his fingers in mine, his hold tight. "You won't be able to hurt me. Do not stop. Take from me whatever you need."

"But I..."

"You can and you will. I believe you can do anything. Do you understand? I believe we are greater than our weaknesses. That we can use our powers for good no matter what they may be. I believe in you, Savina. I always have. From the moment I knew you existed, I had faith."

I nodded as a knot formed in my throat the size of a cantaloupe. Conleth spoke as if he knew the depths of my capabilities and thought I could fight them, as if this was not his first day learning of all I could do. But that didn't make any sense.

"You cannot kill me. I promise."

"Listen to him, Savina. He'll be fine." Ketner touched my elbow. "Keep trying."

Ketner's words helped soothe me. He'd known me all my life. If he believed, so did I.

Anger fueled my powers, not always for the greater good. But emotions worked like oils to fire, spreading through my veins like lava. If I tapped into that emotion, maybe I could build more healing energy. I allowed my anger toward Zeus to spring free. *Transfer my life into his.* I repeated this as I ate from Conleth's strength and fed into my powers.

A small whimper escaped the man on the table. Conleth and I looked down toward the sound. The man's eyes flickered until his brown-black irises stared back at us. His lips parted as he gasped for air. His rib cage expanded like a balloon. The skin around his wound snaked toward the center until skin covered the hole made by the bullet. Blood clotted until it ceased to spill.

"Vanden," Conleth uttered. "My old friend. How are you feeling?" Conleth released the hand that had been interlaced with mine and I began to wobble. His strength held me together, but with the lack of it now, my knees started to give out. The tension stabbing my temples started to fade, leaving me with a woozy sensation.

Before I even knew I was falling, Conleth reached out and took hold of me, catching me in an embrace with lightning-fast reflexes. He stared into my eyes as if he stared through me, into me. "It's nice to know I have that effect on you." Conleth smiled and although he spoke with words of arrogance his tone held unspoken gratitude. His face softened with relief and something else I wasn't quite sure of. Maybe confusion.

Conleth helped me to stand but didn't let go. We stayed locked in an embrace, our eyes searching. The pressure of his hands grew as he started to pull me in. His eyes gazed down to my mouth. Heat flared all over my body. My chest tightened.

My lips parted to speak. "I..." But nothing else followed. Instead, my mouth formed the shape of an olive. There were no words to explain what passed between us. For a brief moment, I wondered if he'd kiss me. My body leaned in, growing warm all over. Did I want him to?

Conleth used the pad of his thumb to brush across my bottom lip. My tongue slipped out and swept across his finger. He lowered his lips to my ear. The heat of his breath caused me to shiver. "Wouldn't want to catch a rogue fly, would we now?" He lifted my chin, closing my mouth and pulled away so fast, it took me a moment to register what he said and did.

Fire ignited in my throat. All the gooey sentiments slithering around in my stomach hardened. Conleth once again mocked me. It was exactly the cold bucket of water I needed to knock some sense into myself. I pushed him away and stepped back. My emotions varied in his presence like a broken compass that couldn't find north. How easily I could volley between anger and interest burned me to the core. I wanted to hate him, but at times he made that task impossible. Energy surged through me, and my vision cleared. I stared down at the man I saved as Conleth helped him sit upright.

"Thank you." His umber brown eyes held moisture. Color had returned to his cheeks. His breathing steadied.

"You're welcome."

Conleth turned toward Calli. "Where's Henrik?"

Calli shifted from one leg to the next. "I had to knock him out. He was acting like a wild animal trying to escape."

Conleth nodded. The lack of surprise he held told me he knew why.

"He was under the sirens' spell." Ketner handed Vanden a vial from his pocket. The same brown concoction he'd often offered Henrik after his matches with Calli. "They helped us out of this mess."

"The sirens?" I shook my head. "But how? Where are they? Swimming around the port?"

Vanden looked to Conleth as they shared an unspoken thought.

"Well?" I placed my hands on my hips. My lips thinned. From the moment I met Conleth, he had been conspiring with the sirens. And now conveniently the clan swam in the waters by the Cava docks? That couldn't be a coincidence. They never ventured this far from their isle to our lands.

Conleth turned around, giving me his back. "Ketner, can Vanden borrow clothes to wear back? I don't want to cause suspicion when we return to the castle."

Ketner nodded and headed toward his bedroom.

My anger ignited. "How dare you ignore me?" I tapped Conleth's shoulder with more force than necessary, my nail poking into his tunic. "Answer my question." I spoke through gritted teeth.

Conleth turned, a smug smile plastered on his face. "Trust me, ignoring you isn't as easy as you think. I've been trying to do that very thing since the day we met." In a lower voice, he grumbled, "It's not working."

My hands returned to my waist, griping my hipbones as if they were his neck. Was he mad? Acknowledging his blatant dismissal of me? "Tell me right now why the sirens are here, so close to Cava's coast."

Conleth stepped forward. "My darling, as your fiancé it is my duty to protect you. That extends to knowledge as well as physical protection." His gaze raked up and down my body. "Although I know I'll enjoy one more than the other, they are both my responsibility. Please let me do my job."

"You are a swine."

Conleth's hands covered his heart. "Your tongue waggles with insults with such ease." He smiled.

My lip curled. "You are insufferable."

Conleth dropped his hands. "I can be. But I do hope you will love me anyway."

My skin crawled at the idea. "I will never love you. This isn't anything but a forced marriage. I wouldn't choose to marry you if you were the last man in all the lands."

"Savina," Ketner warned as he walked back into the room with trousers and a long-sleeved gray tunic. "I understand emotions are high, but Conleth's kingdom has as much of a choice in this decision as you do. None. Your brother requested and the request either is granted or there's war." He handed the clothes to Vanden, who dipped his head in appreciation and took off to get changed.

My mouth dropped. "What?"

"Really?" Calli asked from somewhere behind me. "Guess my theory that he won't force you to marry him is off the table."

"Thanks, Cal," I groaned.

Conleth's brow lifted. "You were going to ask me to back out of our betrothal?" If I didn't know his dislike for me mirrored mine for him, I would have almost thought he sounded insulted.

"Yes." I placed my hands on my hips.

Conleth's lips twisted, but before he could respond, a hammering of multiple fists at the front door silenced us all.

"Princess, open up! Now!"

CHAPTER SEVENTEEN

CONLETH

Vanden had been taken by the king's doctors to treat his superficial wounds while Savina and I were escorted into the empty library by the Sottom brothers and a woman, Krinny, who I learned was Savina's personal guard.

The female sentinel marched right up into Savina's personal space, her eyes so black I couldn't find where her pupils started and irises ended.

"You've never lied to me before. And now you broke the trust we had." She shook her head, the veins popping in her neck. "It will take a lifetime to get it back." And with that, she spun on her heels, hauling Calli by the arm with her out of the room.

Savina's bottom lip trembled as a single tear fell from her eye. I fought the urge to go to her and wipe it away. What had gotten into me? My mission was not about one girl but about the people of the land, all the people.

I needed a distraction. My eyes flitted around the quiet space. I hadn't a clue what we'd be walking into, but by the terse commands of the Sottom brothers who caught us at Ketner's home, I knew it wouldn't be a welcome return.

Minutes passed as Savina paced, playing with her nailbeds. She walked from one bookshelf ladder to the next, then turned around and took the same path. Her eyes were downcast, as if memorizing her steps. Although she never spoke, I could see the wheels in her head spinning. I was just about to suggest getting our stories straight when I heard thunderous footsteps approach.

I whirled to find the king standing at the entrance, his breath ragged and his face red with either exertion or anger. His fingertips coiled into his palms at his sides. His sleeves, crinkled at the elbow, exposed his pulsating veins along his forearms.

"You," he growled in my direction. But before he could muster up more words, the door swung all the way open, hitting the adjacent wall with a bang. Three men strode in.

The one I noticed first snickered. Hermes. But the two by his side gave me pause. The older man reminded me of a soldier from the Trojan War. His shorn salt-and-pepper hair signified wealth and superiority in the ranks. His wrinkled milky skin shone pale in contrast to his dark features. His cobalt eyes flared wide as he took us in while his Prometheus's apple bobbed.

With the speed of a god, he rushed toward Savina. His hands grabbed her by the shoulders, gripping a little too tightly for my liking. She sucked in a breath as he pulled her into his arms. "Thank the gods you're okay." But the words didn't match his tense shoulders. Anger radiated off him like steam from a hot spring. His little show of comfort seemed to convince no one else in the room either. Rylander's lips curled while Hermes tried to hide his eye roll.

Savina nodded while the rest of her body froze.

"Zenith," the other man I hadn't met said. He stepped forward, placing his hand on the older gentleman's shoulder, pulling him away from a now shivering Savina. "She's fine. Our prayers to the gods have been answered." His thick blond waves curled over his ears, and his ruddy complexion made him appear young. But his tone grated as if he were older than everyone in the room.

The soldier released Savina and glared at the man who spoke.

He stepped forward and extended his hand to me. "I am Arlo, and this is my father, Zenith. We are noblemen and advisors to the palace. We've watched the princess grow up and are close with the royal family. When news arrived of Calli and Savina's disappearance, we shared in King Rylander's concern, as you can imagine."

I placed my hand in his and he squeezed. His grip reminded me of Hermes's hold the first time we met, but the glint in Arlo's eyes told me he wasn't hiding his godly nature. He wanted me to know and that had me curious.

"The Duke of Eloqua." I hardened my voice. With a curt nod, I dropped his hand. I didn't believe for one second they were noblemen of the court, but I couldn't be sure what god or demi-god they were without further examination.

Zenith watched me, cataloging my reaction to his son. His hand stroked his short beard.

"Well, now that the introductions are over." Hermes leaned back on the desk and crossed his arms. "Mind telling us what in the underworld happened?" He scowled.

Savina stepped forward. She wrapped her fingers around my bicep, drawing me in. The surprising touch caused my breath to hitch. She had never taken hold of me before, nor had she touched me in a protective gesture.

"This was all my fault. Conleth was already in town exploring with his men when I went looking for him." She threw me a small smile like she cared for me and had wanted to spend time together. "I rode with Calli into the square to find him and bring him back to the castle. It's such a lovely day." She motioned to the long windows where the sun shined through the stained glass, casting colorful prisms of light onto the marble floor. "I thought it would be nice to show him the gardens."

Rylander shifted. As expected, he hadn't bought her lie. He waved his hand. "And you thought Calli should join you for what reason?" He rubbed his temple as Savina frowned. "How did you both get out of the castle undetected?"

I placed my hand over Savina's and squeezed. "I believe that Lady Calli was trying to be a smart and capable companion to Princess Savina. You wouldn't want her to go into town by herself, after all."

"That's what we have royal guards for," Rylander said with a clenched jaw. "But for some reason, Savina's personal guard was under the impression my wife was in danger and relinquished her post."

My eyes widened. That was news. No wonder Krinny regarded Savina with such ire. But still, if the king and queen knew...then it dawned on me. How were the tables turning when it was this magistrate who had ordered the bloodshed below in the town? Two runaway royals stood to be a lesser crime in my eyes.

"I believe you were all endangered considering the mess in town could have traveled to this very castle if not thwarted," I snapped. My calm exterior cracked as I remembered the scene at the fountain. So many dead, all at Rylander's command.

Rylander stepped forward. "We had a situation that needed to be dealt with."

I stood straighter, my shoulders drawn back. "I assume you mean the two pirate ships being docked at the same time at Cava's port?" I lifted a brow.

Hermes cursed from behind. Rylander held up his hand like a king silencing his subject. "Yes, that situation needed to be de-escalated before we had a war on our hands."

A knot in my throat formed from the rage boiling inside of me. The fire within begged to be unleashed. "De-escalated?" What madness! "You thought caging in innocent townspeople and pirates then unleashing all hell on them was the proper way to deal with a possible battle? That's what this kingdom deems de-escalation?"

Savina gasped.

Zenith's blue eyes slid in my direction. The pleased smile twisting around his lips caught me off guard.

"What are you talking about?" Rylander's gaze volleyed from Savina to me. "I never—"

I moved forward out of Savina's grasp. The place her hand held immediately felt cold and I wanted back in her touch, but I stayed on course, cutting Rylander off. "You ordered your men to attack anyone in town square. Civilians died trying to escape. Children. Women. Elderly. My own man suffered a bullet wound. We watched many innocents murdered by your guards' hands."

Rylander's mouth opened, then closed, then opened again. Confusion lay in the creases around his eyes. But before he could speak, Zenith moved forward. "We are lucky to be ruled by such a proactive king. Thank the gods he did what was necessary to stop the unlawful brigands from disrupting the peace of our nation. Unfortunately, in war there are casualties. I'm sure if he hadn't commanded his sentries, we'd have lost more people." He clasped his hand on Rylander's shoulder and squeezed. The action spoke volumes to who really gave that order. If this command hadn't come from Rylander, then the only deity who'd encourage the pointless death of humans and ruled above all other demi-gods and gods had to be...Zeus.

A chill pricked my spine. The man before me, my torturer, smiled. My hands clenched at my sides, but there was nothing I could do. I had to stay the course.

"We still haven't heard where you were with the princess and her niece." Hermes interrupted the tense conversation and my thoughts.

"We were at Ketner's," Savina spoke. "Once the guards barreled into town, Conleth and his men hurried us out to safety. Calli and I thought that would be a good place to take them until the path back to the castle was safe to travel."

Savina joined me, again. Her shoulder brushed mine. The heat radiating from her sent a wave of protective emotions through me I hadn't known existed. Stealing her away from Cava was supposed to be for the good of humanity, but right now, all I wanted to do was save her from these gods who wanted to use her as a pawn, especially Zeus. I bit back the response teasing the tip of my tongue and waited for Rylander to speak.

"How many died?" His voice wavered. His body strained under Zenith's grip.

I crossed my arms, digging my fingers into my skin. "Too many," I gritted out.

Rylander grimaced. His colorless eyes darted from me to Arlo. An unspoken thought passed between them. If there was discord between Rylander and "Zenith," perhaps I could use that to my advantage.

"Smitter, call in the Sottom brothers. I'd like the death toll and confirmation that *The Black Hallow* will be leaving port tonight. Might you also let *The Serpent's Snare* know they are no longer welcome here as well, and to depart within two moons." He regained his steely calm. Zenith appeared pleased with his response and took a step back, aligning himself with Arlo. "As for you, Your Grace, you and your men will not leave the castle again. It is our responsibility to protect you."

A muscle in my jaw popped. "Are you imprisoning us? In a country that I am to run soon?" I breathed deep to stamp on the violent impulses surging through my veins. Not that we'd still be here then, but Rylander didn't know that. Heat flickered at my fingertips and the promise of my godly powers sizzled under my skin.

Savina moved in closer to me. She pinched the skin around my elbow, her hand hidden from the others' views. "Thankfully everyone is safe now. Why don't I take Conleth to the gardens like I originally planned?" Her arm threaded through mine and she squeezed, pressing her chest against me.

I didn't dare look at her, but I wanted to. Part of me yearned for her affection, while the other part knew it was a show put on for our audience.

Zenith clapped his hands. "They are getting along so nicely. It's wonderful. I think that's a great idea. Don't you, Rylander?" The bite of Zenith's tone hadn't been missed by the room.

Rylander nodded, but his lips pressed down as if he were holding back his words.

"I shall join you. I am walking that way as it is." Arlo proceeded to the door.

Savina kept me in her hold, following the young man.

I bowed my head to the rest of the men in the room before leaving. Hermes barely acknowledged me. His cheeks
had been stained a permanent red since he entered. Zenith,
who I now believed to be Zeus, dipped his head, a silent
goodbye.

Savina dragged me forward. As we turned down the corridor toward the side exit, Arlo spoke. "Conleth, other than
today's events, how are you faring here?"

I ground my teeth before taking a cleansing breath to
answer such a cavalier question. "I'm finding Cava to be
more interesting than I had expected."

Savina's grip tightened in warning, but I ignored it and
focused on the heat from her body. A tight sensation
gripped my emotions like a viper around its prey. The hold
reminded me I couldn't allow myself to relax in her false
comfort.

"And the princess?" His blond barely-there brow rose.
"Are you finding her company enjoyable?"

"I find this questioning a bit odd coming from a noble-
man." I tilted my head, studying the man before me. "How
long have you known my intended?"

My left hand lifted to grip Savina's arm where it was still
threaded through mine as if I couldn't get enough of her
warmth. Her brow lifted in question, and I shrugged. Why
couldn't I act as the doting fiancé if she could?

"All her life."

I nodded. My eyes darted around to find a distraction. I
didn't want to overplay my hand. Mosaics of griffins, the
same creatures that sat on the Cava flag, sprawled into the
etching of the floors. My eyes squinted as I realized this
was another one of Apollo's doings. That was when it hit

me. If Zenith was Zeus, then Arlo had to be Apollo. I stared into his blue eyes and blond hair and the memories of him returned. Like me, he presented a rather close version of his godly visage. The only difference lay in his age and stature. The Apollo I knew was a tad bit taller, wider, and older.

Arlo's gaze followed mine and he chuckled. Whether he knew I had an idea of who he was, I hadn't a clue, but something told me he wasn't trying to hide it from me either.

"Have you ever seen a griffin in person?" Arlo asked.

My head twisted in his direction. "Have you?"

Arlo's smile widened. His bright white teeth sparkled. "If I said yes, would you believe me?"

"Yes." The sparkle in his eyes told me he was pleased by my answer. But why did he want me to know who he was, and did that mean he knew who I was? His strange question alerted me to one thing. He didn't want me acknowledging it in front of Savina.

"Not that anyone asked me, but I've never seen a griffin," Savina huffed. She released my arm and pushed open the glass doors to the veranda. The setting sun cast the sky in an orange glow. "But I've always wanted to," she whispered, as if the last admission was truly just for herself.

Arlo turned to us and stopped.

"Are you leaving?" Savina's voice sounded desperate and sad.

"For now." Arlo frowned.

Savina moved forward and wrapped her arms around him. Her fiery red hair covered her face, but the sounds of soft sobs filtered through. Arlo kissed the top of her head. Her actions confirmed this was indeed Apollo, her father. I was surprised she allowed me to see such affection.

"It was a pleasure meeting you, Your Grace." Arlo bowed his head.

My mouth twisted. The polite response died on my tongue. Savina's eyes narrowed at me.

"It's been—"

Before I could finish, Arlo pulled me in for an embrace. His lips grazed my ears as he breathed so low, I wasn't sure I heard correctly. "Stay the path. You are guided by the right light. You will need it before the darkness."

CHAPTER EIGHTEEN

SAVINA

C onleth offered me his elbow. Now that we were alone, I scoffed and took off in the direction of the garden, throwing, "I'd rather walk on hot coals," over my shoulder.

My persistent betrothed jogged to catch up to me and chuckled. "I was wondering when the performance would fizzle out." Conleth clapped slowly. "You were impressive back there. You even had me fooled."

"Well then, if leading the nation as queen doesn't work out, at least I could enter the arts. Cava has a wonderful theater troupe." I threw a fake smile Conleth's way.

He stopped short, causing me to do the same. His mouth opened, his eyes twinkling with mirth.

I squirmed under his ceaseless stare. "Why are you looking at me like that?" I circled my pointer finger, outlining his face.

"Did you just make a joke?" His brow quirked.

I rolled my eyes. "I can be funny." I tromped on ahead. His surprise bothered me. I might not be as entertaining or adventurous as Calli and Henrik, but did he really believe I was such a bore? It wasn't my fault between the three of us, I had to carry the weight of responsibility. For I knew neither of them would.

Conleth nudged me in the side. "I like it. In fact, I'd like to see more of it."

I put on a coy smile. "Humor and adventure. Is that what you seek?" I beckoned him with a finger, then twisted toward the equipment shed at the far end of the garden. "I have many talents." He thought me a bore who spent her days following around her more interesting relatives and wandering my castle like a spinster? I'd show him he'd mistaken a phoenix for a timid songbird.

"More than singing?" He chuckled to himself.

"Very funny. Maybe *you* ought to join the arts."

The large shed stood just outside the gate. Rather than use the swinging picket door, I hopped the low stone wall and turned back to waggle my brows at Conleth.

"You're practically feline," he said with a gravity that cracked around the edges.

"And yet you doubt my claws." I let a half-smile slip on my face.

His laugh followed me into the dark storage area. Using the light from the doorway, I located my longbow and arrow, stringing the bow as I pushed past him and back outside.

"Don't you need a target? They're just there." He tossed a thumb at the sacks painted with bullseyes.

I scanned him top to bottom. "Oh, but I have one already. A pretty one at that."

He squinted one eye. "I'm not sure whether to be intrigued and flattered or to run and scream for help."

"For this trick, it's best if you stay very still."

"Ah. Should've chosen to run!"

My mouth quirked without my permission. "Probably."

The manicured field between the garden and the stable acted as a training yard where I'd set up many an archery pitch. But I led Conleth across the now-empty field to a grove of fruit trees planted by a long-ago queen. I paused about a hundred yards from an apple tree and shot Conleth a ponderous pout. "You look nervous."

"Do I?" He wiped his forearm over his brow.

Men could be so dramatic. "How about I instill some faith before I make you play target?"

He bowed out of the way. "I'm all eyes, princess."

I readied two arrows in my hand, but only strung one. Drawing back the fletching to tickle my cheek, I released the first and nocked the second as it flew. The first arrowhead sliced through the slim branch holding a green apple just as I let the second fly. With a juicy *kathunk*, the falling apple burst apart and my arrow sank deep into the trunk behind it.

Conleth clapped two slow beats. "Impressive! So this is what occupies your free time, hmm?"

"When I can." I practiced every now and again, certainly, but with the blood of my aunt, Artemis, in one's veins, the basics came rather naturally. "I find it relaxing."

"You find piercing things with arrows relaxing?"

"Some things more than others," I said around a sly grin, then jerked my head toward the tree. "Go on. Try an apple. They're a little tart right now, but still delicious."

He plucked an apple without trouble, took a hulking bite, and scrunched up his face. "I think you may have understated the tartness, my little songbird."

I snickered. "If it's unsuitable for eating, why don't you place it on top of your head?"

"I'm regretting my decision not to flee more and more, but if you insist." He obeyed and stood like a prisoner awaiting execution, hands behind his back and a morose frown on his face. "I suppose I have no choice but to trust you now."

I contained my chuckle and drew three arrows from my quiver. "Take two steps back, please."

He obliged, balancing the apple all the while.

"There! Perfect," I called. Nocking all three arrows, I lined up my shot. "Hold still now."

"You'll bid my men farewell, won't you? Throw a beautiful ceremony for my passage across the Styx?"

I snorted, then completed a steadier exhale and let the arrows fly. Conleth's hair swished in the breeze made by the passing fletching as the apple vanished from his head and reappeared, along with two others snatched from the branches, speared to the tree trunk. The trio formed a perfect vertical line—though not every fruit had survived in perfect shape—that Conleth admired before freeing his bitten apple and indulging in another nibble.

"I think I'm coming around to them!" He jogged to rejoin me.

"Are you also coming around to the realization that your betrothed is not to be trifled with?"

"Indeed," he said. "But as I'm sure you've noticed, I don't often act in my own best interest."

I rolled my eyes and turned away to hide my smile. "Come on, let's head back."

We deposited the bow and quiver in the shed, then took the gate back into the garden. I'd proven my point; no need to snag my trousers on rough stone.

Conleth picked a rose from the first bush we passed and handed it to me with a bow. "For sparing my life, fair warrior."

With a smile, I leaned in to smell the blood-red petals and a memory blossomed like a fresh bud.

My father and I walked through the palace gardens and stopped by the rose bushes. I couldn't have been older than four. I vividly remembered being angry, crying and throwing a tantrum because I wanted to play with my dolls inside, and Father wouldn't let me in the house due to an ongoing ball Zeus attended. He'd grabbed my hand and led me to the gardens.

At the time, I wasn't permitted around anyone other than trusted staff and family. Rylander's visits had become my favorite salvation. Until Galen, in all her rapscallion glory. I'd had more adventures with her in a fortnight than any other time in my life, right under my keepers' noses. But that was horribly short-lived. I'd never know if she would've accepted my invitation to join Rylander's crew and travel back to Cava with us, where her disguise wouldn't be necessary and where I could see her more often.

I'd lost the one light in the crippling void of isolation of my youth. Not that much had changed over the years, but as a child, I'd been deprived of real relationships with peers. I got lost in fictional friends, fairy tales about romance and heroes. I dreamt my future would be filled with similar narratives, and when Galen appeared, I believed for a moment my fantasies would be realized. She'd seemed plucked straight from a nighttime tale of daring deeds and happy endings. Older, braver, free to bounce from isle to isle at the whim of the winds. Until Zeus stripped that whimsical idea away from me. No one could withstand the gods' iron will over my future. Not even a real-life hero.

But my walk through the rose bushes had occurred before I'd crashed into Galen on a Jacarian wharf. My small hand reached for a perfect rose sticking out from the bush as my father guided me along the path, explaining the importance of my sheltered life.

"Savina, I don't enjoy keeping you hidden. I do it for your safety. I worry about how your grandfather views all his grandchildren, but especially you."

I sniffled.

"Grandfather loves me."

Father cupped my face. "He does, my darling. But power, greed, betrayal, ego, they are very influential things to the God of the Sky. I need you to stay away from him. Do you understand?"

"No. I don't." I moved out of his embrace and my free hand brushed against the satiny petals, so delicate and soft against my skin. Not even its loveliness could soothe my fury and sadness. My power surged through my caress. The flower drooped and darkened to brown. I stepped back and gasped. Apollo's eyes widened. Within minutes, the entire rose bush wilted and blackened. I started to cry, my sobs loud and angry. Apollo took me in his arms and held me tight. His warmth wrapped around me like a blanket. I clung to him.

"Shhh, it's okay." He rubbed my back, brushing his fingers through my hair. "All you have to do is use your powers to reverse it." He pulled back enough to wipe the tears under my eyes with his thumb. "For every disease there is a cure. Sometimes we don't see it right away. But you possess the magic of both life and death. Don't ever forget that. In your darkest hours, your gift has the power to give back the light you've taken." He returned me to my feet on the stone path and encouraged me to approach the flowers. "Go ahead. Try to reverse it."

I stepped forward on shaky legs and pressed my un-marred fingers to the crinkled petals and summoned the feelings I experienced in my father's or Rylander's arms: security, warmth, and love. My skin tingled. Slowly, the petals lightened to burgundy, then startling red. Not all the colors came back, not all the flowers survived. Many a bud had to be clipped by the gardener later the next day, but for a select few, my magic reversed the disease I had inflicted.

Apollo knelt on one knee. He picked me up and sat me on his thigh. My feet dangled. "Do not ever be afraid of who you are. Your powers are greater than you know. Others will fear you or want to use you. It's why you need to listen to me and stay within the safety of these walls." He tapped me on the nose. "You are the most important person in my life. Do you know that?"

I shook my head, wiping leftover snot onto my forearm.

"From now on, I shall call you Little Rose to remind you of all the beauty you inspire."

The memory faded into the dusk like the sun setting on the horizon and my fears of the future tumbled to the forefront. If Zeus was encouraging me to wed, and now to be in the public eye, what did that really mean for me? Who would I become in order to serve his dominion?

CHAPTER NINETEEN

CONLETH

My eyes crinkled with concern as I gripped Savina's hand. She appeared to have left me, lost in thought. "Princess, are you okay?"

"Sometimes I forget why I haven't been allowed much freedom. Why my life has been one big prison. And yet, when I remember, I'm still confused."

My voice grated in my throat, recollections taking the shapes of blades as I recalled my own prison on top of the mountainside, my guardian a crazed bird with an iron beak. But why had Savina been imprisoned? What had threatened Zeus to keep her so caged? "I'm not sure I understand."

She waved at the surrounding castle grounds. "I'm rarely allowed out of these walls. My subjects have never witnessed their princess in town unless disguised as a commoner."

"And why is that?"

"My powers, I assume. No one has ever told me." She let out a dark chuckle. "And because of the threats made on those I love, I've never questioned. The one time I disobeyed, a friend paid with her life."

I squeezed her hand before dropping it and settling onto a wrought-iron bench. I patted the seat next to me, and instead of fighting me, she lowered into it. The heat of her body bathed mine, helping ease the chill in my bones left by the memory of my capture.

My gaze traveled along Savina's profile as I memorized her heart-shaped face, her cheeks indented with the sweetest dimples. They were always there, but when she smiled, they danced in tandem with the apples of her cheeks. Currently, they sat dormant, just as still as her body.

"I thought you could heal and control light. What's so dangerous about that?"

She laughed, tilting her chin to the heavens. "I wish those were my only powers. That it was as simple as that." She bit her lower lip, clenching her jaw tighter than the lock on the Titans' ancient prison. The uncomfortable silence added to the already crushing feeling inside my chest.

"You don't have to tell me." I tucked a rogue curl behind her ear and she shuddered. The temperature of her skin warmed my insides. How I wanted nothing more than to caress her, calm her with promises of the future. But I couldn't. What I could offer her was an outlet to the present. "If you want to, I'll keep your secret in here." I touched my chest above my heart. "We don't know each other well, but I'd like to change that. In fact, I'll give you one of my own. An even trade."

Her lips parted but nothing came out. For a long moment, we sat staring at one another. Her oceanic-colored eyes traced every inch of my flesh. I began to feel warm in places that had no purpose in such an innocent situation. We were tethered together by circumstance, not by anything more.

She gripped the fabric of her trousers like she was trying to hold on to something. This moment, her thoughts, her fears. I had no idea which, but I itched to calm her, to make her feel safe and cared for.

When she gazed up at me, my breath hitched. "How did you change the color of your eyes? I vividly remember an array of reds and oranges, like a dancing flame."

My brow rose. "Princess Savina, that sounds as though you fancy me."

She glared at me, making it hard not to smile. I held up my hands. "I'm just teasing." I crossed my ankle over my thigh and leaned back. "The truth of my shifting eyes is the very secret I had intended on sharing. Do we have a deal?"

My heart thudded inside my chest. I was taking a chance trusting her. She knew little about the god Prometheus, as did many of Zeus's offspring. But maybe she believed the story I told at dinner the other night and would find refuge in knowing I, too, had been caged by her grandfather.

Her hands fidgeted in her lap as her gaze settled downward. I enveloped her hand and threaded our fingers together. "How about this? I'll tell you mine regardless of any deal. If you deem my secret good enough to meet yours, you tell me. If not, I trust after all we have been through together that you'll keep my information to yourself." I gave her a light squeeze.

She looked up and her eyes shifted, like the uncertainty and fear she felt had drifted away and were replaced by something else.

I slid closer to her, and her chest started to rise and fall in quick succession. My eyes zeroed in on where her tongue snuck out to lick the corner of her lips. I doubt she even knew she was doing it. Heat stirred inside of me, desire I knew had no place in this moment. I cupped the side of her face, my thumb brushing her soft skin. The war inside of me stirred, tugging between telling her the truth and forgetting everything entirely and devouring her mouth with mine.

"The reason the color of my eyes—"

"Your Grace."

Savina jumped away from me as if my powers had burned her.

From the shadows, Flick appeared under the hanging oil lamp. His gaze volleyed between us. "I am so sorry to interrupt. You are needed. Vanden..."

I stood. "Is he all right?"

"I think it's best if you speak to him." Flick bowed his head.

"Of course." I swiveled back to Savina. "Another time then." I hoped with all my heart another opportunity like this would arrive. Savina had threaded herself into my life and wrapped so tightly around me, sometimes it was hard for me to breathe in her presence.

Her eye lashes lowered. "Another time."

Flick stayed quiet until we entered the hallway and rounded the bend. Our guest chambers came into sight, and I headed straight for Vanden's.

"Pythia warned you. She warned all of us." Flick's hard tone halted my feet, and I spun on my heels in surprise. "If we don't get her to the sirens' island, you will have no choice but to kill her. And if you tell her your true identity, you risk all we have worked for. Who can predict how she might take your deception? Have you gone mad?"

My jaw hardened. "You dare stop my conversation with a ruse?" I looked toward Vanden's door, then back to Flick.

"Yes, and I would do it tenfold if it saved you from having to murder the woman you care about."

"He does not wish to see me then." It wasn't a question. I knew I had been fooled but still wanted his admission said aloud.

"Of course not. He's already snoring like the bore he is." He sighed. "I went looking for you to tell you what I witnessed while you were gone, and I saw her take your arm. She was protecting you."

"She was playing me, or rather the part. It was all for show." I waved him off, not wanting to get into what I already knew was a complicated situation.

"No, it was not. Then I nearly tore out my eyes for traitors when I saw the way you looked at her. You were going to...you had this look..." He averted his gaze.

"Oh, just spit it out."

"You cannot fall for her, Conleth. She is a weapon."

"She is a woman."

Flick thumped a hand on my shoulder and squeezed. "It is a foolish sheep who makes the wolf his lover."

I knocked off his arm. "I am not, nor ever will be, a sheep. But your message is clear, friend."

Without another word, I continued to my room, Flick's warning weighing on my heart. If my feelings turned into more, could I really betray her? I feared not. But to save mankind, I'd have no choice but to follow through. Her hate would never expire, and no matter what we shared, she'd toss me aside when she learned the truth. Flick was right. No matter my heart's desire, loving Savina would never be my future. It would bring my end on swift wings.

CHAPTER TWENTY

SAVINA

I had no idea what just transpired between Conleth and myself. Before his steward interrupted us, we'd teetered on the verge of swapping pieces of our souls, or so it felt.

The interference might have come at the perfect time. Sharing the truth about my powers would only make things worse in the long run, and knowing his secret would tie me to him in irreversible ways I didn't wish to commit to.

Yes. It is for the best.

I pushed off the bench and started for my bedroom. A long night's rest sounded perfect right now. But as I passed the office doors, I heard my grandfather's voice roar, "He's here. I knew if I started killing innocents, he'd intervene, and he did. The easiest way to get him out of hiding is to slaughter his precious humans." Zeus clenched and unclenched his fists. "How does he know my plans? What oracle speaks with lax lips? I want them found. And killed. Now."

"Knows what plan?" Uncle Hermes scratched his head, mussing his blond hair.

"Prometheus stopped the war I started between the guards, pirates, and townspeople. That was the work of a god. Did you hear the guards talking about how the square was lit up with fire to heights they've never seen before? Who else has the power to wield an element to that extent?

There's only one god I know of and now he has come to kill her." Zeus pounded his fist against the wall, and I jumped. Flecks of white paint rained down to the floor like snow.

Grandfather paced the room while my uncle sat with his back to me on the edge of Rylander's desk. Was it just the two of them?

"We need to find him. I want all your brethren searching." Zeus tapped his lower lip. "Well, except perhaps Apollo. He might not understand."

"Father, you're not making any sense." Hermes crossed his arms, the muscles on his back scrunched under his tunic.

"You foolish child. Why do you think I've protected her all these years? Do you really think I care for one lowly demi-god when I have thousands at my beck and call?"

Hermes tilted his head. "Savina?"

Zeus rolled his eyes, huffing like a bull at my uncle. "Yes, Savina."

Me? What was grandfather talking about?

"She will make certain Prometheus surrenders himself to me again. I will put his arse right back on the mountain and get two eagles this time. But if he gets to her first, he will kill her." Zeus pounded his clenched hand against the headrest of the chair. The wooden backing split in twain, and I sucked back a gasp.

"You're using Savina to lure Prometheus out of hiding? But why would he care? What can she..." My uncle stopped talking as if Zeus had robbed him of speech. He hopped off the desk. "What can she do on her eighteenth birthday that makes her of special importance to you?"

Zeus's lips peeled into a grin so cold, chills ran up and down my arms, puckering my skin. "She has the power to kill them all."

My hands covered my mouth as the weight of his words settled like stone in the pit of my stomach. I fumbled back a step, almost tripping over myself. My arm shot out to steady me, but nothing was there.

"Because of Prometheus's escape, you would kill all the people of Cava?" Uncle Hermes stepped closer to Zeus, blocking my view of him.

"No. I would kill everyone from all five lands to punish that swine. Maybe this time, he'll accept his place. What I did to the townspeople today was nothing compared to what I will do to the world with Savina's powers."

My heart leapt in my throat as my feet fled the awful confession. What started as a brisk walk turned into a jog. As I rounded the corner, I ran right into Krinny. She steadied me by the arm.

"Where have you been?" Her face tightened, replenishing the angry timbre she'd turned on me earlier.

"We need to get to my brother." I grabbed her shoulders. "No. We need to get my father. Zeus is planning to kill..." I closed my eyes. Admitting the next word out loud would make it real. "...everyone."

Krinny removed my hands from her body and stepped backward, putting distance between us. "I do not have time for your hysterics. You need to get to your room. Per the king's orders, I will be standing guard all night, every night. You will not venture out of my sights until the wedding, and even then, I plan to stay very close." Her dark brow lifted. "Do you understand?"

"I am telling you the truth. He plans to use me, my powers, to kill all five kingdoms. All the humans." Terror pitched my voice. "You included."

The creases around her eyes crinkled as she narrowed her gaze. "What proof do you have to back these wild allegations?"

Proof? What proof could I possibly give her but my word? Trouble was, my word meant little to her now. But I had to try.

"Zeus is here. He comes to Cava in the form of Zenith, the advisory council member." I blurted out a truth I was never supposed to admit to any human, especially ones who lived in the castle. But desperation called for desperate measures.

Krinny's brows pulled together. "That's enough, Savina. I don't have time for more lies. I'll not be led on another false quest." Krinny turned me by the shoulders and pushed me forward. "To your room. Now!" With a hand at my back, she guided me all the way there in silence.

I chewed the inside of my cheek. She'd never believe me. Why waste my breath only to anger her further? I'd have to find a solution without her help.

She entered my chambers ahead of me. "Let me check the room and make sure none of your accomplices are here."

My nose flared as I bit back the defense perched on the tip of my tongue. She had every right to be mad, but this accusatory room-searching act was beyond ridiculous. Krinny walked a circle in the bathroom, checked beneath the bed, opened my armoire doors, then strolled onto the balcony.

I stood in front of my ottoman with my arms crossed against my chest. When she came back inside emptyhanded, I smirked. "Are you happy?"

She shut the veranda doors and clicked the lock shut. "There are guards below your balcony just as there are guards below Calli's. Do not try anything. You will be watched at all times."

"What a lovely prison you've provided."

Krinny's face fell for a mere second before the mask of indifference returned. "If you believe this to be a prison, remember it is one of your own making."

My eyes watered, but I refused to shed a tear. If she wanted our relationship to be like this from now on, there was nothing I could do, but she did deserve a partial truth. "For what it's worth, I did what I thought was best for my family."

Krinny's shoulders tensed. "Sadly, I had believed to be included in that category before today. My mistake." Her jaw ticked. "Calli will no longer be seeing Henrik. In turn, you will no longer need to protect either of them."

My mouth opened. She knew.

"How dumb do you think I am? I've been shadowing you since you were eleven years old. I've followed and watched you from a distance for years as you've explored Cava's streets." She shook her head. "It's only within the last year I stopped tailing you, giving you the space I believed you deserved because I trusted you. Ketner and I had an agreement. He'd watch when I couldn't. And no matter what Calli did, you told me the truth about where *you* were. But today you changed that, and thus the course of your protection detail. From now on, this will be your life. Don't cast blame on me." She pointed to the mounted mirror inside a gold floral frame. "Take a look in there, and you'll find the person who did this to you."

With that, she left, slamming the door, and locking it from the outside.

Warm tears beaded along my cheek and chin on a path to the floor. I tossed myself onto the bed and buried my head into the pillow. What was I going to do? I had to escape, but how? In less than a fortnight, I turned eighteen, and then... How would I end up killing everyone? And what about Prometheus? If he was here already, he'd be coming for me. To kill me.

"Well, I didn't think I'd find you sewing in here, but crying feels a bit dramatic. How much did Krinny yell at you?"

I jackknifed up to see my niece slipping through the curtains from my now opened veranda doors. The wind at her back blew her blonde hair over her shoulders. She smirked and her dimples popped.

I ran to her and threw my arms around her. "They know about Henrik."

"I know. It's why I am here." She squeezed a little tighter before relaxing in my hold. "I came to say goodbye."

"You what?" I pulled away and stared at her. The glint that lived in her amber irises had dulled. "You can't."

She lifted one shoulder and let it drop. "More like I probably shouldn't, but I won't stop seeing him. He's already waiting for me." She swallowed. "I must go. If not now, I never will, and my life without him would be nothing."

I cupped the side of her face, and she offered me a sad smile. They would leave Cava and never...a fresh idea tumbled out of my mouth. "I will leave with you." It made sense. If I went with Calli and Henrik, Prometheus wouldn't be able to find me, and neither would my grandfather. No one could use me as a weapon. I wouldn't let it happen. And no god would kill me. You couldn't slay what you couldn't find.

Calli bloomed, standing straighter, her eyes crackling with vitality again. "You will?"

"Yes. But I am not sure how you intend to sneak out of here unnoticed." I squinted. "Wait a minute, how did you get to my room?"

Calli winked. "I knocked out the guards. We probably only have a couple hours before the change, so..."

I yanked her by the arm. We ran to the balcony and leaned over at the same time to study the prostrate form in the grass below.

"He's still out cold." I squinted down, making sure his eyes were closed. "We must be quick." I grabbed the drapes Calli always used as rope and handed them to her to go first.

"*The Black Hollow* leaves soon, so we have no choice but to move fast." Calli reached for the hangings, but I pulled them back.

"The what?"

She shrugged. "That's our escape. You ready to live the life of a pirate?" Calli chuckled.

Lou would be so proud to hear Calli's enthusiasm for the idea of living on the high seas as a brigand, but only for a moment. When she found out her daughter had joined the enemy's ranks, not even Cava's army would stop her from exploding. But what choice did I have but to support Calli's decision? If I wanted to stay alive and keep humanity safe, too, this was my only option.

"Ready as I'll ever be."

I took one more look at my room. My gaze traveled over the wood carvings my father had etched into my bedpost to depict one of my favorite stories: how the Goddess of the Sun saved the people of her nation while falling in love with the man who helped her claim her rightful rule. If only fairy tales like that existed. I sighed and turned around, following my niece into a new life.

CHAPTER TWENTY-ONE

SAVINA

Calli and I made our way toward the harbor where Henrik waited. I hoped he'd be okay with two stowaways rather than one.

Shopkeepers filled the small strip of shoppes in this part of the village, and the dockworkers were still unloading the seafood inventories that had come in earlier that day. It was almost as if the morning's chaotic slaughter had never happened. Business went on as usual. The overwhelming fish smell made me cough. I'd never gotten used to that stench, but I guessed with our new life, I'd have no choice but to endure what would become a daily nuisance.

"We're almost there," Calli whispered. I reached for her hand and interlaced our fingers to keep her close. "We have to stay away from the lanterns." We crouched and hid behind the shadows of the buildings as we continued onward.

As we neared the crest of the hill, I spotted the top of *The Black Hollow*'s mainmast waving in the evening's breeze. From here, the men looked like rodents, hauling supplies across the decks. Some drank grog, loitering at the rail like they were at the tavern. My gaze traveled out to sea. It looked black. If not for the moon, it would have blended into the night sky.

"Are you ready?" Calli asked.

As I took a confident step forward, a hand shot out from the corner of the next building, ripping Calli's hand out of mine. Fists bunched in our tunics and tugged us both backward into an alley.

Two flaming irises roved my face as if seeking signs of madness. "What in the gods' names are you both doing?" Conleth's low admonishment maintained a steady pitch, unlike my erratically beating heart.

I rolled my shoulders back, beckoning my inner strength. "We need to leave town."

Conleth released us and leaned against the stone wall behind him. The unnerving calm on his face didn't waver as he lowered his chin to look me in the eyes. "I am going to regret asking, but why do you need to leave town, and why are you two slinking around in the middle of the night when gods know what could happen to you both out here alone?"

Calli stepped forward. "My parents won't let me see Henrik anymore. I'm fleeing with him aboard his father's ship."

Conleth's eyes widened before volleying to me. "You're accompanying the lovebirds' escape? Why?" He cocked a skeptical brow. "In protest?"

"No. It's more than that," I said through clenched teeth. When I'd tried to tell Krinny, she hadn't believed me. I imagined the conversation with Conleth would be no different.

"I'm waiting." Conleth waved a hand, urging me to continue.

"Yeah. Me, too. I thought you were leaving the castle because of me." Calli squinted.

I closed my lids and sighed. When I fluttered them open, I drew in a courageous breath. "You both might not believe me."

Calli's lips thinned. "It's like you don't even know me."

"I overheard Zeus and Hermes today at the castle. When I turn eighteen, Zeus believes he'll be able to use me as a weapon to massacre every human in the Five Isles. He's baiting Prometheus out of hiding to save the people." Calli gasped, but Conleth didn't even move a muscle. "Apparently an oracle already told Prometheus of Zeus's plan, and he's now on his way to Cava to kill me."

Conleth pushed off the wall and moved into my personal space. He was so close I could feel his breath on my nose. "Then we need to get you out of here, and fast."

My forehead crinkled. "You believe me? About everything?"

"I believe you." Calli tossed a thumb in Conleth's direction. "But I'm surprised he does."

Conleth chuckled. "I've known Zenith is Zeus and Smitter is Hermes since I met them. I imagine with them cavorting around the castle, it'd be easy to stumble upon their conversation, and since you believe it to be true, then I believe it." He reached out and squeezed my elbow. "I will help you."

"How did you figure that out that they are gods?" Calli's brows raised to her hairline.

Conleth released my arm and turned toward Calli with a smirk. "Part of my intuition."

My tongue failed me. I didn't really understand Conleth's powers, but I also hadn't asked much about them. I guessed that made sense though.

"Wait." My head twisted back and forth. "Why are you here?" Did he follow us, or was he here...

Encroaching heavy breathing made Conleth push us behind him. "Who goes there?"

"It's me," Henrik whispered.

Calli pushed Conleth out of her way and threw herself into Henrik's opened arms, wrapping her legs around his torso. Henrik kissed her with the hot passion of Ares, and she kissed him back—his forbidden Aphrodite. My mouth flopped open. I'd never seen them this way before. A sliver of jealousy slinked into the pit of my stomach. How I longed for someone to love me the same.

When they broke apart, she breathed, "I'll never let them take you away from me."

He placed her on the ground and kissed her nose. "Nor will I, my little sphinx."

I looked back to find Conleth smiling. "Young love is so refreshing." He threw his arm over my shoulder and pulled me in. "I hope we're much the same in our early days of marriage." He chuckled.

I tossed his arm off me. "You'd delight in that, wouldn't you?"

"Very much, princess." His eyes held mine and for a brief moment, I truly believed he meant what he said. "But for now, we need to get you to safety." His hand steadied my lower back.

"Safety?" Henrik questioned over Calli's shoulder.

"Henrik, how were you getting Calli aboard your father's ship?" Conleth's gaze traveled to the fluttering black-and-white skull and bone flag of the boat anchored at the nearest dock.

"I made a deal with our cook. I'd bring her Ketner's healing potions in return for her letting Calli stay in the kitchen quarters."

"Does she know what Calli looks like?"

Henrik shook his head.

"Good." Conleth turned to Calli. "I know you want to leave with Henrik. But I need you to look at the bigger picture. Savina will be killed or forced to kill if she stays. She needs to set sail tonight, and this is the only way. I also need you here in Cava to bring word to my men."

I pushed Conleth's chest, but he didn't budge. "You can't ask her to do that." How dare he request Calli forfeit the love of her life so that I could have a future? Well, so the world could have a future, I supposed...but still. I would never ask that of her.

"Yes, he can, and I will." Calli stepped out of Henrik's hold and came to clasp my hands in hers. "You've saved me and Henrik's lives time and time again. We not only owe you, but we love you, and we'd do anything to keep you safe." Calli peeked back at Henrik, who nodded, wearing a frown that aged his boyish face.

"We would do anything for you, Sav. You're the only reason we found each other in the first place, and the only reason we have been able to continue to see each other. Without you, we'd never have had the chance at love." He looked up at Conleth. "I assume you want to escort her."

"Yes."

Henrik shook his head. "I don't have a way to get you on, and they check everyone as we board. You could probably blend in if you could figure out how to—"

Conleth placed his hand on Henrik's shoulder. "Don't you worry about me. You get her on the ship, and I will meet you both in the kitchen before we heave off." Conleth looked between Henrik and Calli. "Say your goodbyes now. Time is of the essence. I will walk Calli back some of the way and let her know what to tell my men. But it's important Savina gets on right away."

Henrik's mouth turned down. "I hope you know what you're doing, Conleth. If you get caught, they will kill you."

Conleth smiled. "A man like me is hard to kill. Go on now. Say your goodbyes."

Calli smiled, but it betrayed her as tears streamed down her face. She pulled me forward into a hug. "You'll stay alive, right? Promise me, Sav, one day I will see you again."

A soft sob escaped me. "I promise. I love you." I pulled back and cupped her cheek, my thumb sweeping away her sorrow. "You are my sister, and you will always live here." I grabbed her hand and placed it over my heart.

Calli turned around and glared at Conleth. "You'd better protect her from Prometheus and Zeus. If either of them gets their hands on her, I will blame you."

Conleth swallowed. "I will protect her with my life and keep her safe. That is the only promise I can offer."

"That's fair." Calli threw herself at her beloved. She wrapped her arms around Henrik's midsection, her face buried in his chest. "I love you. There is no sea nor war that can keep us apart in our hearts."

Henrik kissed her head. "I love you, forever and always in this life and the next. You will always be my little sphinx."

When she pulled away, he kissed her. Their passion and vulnerability fractured my own heart.

Conleth threaded his fingers into mine and pulled me to his side. Warmth radiated between us, providing me a small comfort in my sadness. "They will find each other again."

"How do you know?" My words were barely audible in my stuffy head.

"Exchanged hearts always find their way back to each other. Even death cannot divide two souls bound together."

It was a lovely sentiment that I wanted to be true, but I had seen firsthand how the gods liked to toy with star-crossed lovers like Orpheus and Eurydice, or with mysterious heroes like Galen...or Conleth. Especially those who gave over their heart or their time to me. Higher powers made sure none of it was ever real. Maybe my death would solve the world's problems.

"Do you think I should let Prometheus find me?"

Conleth's eyes widened as he stepped back—my heart beat erratically waiting for his response. But he never answered.

CHAPTER TWENTY-TWO

CONLETH

C alli smacked her aunt's arm. "This is no time to be a martyr."

Savina's red locks glowed like twisting flames framing her porcelain face. She blinked back tears, her blue eyes as clear as the Caviar Sea. Even with fear and sadness etched in her features, her beauty stole my breath away.

"Your niece is right. What we need to do is focus on getting you aboard. You'll need to pin up your hair and perhaps roll around in the dirt to blend in better." I pointed to the moist ground covered in morning dew. She might not be able to hide behind the filth, but she'd have to try or she'd be dead before dawn.

"Conleth's got a point," Henrik agreed. "You'll draw too much attention this clean and pretty."

My little songbird huffed but bent down and did as instructed. Her petite hands pressed into the soft mud, then coated her pants, blouse, and cheeks. Without removing the grime, she pulled up her hair and twisted it into a bun. Dirt-caked strands stuck to the side of her face as she glared at us with an *are you satisfied now?* grimace.

Henrik pointed to her mouth. "Maybe we should pull a tooth or something. Not many sailors have all their teeth."

Savina gasped, fingertips pressed against her sealed lips.

"He's joking." I grabbed Henrik by the neck and squeezed. "Right?"

Henrik shrugged.

Whether he spoke out in jest or not, I imagined the princess would not find humor in the monumental if not impossible task of disguising her. I just prayed to the gods we'd make it close to Anthemusa and that I'd have time to figure out the rest before we were caught.

"You need to go now." I gently pushed Henrik.

The young boy turned and planted one last chaste kiss on Calli's lips before spinning back to the path he came from. He waved to Savina to follow. The princess's gaze roamed over her niece before it settled on me. "Thank you," she mouthed. Then she took off after Henrik, who was now cresting the hill.

Soft sobs sounded next to me. "Will I ever see them again?" Calli whispered. Her eyes stayed fixed on the hillside even after they disappeared down the opposite slope.

I wrapped my arm around her shoulder and pulled her in to my side. "I vow you will be with them again."

She looked up at me, her amber eyes glassy with unshed tears. "You mean in Elysian Fields, don't you?"

I smiled. *Smart girl.* "I hope before then as well."

Calli buried her face in my chest and released a mournful cry that cracked open a larger dam. I held her close, knowing her sacrifice all too well. Over the years, I'd stopped saying goodbye to those I cared about. It had become second nature to lose the ones I loved. The pain now felt like numbing ale rather than piercing arrows. But to Calli this was as raw as a butcher's fresh kill.

"Come on. There's someone we need to see before you get back to the castle and tell my men where I have gone." I kissed the top of her head and released her.

She nodded, sniffling into my shirt before letting go.

We moved through the shadows, climbing over swells of rocks, dry brush, and yellow blooms until we reached the worn cobblestone streets leading into town. I had been headed to meet with General Ballas next to the fountain outside the tavern when I saw Savina and Calli traipsing along the edges of the path I had just taken. I followed until I realized they were going to the docks. Then I abandoned my own course entirely to capture and question them.

"What are we doing here?" Calli looked around, as if the answers lay in the scenery.

I placed my finger across my lips. The last thing we needed was to draw attention to ourselves. The townspeople had little clue what Savina looked like, but Calli might be another story. She had no reason to hide in the castle all day like the princess. Whispers of any kind could be dangerous.

Out of the shadows, Ballas appeared, toying with the end of her elegant, red-black braid. Her oversized hat didn't hide her high cheekbones, scrunched nose, or the perplexed tilt of her mouth when her diamond-colored eyes traced over my new companion. "Conleth, are you mad?"

"Ballas?" Calli gasped as she took in the siren on dry land.

"Shhh," Ballas and I said in unison.

"How do you two know each other? Oh, my gods..." Calli's hands clasped over her mouth as her eyes trailed down Ballas's blue ruffled silk blouse to her newfound legs sporting a pair of fitted brown trousers. "You are walking...on two feet...and wearing pants," she said, her words muffled by her palms.

Ballas grabbed Calli by the arm and led her around the back of the tavern. I followed. Not many townspeople were out besides shop owners and drunks, but it only took one soul to question our trio and for the guards to be alerted.

Ballas didn't release Calli until we were under the stables, surrounded by hay and horses. The general drew back from the girl as if giving space for her anger to stand.

"When did you get handsy?" Calli leaned up against a stack of straw, her arms crossed, her chin held high. "Did the new legs come with a bad attitude?"

Ballas sighed. "I apologize for the force. I just..." She turned to me. "Conleth, what in the underworld is going on? Why are you with royalty in the middle of town at this hour?"

I rubbed the arch of my nose. "Plans have changed. Apparently, Zeus is already here in Cava preparing to use Savina as a weapon against the land. The pirate boy got Savina onto his ship so she could flee for safety." I frowned at Calli, but it wasn't my place to out her original plan to run away with Henrik. And considering she gave her aunt her position without an ounce of argument, I owed her a debt of silence. "The girl came to say her goodbyes to her loved ones. She will be fine."

Ballas's mouth opened to accommodate her extending fangs, droplets of venom shining on their tips. A siren's reaction to anger was as instinctual as a human holding their breath when they stubbed a toe. I knew she couldn't help the response, but it had me sidling closer to Calli regardless.

"This is not safe," she hissed.

"That's an understatement," Calli mumbled.

I stepped between them. "No, it isn't, but I will be accompanying the princess on her journey. No harm shall befall her. As for Calli..." I stared at Queen Lou's miniature, her shoulders thrown back, curling fingers already itching to fight her way to the castle if needed. "I know she'll be able to escort herself back home without trouble." I emphasized the last word, hoping the girl would take heed.

"I can handle getting back to the palace. I sneak in and out all the time." Calli waved a hand. "Easy as rolling out of bed."

Ballas removed her hat and wiped her forehead with her sleeve. Sweat trickled along her brow. "I don't like it." She glared at Calli. "Any of it."

"You don't have to like it, but you will help me," I said with finality, then turned to Calli. "I need you to make haste back to the citadel and alert my men. Tell them the princess and I have snuck onto the pirate ship. They are not to leave Cava until they hear from me."

Calli pushed off the haystack, eyes narrowed. "How will they hear from you if you are sailing around the isles for the next three months?" Suspicion emphasized and slowed each word as she took one swaggering step toward me. "Captain Fredrick doesn't visit Cava more than four times a year."

Telling Calli the truth wouldn't ease her worry, nor her pain. Savina wouldn't be coming back, but as a god, I could pop in and out of any place with the snap of my fingers. She would figure out my powers soon enough, but for now, it was better to keep her in the dark. I placed my hand on Calli's head and mussed her hair. "You're too smart for your own good."

She swatted my hand. "I'm not a child. I'm thirteen, fourteen in a couple months, just like Henrik. I could very well be a pirate already if my mother still had her ship. Then how would you treat me?"

"The same as I do now. If you seek the pirate's life, then you need to start learning how to take orders. That's what a good brigand does when their captain asks something of them." Her lips pursed, but she stayed silent. "Just tell my men what I said."

"Fine." Calli's nose wrinkled. The fresh pain of watching her beloved walk away, perhaps to never return, was a knife wedged between us. "And what would you like me to say when the king and queen figure out Savina is missing? You know everyone will assume I know something, and with you gone as well, they'll first assume you kidnapped her. You know that, right?"

"Don't worry about me. Just feign innocence."

Calli rolled her eyes. "The last thing my parents will believe."

Ballas stepped forward. "Maybe she should tell her father..."

I raised my hands, my anger getting the better of me. Flames rippled along my palms, and both women gulped. With a steady breath, I quenched the fire. "Tell your father nothing. I mean it, Calli. Make an excuse worth believing. If you ever want to see Henrik and your aunt again, you will lie, and it *will* be believable. If your family knows where they are, what Henrik did, everyone you love could step into death's path."

Determination hardened the youthful lines of Calli's features. "I won't tell a soul. Ever!" She looked out toward the dock with worrisome eyes. "I'll figure something out and throw them off your trail."

"Good. It's time to go."

Calli exited the stable but stopped before she reached the troughs. I was just about to ask her what was wrong when she pivoted and ran to me. She threw her arms around my waist. This time she didn't shed tears, she just hugged me with a grip so fierce, I held my breath.

"I might not understand everything that's happening, who you are, why the sirens are here *walking* around, or anything my great-grandfather is doing, but I believe you will protect my aunt and that is all I care about. I trust you, Conleth. Don't make a fool out of me." And with that, she turned and ran into the darkness, taking a piece of my compassion with her.

"I worry her heart is too exposed. That she trusts too easily. Blind faith is a weakness." Ballas spoke more to herself than me, but I allowed the words to permeate my mind. Calli's heart did trust with ease, not because she was weak but because she was strong, resilient. She'd make an excellent warrior one day, maybe even a leader of her own ship. Of that I was certain.

"What shall we do next?" Ballas's squeezing talons nipped at my shoulder through my tunic.

"Gather your forces and get in the water. Follow *The Black Hollow*. Keep it surrounded at all times. Then wait for my command."

"Just how many of the sirens do you want in the water?"

"All of you."

CHAPTER TWENTY-THREE

SAVINA

H enrik chuckled under his breath as we hurried down the hill to the narrow trail leading toward the beach.

"What?" I barked, finding nothing about this funny.

"Your family turmoil makes my father look like a kitten. I mean, your grandfather wants to use you as a weapon of war against another god who wants you dead. How twisted is that?" Henrik ducked under a tree branch and held it for me to follow.

I groaned. "I'm aware of my family issues, thank you very much." I plucked a nearby cherry and tossed it at his back.

Henrik smirked over his shoulder. He continued, making haste with his stride as the trees cleared. "We've all got 'em. Can't outrun your own blood." The pounding of his boots hit the rocky path ahead of me like a racing pulse. Henrik was right. Even if I made it out of here, I'd be dead one way or another. Either by Zeus's manipulation or Prometheus's blade. My blood would find me one day. I just hoped it would be at a much later date.

But then again, who knew what Conleth and I were about to get ourselves into aboard *The Black Hollow*? What if a worse fate lay in wait within the ship's hull? I pressed my thumb and pointer into my temples, trying to release some of the tension building from all the uncertainty.

The sky and the sea blended like a black canvas, the moon a silver flame. I'd never feared the dark because I could always control the light, but my foreboding imbued the landscape with a different kind of dread—the fear of falling into a void and losing control of myself. If Zeus thought I had the power to end every life that tread upon this land, then what sort of fate could I possibly have? I imagined just like the night sky, my destiny would be dark, lonely, and terrifying.

Henrik stopped short, pivoting to face me. I nearly barreled into him. He grabbed my shoulders to steady me. "I almost forgot. I gave the crew your name, Savina, to hide Calli's true identity."

I knocked his arms away and pushed him aside. "If you weren't saving my arse right now, I'd pummel you for that." I drew in a deep breath. At least no one had a clue what the princess of Cava looked like, especially not the likes of pirates. "At best it'll be easy to remember."

"Right?" Henrik bumped my shoulder and chuckled. I shoved him back and shared in his laughter.

Trying to give Calli something to connect her to home was almost sweet. I wished Henrik thought things through more, but that would be like asking the gods to leave humans alone. A pointless waste of breath.

We snaked our way down the mountain, hiking dirt trails made by other travelers who took the beaten path rather than cut through the town. Mostly thieves, brigands, or vagabonds, those that kept to the shadows for fear of being found. Salty humidity thickened the air as we reached the bottom. I watched a fisherman carry a metal cage filled with crabs from a ship to the dock. The sea creatures scrambled over each other, locked in desperate squabbles with fellows and the bars of their crated prison. I knew the feeling.

I looked up, sensing eyes on us as we stood below *The Black Hollow*.

"Keep walking and stop staring. You're drawing attention to yourself," Henrik said in undertones. "You look like you're guilty of something."

Of course I looked crazed. Fear hung around my neck like a noose and wreaked havoc in my stomach. One false move and any one of these pirates would behead me.

"Relax your face."

"Stop fussing over how I look and just get me onboard."

Henrik's gaze drifted over to me and he smirked. "Not fun being on the receiving end of orders, huh, princess?"

I pushed his shoulder hard enough to stumble him, but he recovered quickly, snickering under his breath.

The crew on the deck tended to their chores. Several men raised the sails, others boarded barrels of supplies onto the ship. A man shouldered around us on the gangplank with a deer hung around his neck, the blood dripping onto the wood.

Ick.

When we reached the main deck, a large older man with rolls in his chin and neck like an old bulldog shot his hand out, stopping our progress. "Where in the underworld have ya been, boy? Yer father been looking all over the ship for ya."

Henrik tossed his thumb over his shoulder at me. "Fretta asked me to grab extra hands."

The man who looked like he ate his weight in dough trailed his eyes over me from head to toe. "Something of a looker under all that dirt, ay?" He smiled, showcasing his missing teeth, at least five between the bottom and top row, which made me think twice about Henrik's joke.

The boy feigned innocence, lifting one shoulder and letting it drop. His face settled into a bored expression, more relaxed than I'd ever seen it, while my insides were buzzing like a swarm of bees.

"Fretta said get hands. She's got hands. Figured she'd work."

The big guy nodded. "Get her to the kitchen and then get yer arse to yer father's cabin. Ya hear me?"

Henrik grabbed me by the elbow, and we surged forward. "Keep your head down. Do not make eye contact with anyone on this ship."

My eyes stayed fixed to Henrik's boots and the chipped floorboards of the ship until we took the stairs down to the first level. We continued through a narrow hall and stopped at the end in front of a slim door. Henrik knocked twice before opening it and strolling in.

A woman no older than Lou stood in the middle of the small kitchen, her hands propped on thick hips wrapped in a soiled apron. Her eyes cut to mine, her mouth pressing into a hard line that matched the scar trailing across her cheek and to her hairline.

"I'm Savina," I said with a small wave.

The woman drew a deep breath, looking from me to Henrik before she shook her head, cursing under her breath. She grabbed three shot glasses and placed them on the counter in a row.

"I know she's not exactly what you thought, but..." Henrik stuttered.

The woman who Henrik called Fretta held up her hand. She stood on her toes to grab a bottle of bourbon from the shelf. With her thumb, she flicked the cork out of the bottle. It landed on the counter and rolled until it settled against a pot. She poured all three glasses.

I reached out to grab one, but Henrik smacked my hand. I growled, but he ignored me and nodded with his chin toward the woman. I watched as Fretta picked up the first one and tossed back the liquor in one gulp. She then made her way down the line until all three were emptied. Heat burned down my throat and settled into my stomach as I swallowed back my mounting nerves. This couldn't be a good sign.

"I don't want to know who you really are, and I don't want to know how you know the boy." She glared at Henrik, even though her words were for me. "You help me in the kitchen, but other than that, you stay hidden in the pantry. No one must know you are here." She refilled one glass and threw back the contents, making that a total of four shots. "You will get off this ship at the next port." Now her gaze turned toward me. "I won't have you bring about the boy's death."

"But, Fretta—" Henrik stammered.

"No 'but, Fretta.' She ain't no pirate. She ain't no commoner either, which can only mean she is..." She shook her head. "It don't matter to me. She's in trouble and you say you care about her. That's all I need to know." She moved around the table and got in Henrik's face. "But I swear, boy, you better never ask anything like this of me again. Ketner's vials are not worth the blood." She waved her finger around his nose. "You hear me? I ain't looking for a matching scar." She traced the crooked line from her ear down her cheek to the corner of her mouth.

"Yes, ma'am." Henrik looked at the floor as he shuffled his feet. Whatever had happened to this woman, Henrik felt responsible.

Fretta shooed him with both hands. "Now get. Your father's been looking for ya. I told him you'd be helping me like the good boy you are, preparing gruel for tomorrow's breakfast."

Henrik looked up and smiled, showcasing all his teeth, including the one I'd healed. "You're a goddess, Fretta, you know that?"

The older woman blushed. "Now hush and get." With a final shove out the door, Henrik waved goodbye.

Fretta spun on her heels. "I ain't got no good feeling about ya." Her lips pulled upward, into a surprising grin. "Then again, I ain't got no good feeling about anything when it comes to *The Black Hollow*." She moved close enough to cup my face. Her calluses rubbed my cheeks. "You must be in mighty big trouble to come here for solace. This is a place people come to die, not for refuge."

A tear streamed down my cheek, one I hadn't willed but couldn't stop.

"Ah, don't let 'em get ya down. Tears are wasted prayers on those who ain't deserving of them." She wiped the wetness off my cheek. "Those deserving will never make ya cry." She smoothed down her apron and began to put away the glasses. "You'll be just fine so long as you stay out of sight. Plus, I could use two extra hands. We've got lots of mouths to feed. You'll stay busy." She popped the cork back on the bottle and motioned for me to follow her with the flick of her hand.

We walked to the other end of the kitchen where a small door barely on its hinges stood ajar. "It ain't much, but it's all I got." She pulled open what Hannah, our cook back at the castle, would call a pantry and ushered me inside. But in the place of stacked spices was a wooden bench with a thin mattress. Feathers stuck out from the ends as if the birds inside were trying to escape. A thin blanket rested on top of a single pillow. My legs barely fit in the small space as I walked farther inside. How in the gods were Conleth and I...

"Savina." Conleth's voice plucked me from my thoughts. "Savina, where are you?" My hand covered my mouth as I gasped. Henrik never told...

"Who in the underworld are you?" Fretta stormed out of the closet. She grabbed a knife from the counter and, before I could utter a syllable, held it to Conleth's throat. "You have two seconds to explain yourself before I use your innards for tomorrow's supper."

Her gaze traveled down his body. His pristine body. Why hadn't he rubbed dirt on his face and shirt like I had? And how, in an outfit that screamed Eloquan royalty, had he even gotten aboard without being butchered?

"How did a pretty thing like you board a ship like this?" Fretta asked the question swimming in my mind. Her gaze traveled back to me, then Conleth. As if lightning struck, her eyes widened. "Damn Henrik to Hades's dominion." She released Conleth and swiveled the tip of her blade between us. "I assume you're a set?"

Conleth straightened his shoulders. "This is my wife."

My mouth dropped open. "We are not—"

"—here to do you harm. We are just two lovers in need of sanctuary." Conleth finished my sentence. My face burned hot. Of course he'd lie with an absurd story like that. I shouldn't even be surprised. Anything to ruffle my feathers.

"We are also the reason Henrik remained in one piece after his meeting with Captain Niles."

Fretta laughed. "You think telling me you saved Henrik from a slicing and dicing is gonna win an old bird like mine's heart, aye?"

Conleth smiled and even my own insides melted at how handsome he looked.

Fretta waved her knife. "You are good." She shot me a look. "I can see why you're in trouble. This one is a fine piece of brisket." She shook her head. "Henrik must have a death wish. I swear it." She nodded her head in Conleth's direction. "Why ya best stay with your lady here in the pantry. If either of you are seen, you may as well say your last prayers to Zeus."

I shuddered at my grandfather's name. He sat at the bottom of the list of gods I'd be praying to in the future.

"We'll raise anchor in an hour, and I'll be getting some shut-eye. I suggest you both do the same." She muttered to herself as she left us alone.

Conleth and I wordlessly retreated into the tiny rectangular room with a cot barely large enough to hold me. How in the underworld would we both fit without touching?

"I'd sleep on the floor, but there's no room there. We will have to make do." Conleth grabbed a pricket with a candle atop. He flicked his fingers over the wick, and the small space glowed. "Here." He handed the flame to me as he closed the door. Then he removed his vest and folded it. He placed it on the shelf opposite the cot that held pots and pans. I watched as he removed his boots.

"What are you doing?" My jaw slackened.

His brow quirked. "Disrobing."

"Yes, I can see that, but..." I struggled to find words as he started to unbutton his shirt. Dark strands of hair covered a chest made up of solid muscle. My throat dried like a desert. Conleth stopped four buttons down and stared at the ceiling with an exasperated huff. Was that because I'd stared? Did he think I fancied him now? A blush crept along my cheekbones as I realized how long we'd stretched the silence.

"I will keep my shirt and pants on, but I am not sleeping fully clothed. If you'd like to"—he waved his hand to the cot—"go right on ahead."

A mixture of a sigh and grunt fled my lips. *Did I wish to? No. Would I? Yes.*

I set the pricket on the ground and crawled under the lone blanket, pulling it around me. Conleth stared at me like a deer frozen in the woods.

"What?"

"Are you really sleeping with your shoes on?" He chuckled, not waiting for a response. Then he climbed into bed with me.

"Can you sleep on the other side? I don't like being against a wall."

"Whatever the princess wishes." Conleth moved over me and settled in.

I had never laid next to a man. In fact, the only soul to enter my bed and snuggle up to me like a cat had been my niece. Sometimes she'd do it out of laziness rather than going back to her room, but on nights when Henrik left with his father's ship, she'd find her way under my sheets and cry herself to sleep by my side.

A knot formed in my throat, knowing tonight would be the first time she'd have to deal with that pain all alone, and instead of mourning the loss of Henrik, she'd mourn the loss of both of us.

CHAPTER TWENTY-FOUR

CONLETH

I stared up at the ceiling, exhausted to the bone. Maybe that was the reason I'd almost forgotten about the scars on my lower abdomen. If Savina hadn't gaped at me with such innocence, I might have removed my shirt, exposing my wounds, and then what would I have said? Certainly, she'd have questions. And what if she asked to heal me? No blemishes left from a divine animal of Zeus's creation could be erased. No, she'd figure out my true name and lose all trust in me. She'd believe the wretched lie that Prometheus had set out to kill her. And after such a long deception as Conleth, her betrothed from Eloqua, why would she trust my new tale?

"Why did you come with me?" Her words sounded like the wind, brushing against my ears.

"You couldn't flee on your own," I answered, gruffer than normal. Being in such close proximity and not touching her felt more wrong than letting my betrayal fester between us while I held her in my arms and sealed our lips together.

"I'm not alone. Henrik is helping me. Why not just leave him to risk life and limb? Why escort me in my escape and give up your rule, your title, your life of privilege? Why would you go on the run knowing full well my doomed fate?"

She impaled me with question after question. If she only knew our plan had been to get her on a ship from the start. All this unexpected scheme provided us was a speedier timeline and a leg up on Zeus. He'd never think to check a pirate ship, much less the rabble-rousing vessel that started a war in town just hours ago. The thought had me chuckling.

"What's so funny?"

I rolled onto my side and faced Savina, my head cradled in my hands. Even with my back pressed into the splintered wood panel, our noses were but an inch apart as she followed my lead and rotated onto her side.

"That was a lot of questions."

"Well?"

"Henrik is a capable young man, but he lacks powers. I came because I can protect you and him. If he had to defend you, he'd be killed. This way, he can keep his anonymity. As for all those things you believe I have given up, I do not see it the same way. I do not believe those are mine to begin with. Titles, ruling over people, noble luxury all mean nothing to me."

What was a title to a god who didn't believe in such classifications? And what defined a life of privilege? Certainly, sneaking aboard a ship with a woman who stole the very oxygen out of my lungs stood as a better proposition than being mauled every night for eternity. But I could never explain how this moment seemed like Elysian Fields compared to the Tartarus on Earth I'd endured atop that mountain to a woman who could not know my true identity.

For a moment, we just stared at each other, listening to the water sloshing against the hull and the angry howls of the wind. The gentle rock of the ship soothed the guilt that had settled in my stomach.

"And I do?" Savina broke the silence. "I mean something to you?"

The shock in her voice didn't surprise me, but my immediate answer did. "Yes, very much so."

Savina pinched her eyes closed, and my heart constricted. "Why? You hate me. You're always arguing with me."

I cupped her cheek, my thumb rubbing away the dirt I had asked her to smear on her face only hours ago. My eyes devoured the being who had crawled under my skin and claimed me for her own without ever knowing it. "I rather enjoy our friendly debates."

Savina blinked. "I don't know if I'd call them friendly."

"Oh, no?" I chuckled, letting my hand drop.

Savina rolled onto her back and stared at the wood paneling above us while I continued to gaze at her profile. The outline of her dark lashes left a shadow on her cheeks in the candlelight while the plump curve of her lips moved with the rhythm of her speech.

"He'll find me, you know. Zeus. He will never give up. If he truly believes I am a weapon..." Savina lifted her hands and twisted them back and forth, inspecting her fingers like she couldn't believe they possessed the power to kill. "He will never stop."

I knew all too well Zeus's determination to hunt down a target. "I'll protect you."

Savina let out a breath I didn't realize she was holding and turned her back to me on her side. She snapped her fingers, and darkness blanketed the room. In a sleepy voice, she murmured, "And who will protect you?"

Moments later, soft snores encompassed our small quarters. I unbuttoned the rest of my shirt and allowed my hand to trace over the raised skin left by the beak of an insane bird. Through the walls of the silent ship, the flap of the sails raised gooseflesh along my stomach. The sound too closely resembled the beat of a great eagle's wings.

That first night ...

By Mother Gaia, that first night ...

I rattled the chains, biceps and calves straining until the metal cut into my bound joints. The cold, thin wind burned my lungs and chapped my face. But on that hard, barren outcrop, laid flat and gazing into the peachy rays of sunset on this side of the mountain, I feared isolation would be a meager pinprick compared to my real punishment.

It was that smile of his. A grin like a saw-toothed blade. Blue eyes dancing with mirthless delight that seemed to scream, *I have you now. Mind, body, spirit, in the palm of my hand.*

But he'd only feed on my fear. Grow fat on it. Lick his lips and relish it. So, I donned a grin of my own. "Fine metalwork, old friend. Dabbling in my art, are you? Or did you have little Hephaestus sweat over it?"

Zeus only stared down at me, his long white hair whipped by the wind and face unaffected. Creases framed his eyes and covered his forehead.

I twisted the grin sideways. "I suppose the more important question is, how long do you think it can hold me?"

"In your prime? A century or three," he answered, smooth as ambrosia. "But in this state, how I intend to keep you?" His smile went wolfish, gleaming. "Eternity."

Mouth dry, I switched my mockery for stoicism, and Zeus did the same, standing sentry. Until the glow of sunset became the silvery tones of dusk. His hair became moon-light, on a night with little in the sky. His serrated smile returned when the first beat fell on my ear.

A sound like a canvas snapped taut. Once, twice, thrice. A steady beat, with long pauses as the wretched creature glided on air currents. And in those pauses, I tried to deny. No, it couldn't be what I thought.

His damned eagle. Enormous. Ruthless. Ravenous.

And then the next wingbeat slapped the air, and the bird blotted out the stars.

I thrashed, all stoic dignity gone as the eagle circled, head cocked so a golden eye roved my exposed chest. My heart pounded in my ears. I heard my breath inside my head—short and frantic, undercut with sporadic, feral grunts like feeble war cries to try to keep my nerve. But it had already failed me.

"The fat and the bones," Zeus rumbled, a low purr of unforgotten rage and savage pleasure. "You'd give me fat and bone, and let those worms have their fill?" He rose up to loom over me once more, voice rising until it shook the mountain beneath my back. "I, who delivered you from the tyranny of our fathers. I, who took you into my arms and into my confidence when you crossed the battlefield lines." His spittle hit my face as his eagle's massive feet slammed into the rock on either side of me, beak clicking. "Fat and bone! I don't even feed my pets such scraps." He reached up to stroke the eagle's neck, and it ruffled russet and brown feathers, head twitching this way and that, looking for the perfect spot to dig that wicked, hooked beak. "No. Tonight, and every night, he shall feast on a choice delicacy."

"No." My cheeks puffed with bull-like breaths, muscles tearing as I fought to break free. "No. This? This for a nick to your pride? This because you cannot see that the only difference between you and a reviled human king is a little bolt of—"

Zeus stepped back, snarling. The eagle's head dove down. And the world went black and red. Embers crackled at the edges of my vision. Agony so searing nothing else existed. Heat. Fire turned against me. The world smeared into dark colors. Flashes of sky. Cries for death, for vengeance, for mercy all tumbled out of my mouth in a nonsensical jumble. A flash of yellow as the beak tore a sliver of something loose, tipped back its head, and gobbled it. Cracks fissured the world and my will to live. And through it all, Zeus laughed.

He never returned after that first night, but his eagle did. And sometimes, when I began to forget myself, forget my name, forget my purpose, drowned in the sheer immensity of the pain, I heard the ghost of that laugh on the wind.

Years passed, the crushing loneliness almost as wretched as the creeping dread of sunset. When the light began to fade each day, so did my hope and my resolve that this time I'd break free, or that this time, I'd laugh up at Zeus's heavens rather than give the satisfaction of my screams.

Dusk after dusk. Short of breath in the thin air. Heart in a panicked drumbeat. And then would come that whoosh and snap—the flap of mighty bird wings. Night after night. The terror returned. The pain erased the world I had fought for. But never my remembrance of why I'd taken back that flame.

Now, as I lay crammed in a cot, recalling it all, skin prickling at the undulation of the sails, I did the one thing I could never do on that mountaintop. I moved into another person's warmth. Savina's arm banished the spider-leg sensation running along mine. Her breathing shushed the snapping canvas. As my lids fluttered shut, a smile crept onto my face.

Even in chains, I'd never forgotten why I climbed Olympus. But now, I had a second cause.

To go back to that mountain might break every part of me I'd reclaimed. But for the woman asleep beside me, I'd scale that barren rock and lay myself down for eternity.

CHAPTER TWENTY-FIVE

SAVINA

I woke thirsty, tangled in the cumbersome folds of my dress, and to a room as hot as Tartarus. I realized the culprit the second I tried to loosen my bodice and found a heavy arm wrapped around my center.

Conleth embraced me as if he feared I might run. The thought had crossed my mind. But where would I go on this ship? There was no other place for me to sleep without being uncovered as a stowaway. If I were honest, I'd admit that I'd snuggled closer to him during the night when the ship rocked abruptly, or an unknown noise stirred outside the door—my mind unable to discern if it was a hungry rodent or a pirate who'd discovered us. It didn't matter which. Conleth felt safe, safer than anyone other than my brother. Yet, these feelings were nothing brotherly. Instead, butterflies had taken permanent residence in my stomach at the sound of Conleth's voice. I wished them away, but no matter how hard I tried, they took flight at the slightest provocation. And when he'd admitted to me last night that I mattered to him, I worried my heart had melted like butter, its protections never to be restored.

I stared at his slumbering face. In this moment, he looked like the prince I'd imagined in all my childhood fairy tales, so innocent and vulnerable. His lips, plump and red, emitted soft breaths that caressed my cheeks. A small voice inside of me wondered what they would feel like on mine. Without thought, my finger traced over them.

Conleth jolted awake, drawing a knife he kept on him. He breathed hard and fast.

I snapped my fingers, bringing light to the candlestick on the floor. "It's just me." Heat trailed up my neck, hoping he didn't recall the touch. "I didn't mean to startle you. I..."

Conleth's mouth slanted. "Were you tickling my lips?"

I let out a dismal groan and flopped onto my back.

Conleth raised himself up on his forearms. "Was there a spider afoot?"

I cupped my hands over my eyes. "Can you not tease? Not about this."

Conleth pulled my hand away. "I won't if you tell me what you were doing. You have my word, no insect jests." He crossed his finger over his heart.

I sealed my lips. How would I even explain my actions? I'd sound like a deranged, lovesick adolescent if I admitted I had always wondered what the passionate first kisses between heroes and reluctantly besotted maidens felt like, tasted like. Would it be how I dreamt or fall short?

"Oh, come on now. I gave you my word. Surely a man who followed you aboard this floating coffin deserves the truth about why you've ravaged his lips."

I dropped my hands with a frustrated smack to the mattress. "I was not ravaging your lips."

"If not that, then what?"

I tilted my head to the side, staring into his glittering violet eyes. "I was just...curious." My cheeks heated.

"Princess, dare I remind you? You have your own mouth to stroke." A teasing smile stretched across his face.

"I..." Why were words so hard? Maybe because I knew they'd sound ridiculous.

Thick lashes lowered as he traced my cheekbone, drawing a shiver from me. "You wanted to know what *my* lips felt like."

I nodded, unable to speak.

"Do you want to know how they feel against yours?" His voice deepened, almost breaking at the end, like the idea affected him, too. His lashes lifted, and there was intent in the way his eyes locked onto mine. "Do you want me to kiss you?"

A shiver tensed my body. He'd said it. Words I was too shy to admit, he spoke without embarrassment or shame or ridicule. Did he want to kiss me as well?

For fear of what I might say, I simply dipped my chin.

Conleth leaned in and answered me with his mouth.

His lips brushed across mine not once but twice, soft as flower petals. My fingers threaded through his charcoal locks. They were softer than I imagined, softer than my own hair, like silk. I traced his upper lip with my tongue, having no idea what I was doing but letting my body set the course. With a hand at my chin, he guided our mouths together and deepened the kiss.

The plan was to see what a kiss felt like. To learn if my fantasies rang true. But I could see now this wasn't just about feeling his lips pressed against mine. This was more than that. Conleth had left everyone and everything to protect me, and the only reason someone would sacrifice that was a greater power. Maybe the bridge built between us stood stronger than what our lands wanted. Maybe we were meant for each other regardless of duty and oath to our people. If that were true, then all the resentment and reluctance I'd been harboring were in vain because as I sank into our kiss, I realized for the first time ever, I felt free.

Conleth moved his body to hover over me. Our legs mingled together. I didn't know where he began, and I stopped. The blazing fire of his touch burned my skin. I was practically panting under the pressure of his lips, even when he pulled away. I reached out and touched his face. He turned into the embrace, nuzzling my palm like Winnie, my beloved horse. When his eyes opened, I swore they glowed red.

Neither one of us moved or spoke for a long moment. Conleth's gaze traveled over my face, outlining my eyes, nose, and cheekbones until they settled back on my lips. A slight grimace pulled at his beautiful features.

"What's wrong?"

His throat worked on a swallow. "There's something I need to tell you."

"What?" My gaze searched his face as I drew my fingers over the curve of his neck. Bravery guided my hand, bolstered by the budding feelings in my heart for this man I'd hated only days ago.

Conleth turned his chin, kissing my fingertips. It was such a sweet gesture, I didn't even care that we were fugitives on a pirate ship, running from the gods. Nothing mattered to me but this...him.

"I need to tell you—"

"Are you two done smooching in there? An old gal like me could use the extra hands she were promised." A wood cabinet slammed. "Risking my life and limb so two newlyweds can spend their mornings on lovemaking. Fool I must be."

I giggled, covering my mouth with my hands.

Conleth kissed my forehead and offered me a smile. "I think we should go help her before she comes in and holds a blade to my throat again."

"I heard that, and I wouldn't be opposed to it if you're not swift on your feet."

Conleth nodded to the door. We exited one after the other, serenaded by Fretta humming a tune I'd never heard before, a pirate's ballad.

"Smells delicious," Conleth said, buttoning up his shirt.

"Eggs, spicy sausage, and bread. Be a dove and grab the cider." She motioned with her head to the metal pitcher.

For the next several hours, we helped cook and then clean. Fretta said there wasn't much time before we'd have to start on the crew's lunch, but she wanted to get some fresh air and check on "the boy." After she left, Conleth announced he, too, wanted to go topside and that I was to stay here and out of sight.

"Absolutely not." I stamped my foot.

He threaded his arms through his vest and slipped his feet back into his boots. He straightened his tunic and tucked it deeper into his trousers. "I'll be fine, my little songbird. Trust me."

"I do trust you. It's the unpredictable pirates on this ship that I don't trust." I crossed my arms over my chest, challenging Conleth to disagree.

We were not welcomed here, and no layer of grime could hide his handsome, distinctive visage. I dared not admit that to his face, though, for fear his ego would take flight, but he should know better than to risk his life just for curiosity. We had to be careful if we wanted to make it out alive, and I did wish to live. Now more than ever.

Conleth's violet eyes lit up like I'd just proposed my undying love for him.

"Why are you staring at me like that?" I waved my finger at his face, squinting over his expression.

"You said you trust me."

I rolled my eyes. "Of course I trust you. You sacrificed your life for mine. How could I not?" I shook my head. What an absurd proclamation. I just gave the man my first kiss. Was there a greater trust than that? "Now, will you please stay with me? Don't go above deck. Please."

Conleth stepped forward and wrapped his arms around my waist, drawing me flush with his body. My breath hitched. "I won't be long." He kissed the top of my head, and my body relaxed in his arms.

When I looked up into his eyes, I saw desire in them—the same I imagined painted in my own irises. My hands pressed against his chest as I lifted my heels. I wanted to close the distance between our lips. I wanted more than the brief kiss we'd shared earlier.

But nothing ever came. I blinked my eyes open to see Conleth staring at me. His brows pinched together. My head tilted. "Why aren't you kissing me?"

He sighed. "When I do kiss you again, Savina, you will know everything, and you will still want me." He touched his lips to my temple, then pulled away. "I must go."

Did he just deny me? And for my lack of knowledge about all that lay between a man and a woman? My pride faltered, launching anger from my toes to the tip of my tongue. "How dare you?" I pushed him, and he stumbled back. Embarrassment crept up my chest and neck in flashes of heat. He'd turned me down. I'd been so stupid to believe that maybe we were fated. But he saw me as some young fool. Well, never again.

"Be thankful you ever came close to my lips, for I refuse to allow it again. You had me besotted with your..." I waved my finger up and down his body. "Your daft handsomeness and charm and..." Useless, senseless words continued to pour out. "Your gallant gesture to escape with me. I...I only kissed you out of curiosity. But I won't be mistaken again. Even if you were the last man in all five lands."

Conleth smirked. "You will kiss me again one day, and you will want to." He stepped closer, negating the distance I put between us. He gripped my chin, his hold firm but gentle. It took everything inside of me to not melt into it. "No one will love you the way I do. You are mine, but I need to earn my place in your life first to become yours in return."

My eyes closed as his words replayed like a song. When they reopened, he was gone.

CHAPTER TWENTY-SIX

CONLETH

I 'd never intended on going above deck, but I had a good visage to reuse when needed. I'd gotten aboard undetected by dressing the part of a pirate tasked with checking the men onto the ship at the gangplank. We'd had quite the chat before I tied him up and left him at port. But instead of reprising my role, I transported myself back to the castle and into Flick's room.

"What are we going to do?" Vanden paced in front of the bed, head bent as he wore the carpet thin under his feet.

Flick stared out the floor-to-ceiling window that overlooked the garden. "You heard Conleth's message. Calli said he'd be in touch."

Vanden ran his hands through his long, blond hair. "You want us to wait then, to do nothing?" he spat.

I stepped forward. "I expect you to listen to orders and trust me."

"Milord." Flick spun around. His coffee-bean eyes blended into his widened pupils. A smile curved along his lips, and then he charged forward and embraced me. "We were ridden with fear. The king's daughter had a rather flimsy explanation for your last-minute departure." He pulled away to look at me, his hands clasping my biceps. "You are a sight for sore, old eyes."

I wrapped my arms around Flick and hugged him again. "As are you, my friend."

"A little notice would have been nice," Vanden growled from behind us.

Flick turned out of my embrace and nudged me in the side with his elbow. "I think he's just jealous you hugged me and not him. What do you say?"

I chuckled. "Would you like a hug?"

Vanden pushed the sleeves of his tunic up to his bony elbows. "Neither one of you could be a jester. All I was saying is it would have been nice to be consulted on the matter before you went off to become a pirate with the young lad and the princess."

I tilted my head and smirked.

Vanden's mouth twitched, fighting to hold on to his anger. "Oh, fine, come here." He beckoned me in for a solid, back-thumping squeeze that never came.

Before I could oblige my old friend, the door to Flick's room burst open. The three of us turned to see the Sottom brothers dressed in their red-and-gold uniforms, Zeus in his Zenith disguise, and King Rylander marching into the room, all displaying grimaces.

"Where in the underworld have you been?" Rylander thundered.

My teeth clenched, my fists tightening at my sides, but I didn't dare talk back to the king in front of Zeus. I couldn't risk his suspicion.

A breathless Calli ran in behind them. The second she saw me, she screamed.

King Rylander whipped around to face his daughter. "I told you to stay with Krinny."

Not a second later, Krinny appeared. Black tendrils fell from her tight bun, brushing the side of her ears. Her chest huffed and puffed, eyes narrowing in her pale face when she located Calli next to her father. It must have been a full-time job, running after the princess and her niece. I did not envy Krinny or her role in the royal family.

Calli pointed at me, mouth gaping open like a fish.

I closed my eyes for a brief moment to regain my composure. "It's nice to see you again, Calli. Are you all right? You look a little flushed."

Her arm dropped, but her body stayed frozen, her eyes glued to my form.

"What is wrong with you?" King Rylander grabbed his daughter by the elbow and pulled her to his side.

"I...I told you he was somewhere around the castle," she croaked, catching her breath. "Now do you believe me?" Her words were convincing, but her owlish eyes told a different story. Her father and grandfather shared her surprise, but the Sottom brothers seemed uninterested, while Krinny's focus stayed glued to Calli.

"Where is my daughter?" Queen Elouise bellowed from the hallway.

"In here," the twin with green eyes called back.

Queen Elouise entered, arms crossed, lips turned down into scowl. "You have a lot of explaining to do." I couldn't be sure if she was talking to her daughter or me, but I didn't say a word. Neither did Calli.

Flick and Vanden had flanked me as all the chaos ensued, their bodies warm at my side. Anger radiated off Vanden as he tied back his long hair, a gesture that meant he anticipated a fight. Flick's more subtle displeasure resided in the pulsing vein in his forehead. My fiery powers tickled my skin and tested my control. The space around us began to diminish with the growth of our audience.

"What is this about?" I demanded.

"Where were you last night?" Zenith spoke for the first time, his salt-and-pepper brows furrowed. The tips of his ears burned red.

"Asleep. In my room. Why?" I crossed my arms over my chest, mirroring the queen.

"Impossible," the blue-eyed brother argued. "We went into your room, and you weren't there."

"You went into my room? What right do you believe you had to do so?" My voice deepened as the reasons for my fury piled up in my mind.

"We were under the king's command," the guards said in unison.

I huffed while Rylander confirmed their claim with a slight nod of his chin.

"I went for an early ride on Savina's mare. She let me borrow it. Sometimes I do that when I can't sleep, but I was in my bed until dawn."

The Black Hollow left port before the sun rose, so Calli couldn't have returned any sooner than that. If they had checked my room—which enraged me for many reasons, none of which I'd bring up now—they'd have done so around that time.

"Do you know where the princess is?" Zenith straightened his tunic, flattening the wrinkles as if my answer mattered little to him, but I knew better. This was a test.

"I'd imagine in her room since she's not here with the lot of you." To stay calm in his presence took all my godly strength. While the man inside me wanted to torment him for using my love as a weapon, the god in me knew better than to show my hand, especially while he baited me.

"She is not there. It seems she knocked out her guard last night and hasn't been seen on the palace grounds since." Zenith perused my face, searching for a reaction. Surprise, guilt, anything to gage my knowledge, I was sure.

I held firm in my indifference and turned my gaze to Krinny.

"It wasn't me." Krinny's jaw popped. She stood taller, raising her height several inches above the Sottom brothers. For the first time, I saw the imposing assassin inside her. "It was the man stationed under her terrace."

"Well, I am happy to hear you are fine."

"Thank you," she muttered.

"None of this helps find her." Rylander started pacing. Queen Elouise moved into his path and placed her hands on his shoulders. He stopped, looking at her with worried eyes.

"We will find her, my love," the queen murmured, voice sympathetic and gaze cautious.

Tapping his lips, Zenith's eyes roamed the room and settled on Krinny. The hairs on my arms stood. What was he thinking?

"You are her personal guard, are you not?" Zenith stalked toward her. "You are supposed to be with her at all times?"

"I am." She pulled her shoulders back and looked down at Zeus, whose visage stood about four inches shorter than hers. "But I do not sit vigil over her bed while she sleeps. She's been in my care her whole life and nothing has ever happened to—"

In a blur of motion, Zenith placed his palm on Krinny's stomach, and a lightning bolt shot through her. To the untrained eye, it looked like a gunshot, but I knew better. A yellow spark flashed. Blood splattered onto the wall behind her like paint thrown on a canvas. Her eyes widened; her mouth gasped for air. A crimson trail trickled at the crook of her mouth as her body collapsed to the floor.

Queen Lou's and Calli's screams cut through my men's gasps.

"Get my wife and daughter out of here," Rylander roared as his family wailed.

Vanden and Flick moved forward, but I shot my arms out, keeping them in their place. There was nothing we could do to help, not now. Krinny was dead.

The Sottom brothers grabbed both women and dragged them kicking and screaming out of the room. Lou shouted so many profanities, I feared Zeus might strike her next.

"How could you?" Rylander breathed. The apples of his cheeks darkened into a deep cerise.

The thought of intervening crossed my mind, but how to do so without showing my hand eluded me. What could I even do now to make things better?

Zeus's face purpled. "Be careful, my boy. You may be a favorite of your father's, but you are not mine."

"But he is protected by his father and me," a new voice spoke. Hermes entered the room, dressed as Smitter, and stood guard in front of his nephew. "May I have a word, Zenith?" Although his tone was respectful, he stood rigid in a warrior's stance, chest puffing like a raging bear.

Zeus growled. "He's taken her. I know it. If she dies—"

"A word. Please," Hermes interrupted. This time, he showed his cards with a pleading tone. He knew if Zeus said too much in front of us, he'd kill us, too. Or try anyway. I'd never let that happen.

Without so much as a glance at anyone, Zeus marched out the door, Hermes on his heels.

I returned my focus to the king. Rylander didn't let any of the tears glossing his eyes fall. Instead, he appeared stuck in a fog of his own making. His stare drifted, latching to nothing, his body frozen in place.

"Vanden, Flick, leave us."

"Your Grace?" Flick postured, his eyes darting between King Rylander and me.

"Please," I repeated.

My two friends hesitated for all of a second before following my command. They left the room and closed the door behind them.

"Would you like to sit, Your Majesty?" I waved to the breakfast table next to the window where pastries from Flick's morning meal still sat out next to a pitcher of freshly squeezed orange juice.

Rylander ran a hand through his hair, pulling on the ends, before taking me up on the offer. The creases in his face aged him beyond his years, and I wondered if that came from leading a country or dealing with Zeus and the rest of his deity family members. Did he know of his grandfather's plans? From the way the God of the Sky spoke to him, I assumed not.

I pulled out the chair next to him and lowered myself down. "Are you surprised at Zeus's behavior?"

At the use of his grandfather's true name, his head snapped up. "How do you..."

Without much thought, I took a chance. I opened my palm, and a ball of fire appeared. Flames licked my skin, and I welcomed their warmth. The glowing orb rolled off my fingertip and bounced onto the table in front of us.

"My real name is Prometheus. I am the God of the People, the yielder of fire, the thorn in Zeus's side." I snapped my fingers and the fireball disappeared, leaving but a speckle of embers in its wake. "I am the reason he seeks to use Savina as a weapon against the land."

Rylander's mouth dropped open.

"I have no intention of hurting Savina, you, or your family. In fact, I am why Savina is far away, safe from your grandfather's sights. He plans to wield her power for a war against the land, wiping out humankind. After that, I fear he may end her as well. I intend to stop him."

"How?"

I stood. My original reason for coming back was to inform my men we'd escaped safely and charted a path to Anthemusa, but my instincts—after what just transpired—led me to trust Rylander with the truth. How much of that truth, I was still uncertain. "I do not know what I can say to you without..."

Rylander wrapped his hand around my wrist, showing he did not fear me. A brave move, not necessarily one I would have advised, but one I respected, nevertheless.

"She is my baby sister. She is the first girl I gave my heart to, and she is the first person I swore to protect until my dying breath. If you have her best interest at heart, you can trust me with your life." He stood to better meet my eye. "I will kill Zeus if he tries to take my sister to Elysian Fields before her time, or I will die trying."

I placed my hand over his. "I will never let him."

Rylander released his hold and turned his head to the body on the floor. I watched as he wiped away a tear, his back now facing me.

"Queen Yemma and her people have sworn to protect her. We made a blood oath. I am taking Savina to Anthemusa, as we speak. That is all I can tell you, for now."

He continued to stare at the fallen assassin. "Thank you."

I started for the door to say goodbye to my men and to give them orders to take Ketner with them back to Eloqua as soon as possible. He was no longer safe here in Cava. Of that, I was certain. Now, I needed to get back to Savina and protect her for the rest of my days, trusting her with the truth and earning the love I felt for her in return.

"What do I tell my wife?"

By the way Rylander rubbed his forehead and took a tentative step toward Krinny, I knew he wasn't referring to news of Savina. He meant, how could he soothe his wife's grief for her friend.

"You tell her a true warrior lives not because of the fear of death in front of them, but because of the loved ones they keep safe behind them. She died doing what she loves, being there for her family, your family. You tell your wife that, and you tell her they will reunite again one day in Elysian Fields. I will make certain of it."

CHAPTER TWENTY-SEVEN

SAVINA

When Fretta returned to the kitchen, we prepared lunch for the crew. I asked her if Conleth had been spotted above, and she said no and not to worry. "He's got a good head on his shoulders, that one. You married well."

I groaned, having forgotten about the lie. But she instinctively trusted Conleth, believed in him, just like Ketner, Henrik, and Calli. He commanded faith in people. Even though his denial had bruised my ego, I, too, trusted him to do right by not only me, but everyone else.

The door opened and Henrik strutted in, clutching a green apple. He bit into the fruit, spraying juices. In between chews, he asked, "Where's Conleth?"

I motioned to the deck above us with my head. "Apparently, blending in."

Henrik nearly choked on his food. "Blending in?"

I shrugged, going back to washing the dishes and putting them away. I didn't have more information to share, and I didn't want to focus on Conleth's whereabouts. I just prayed he was safe and would be back soon, the horse's arse. Despite his jab about my inexperience, I didn't want anything to happen to him.

"Well, no one has been tortured today, so he must be doing a good job of pirating. Maybe the life of a brigand is for him." Henrik chomped deeper into the apple. "Plus, the first day at sea everyone acts pretty tame. They got their fill of ale, whores, and food back on land." Henrik paused with a chuckle. "It's about a month in that things get scuttled."

"Is that right?"

My head snapped toward the unfamiliar growly voice.

A pockmarked pirate with a scraggly beard and broken nose glared at Henrik from the doorway. "I wondered where you ran off to, boy." His eyebrow piercing moved with the lift of his forehead.

"Father?" Henrik's voice faltered.

"Who's this?" Captain Fredrick—a man I'd never wanted to have the misfortune of meeting—pointed to me, showing his yellowed, crooked teeth like a snarling dog.

I stepped back, just as Fretta stepped forward and wrapped her meaty arm around my waist. Her strong grip might've brought stability and assurance had her forearm not trembled against my midsection.

"She's them extra hands I asked Henrik to get on shore. Mighty good hands at that. We've been able to cook, feed, and clean at twice the rate." Fretta smiled at me, the strain obvious in the stretch of her lips.

Captain Fredrick grunted. "She ain't no cook or tavern dweller." He strode within a foot of me and grabbed a loose strand of my hair that he twirled around his finger. "Shiny, well-groomed." He sniffed. "Even smells nice." He dropped the tendril with force, and I bit back a gasp. His dirt-caked fingers gripped my chin and pinched the skin as he twisted my head back and forth, inspecting me like a prized stallion. "Face as white as milk." He jerked my jaw to the side as he released me. "Never worked a day in the sun. She ain't common." His head whipped toward his son. "Who is she? Don't make me ask a third time."

Henrik's whole body shook. Fear swam in his emerald eyes. When he didn't answer, Fredrick stepped away from me and backhanded his son. The slap echoed in the small space. I gulped, swallowing any sound that would worsen the situation.

The boy's cheek lit up with the imprint of his father's hand. But Henrik didn't answer. He didn't even cover his face. I'd be a fool to assume this was unusual behavior. From Henrik and Fretta's mutual lack of surprise, I'd guess Captain Fredrick hurt his son regularly.

I stepped forward, hoping I'd cross through a cloud of courage. "My name is Savina." I didn't dare look at Henrik and cause him more harm than good. Just like my father and uncle had taught me to never show an enemy my weakness.

I wiped my sweaty palms on my trousers. "Your son approached me at the tavern when he overheard me asking the barkeep if they had any open positions. Henrik asked if I get seasick, and well, since I don't, he considered me good for the position. I can cook, clean. I even sew. I don't have a home. I've got nowhere to go."

At least I spoke in half truths. After finding out my grandfather wanted to use me as a weapon and a god I had never met wanted to kill me, I had nowhere else to rest my head without them finding me. This was my last hope.

"You ain't no cook I've ever seen, nor maid." A cruel smile covered his lips, giving his eyes a hard shine. "But you could be useful." He stroked his mangled beard. "The crew ain't got no healthy way to let off steam. The boy's right—a month on the high seas leaves the men restless. But if they've got you to warm their beds." He clapped his hands together. "I reckon that will make them work harder, incentivizing them for a taste at your innocence."

"Captain." Fretta stepped forward, shielding me with her body. "The girl is young. She's a pure soul. Let her help me in the kitchen. I could use the—"

She never finished her sentence.

Captain Fredrick removed his blade and swung. The weapon whispered through the air as Fretta's tongue fell silent. Blood sprayed across the room. Fretta's body crumpled to the ground. Her head rolled off her shoulders, pale eyes staring back at me as a red stream flowed from her severed neck onto the wooden floor. Henrik screamed—a blood-curdling sound so awful I covered my ears and closed my eyes.

"We need a new chef." My heart beat so loudly I barely heard Captain Fredrick speak.

My eyes snapped open.

Captain Fredrick stared at the lifeless body. He reached out and yanked his swaying son up by the collar. "If you don't pull yourself together, I'll kill you, too." He pushed Henrik forward, and the boy fell to his knees. He crawled over to Fretta's body and cradled her in his lap. "Get off your arse and bring down two men. Tell them they're on kitchen duty until we dock at the next port. We'll find us another old hag there."

Warm tears streamed down my cheeks, blurring the vision of Henrik rocking Fretta's corpse.

"Why, Father? Why?" Henrik cried, clasping Fretta's headless body to his chest.

"I'm sick of that ole crone sticking up for your misdoings. You'd think that nasty cut across her face would be a reminder she shouldn't get involved in our family business, but even that didn't make no difference." He huffed. "How can I expect a son of mine to grow up a ruthless killer when he's coddled like a babe sucking on his mama's tits? I've let this go on for too long. You need to harden up." Captain Fredrick kicked Fretta's head and it rolled. Her red-soaked blonde hair tangled in wet clumps that stuck to the floorboards.

Bile rose to my throat, but I stamped it back down. The fear over what Captain Fredrick would do to Henrik was the only reason I stayed upright fighting the sensation of fainting.

"She was the only..."

"Boy, if you don't stop blubbering, get off that floor, and go upstairs, I'll ..." He raised his sword again and I stepped forward.

"I can help." My voice shook. "Let Henrik stay down here and clean up. I'll get two men for you." The knot in my throat tripled in size as I watched Captain Fredrick scan my body. He sheathed his sword. In two strides, he stood next to me. His rough hands wrapped around my bicep as he pulled me with him. My feet barely touched the ground as we flew up the steps. I heard boots pounding on the stairs behind us and I knew Henrik followed. Such a brave boy, too brave. I wished with all my heart he never had to grow up with such a brutal father. No wonder he loved Calli. She showed him respect and adoration he'd never experienced before.

Captain Fredrick dragged me up the steps with him to the poop deck. He smelled of ale and sweat, increasing my nausea. He whistled, drawing the men's attention. Everyone stopped and stared. First at their captain. Then at me.

"We've got ourselves a treat, men." Captain Fredrick shoved me forward as if on display. "My son found her, something for us to pass the time and play with." A couple men whistled. Others hollered and raised their fists while I shivered. "However, he did it under my nose without my permission." He glared down at Henrik, who didn't even hide his tears. His red-rimmed eyes shot daggers back at his father. "You know what happens to scurvy dogs when they don't follow orders on this ship."

"Hang 'em from the yardarm!" one man yelled, firing his pistol above his head.

I flinched.

"Make 'em feed the fish!" another joined in.

"Indeed." Captain Fredrick unsheathed his sword and pointed the tip at his son. "But he did bring us a tasty delight. So instead of death this time, why don't we teach him a lesson? You all get a go at him. Fists, no weapons." As if that were a mercy. "Then one of you lucky bastards will get to deflower this pretty little runaway before passing her on to the next bloke." He nodded to his men. "How does that sound?"

Grunts and hollers encompassed me in fear.

Maybe there was a crueler fate than my grandfather and Prometheus, because right now this looked worse than death, an end I would never come back from.

CHAPTER TWENTY-EIGHT

CONLETH

The moment I reappeared in the kitchen, dread crashed over me like a tidal wave. My foot stuck to the floor. When I looked down, my heart lurched in my throat. Fretta's severed head sat not a bone's distance away. Blood pooled around it and under my feet. I lifted my shoe and stepped out of the crimson mess. I spun in every direction, looking for Savina. Instead, I found several sets of red footprints, all different sizes, leading to the door.

They found her.

I waved my hand over my body and changed my visage back to the pirate form that had allowed me to board this ship. Then I stepped into the halls, whispering her name over and over, checking every door I found. Taking two stairs at a time, I followed the sound of men chanting and cheering.

"Instead of death this time, why don't we teach him a lesson?" a man bellowed to the crowded deck. "You all get a go at him. Fists, no weapons. Then one of you lucky bastards will get to deflower this pretty little runaway before passing her on to the next bloke. How does that sound?"

Broad shoulders blocked my view. I pushed my way through them, jeers and cheers battering my ears until I made it to the front where Savina stood in the grip of man atop the poop deck. I watched as the man yanked her toward him by the arm. She shook as if caught in a blizzard. My heart beat so fast, it drowned out all other sounds except her soft whimpers.

"Not so fast, beautiful," the burnt-skinned man said, stroking a long, straggly beard the color of a seal's coat. By his hat and demeaner, I presumed he was captain. He gestured to Henrik standing mere feet from me. "You've got a show to watch. After all, the boy's suffering is your doing." He addressed the crowd. "Who wants first blood?" He used his sword to point at each ruffian in the front. "I should warn you that Henrik, although young and weak-minded, is one tough buck."

My feet moved without thought. "Let me fight the boy."

Henrik's eyes widened, mouth dangling in pure shock.

"That's unexpected, Jacko," said the captain, addressing my false form. "I would have thought you favored my son too well to take the first swing. But the thought of plundering a woman's innocence is enough to spur any man, I gather. Make him bleed, and you shall be the first to bed her."

"No," Savina shouted.

"Not your choice. I own you now," the pirate snarled.

Blood boiled beneath my skin, my power screaming to be set free as I listened to the captain claim my love.

I tried to stay in character. "She is a beaut."

"A beaut?" Henrik repeated, his nose scrunched. "Are you drunk, Jacko?"

I shook my head but didn't dare speak and be questioned more.

Henrik led the way into the circle the crowd made for us. Fresh tears stained his cheeks, but he didn't seem to mind. His brows pulled together as he studied me.

The captain hauled Savina down to the main deck and handed her off to the two nearest pirates. The men grabbed her, each seizing one arm. She struggled in their hold.

Keep fighting, my little songbird. I am coming for you.

"What are you doing?" Henrik hissed so only I could hear as we started circling each other. I'd obviously broken a trust he and this Jacko man had, poor kid. I'd set it to rights.

I held up my meaty hands in a fighting position. "Do you remember when we first met?" I kept my voice low. "And you asked me to become the fourth in your crew?"

Henrik's eyes widened. "Conl—?"

"Stop talking and fight," the captain shouted.

"Oh, I think we're about good and ready," I responded over my shoulder. "Ready to fight?" I asked Henrik.

I hoped he knew I meant the crew and not each other. I spun and he followed in confirmed understanding. Our backs pressed together as we drew our weapons.

At first the crew stood paralyzed, blinking and exchanging uncertain glances. Savina did not hesitate. Out of the corner of my eye, I watched her stomp the foot of the pirate to her left. He grunted and leaned forward, losing his grip. She took that moment to follow through with an elbow to the nose and the man went down clutching his face. The fight was on. Pirates surged into a tight ring around us, steel ringing out of sheaths.

"Take them alive," the captain roared, joining the charge.

Blades clanged. I rammed my sword into the closest pirate, trying to reach Savina as she struggled against her lone guard. I slit the throat of another man coming toward me. Blood pooled at my boot, mixing with Fretta's, and leaving sticky prints behind as I plowed onward. But I couldn't get close enough. Another man was about to grab her.

"Duck," I shouted in my own voice. She wouldn't have to see my Conleth form to know and trust it.

Savina listened and lurched forward, giving me just the right amount of room. I grabbed the knife in my ankle sheath and threw it. The blade glinted in the sun, soaring straight into the eye of the man ensnaring her. He crumbled to the floor, and Savina jackknifed upright.

Her eyes widened at the bloodied form at her feet, but she looked away in favor of searching for me.

"Climb as high as you can. I'm coming for you." I swung my sword into two more oncoming pirates, slicing off an arm and opening a gut.

She threw one last look over her shoulder, trying to find me, then took off. She jumped back onto the poop deck stairs, away from the reaching arms trying to get to her. I watched as two men followed her up, but more bodies obstructed my view. Five men surrounded me and three Henrik. Others pushed their fellows out of the way, craving a taste of us. I had to fight with more than my sword, but it would not only expose my powers, but cause extensive death. I looked at Savina, clambering onto a stack of crates and kicking out at her pursuers, and knew in my heart that I'd kill every soul aboard if it kept her safe.

"How do you look like Jacko?" Henrik yelled, tugging his sword out of his would-be attacker's chest.

"Let's fix that," I said with a flash of a smile.

In a moment, my godly visage appeared, dark flowing black hair, eyes red as a setting summer sun, and broad and chiseled as my rescuer Hercules. I changed into the clothes I donned in my godly form, a loose-fitting silk shirt rolled to my elbows and tailored trousers, unlike the layered purple uniform of Eloqua.

"Holy Hades's gates!" Henrik shrieked. "You're a god."
He swiped his weapon across another man's chest. Blood
seeped from the gash as the man seized his heart.

My sword dropped and fire sprung from my fingertips.
I shot searing balls of it at every man in sight until only a
handful still stood. The smell of burnt skin filled the air.
I climbed up the mainmast toward the crow's nest and
grabbed a sail rope. Wrapping it around my hand twice, I
threw myself into the fight and snatched Savina from the
hands of the pirates after her, including the captain. She
threw her arms around my neck.

"How did you—?" She stared into my eyes. "They're red
again." She hadn't forgotten that detail from our meeting
on the sirens' island. "Who are you?"

"Not now, my little songbird. Let's get to safety first." I
landed on the deck and placed her down next to Henrik.
The three of us were pressed against the rails.

"Looks like we have you cornered." The captain led his
huddle of remaining men, swords and pistols raised. His
head swiveled around. "Where's Jacko?" His gaze returned
to me. "Who are you?"

"I'll give you one chance to surrender. Lower your
weapons and we will leave your ship and never return." I
wrapped my arm around Savina's waist and pulled her into
my side.

Captain Fredrick threw his head back and cackled. "How
about you hand over the girl and the boy and we will make
your death swift?" The captain twisted his head, making
sure all the men understood his command. Many bore
fresh wounds from my blade and Henrik's, bleeding from
their faces, arms, or torsos. It was the ones smoldering in
half-melted puddles, skin bubbling from my fire, that had

my stomach roiling. I never wished to kill man, only to save him. But I'd never regret protecting the ones I loved either.

The captain's forehead crinkled. "I am curious. Before I cleave your head, why don't you let me know who I be sending to the depths, lad?"

I stepped forward, my shoulders pulled back. "I am Prometheus. And the only one going to Hades's kingdom is you."

The gasp behind me and the whispered "no" came from Savina.

I turned my head. "It's not what you think. I am not here to do you any harm."

"A god. On my ship?" The captain laughed so hard, he keeled over, resting his free palm on his thigh. "Absurd. I don't know what game you play, but we don't believe—"

"Not impressed?" I smirked. "Well, let's see about that, shall we?" I lifted a brow, then my hand. Fire shot threw my skin and landed on the ropes holding the tender. The cables snapped, and the rowboat fell into the sea. The men sent up curses and clunky, unpracticed prayers. I then lifted my hand and molded fire arrows, sending them off to tear through the sails, setting the ship ablaze. Orange and red flames—my own personal army—licked the wood, growing in destruction.

"Jump." I turned to Henrik and Savina. "Now."

Henrik tossed his weapons belt onto the deck and hoisted himself onto the rail. Without objection, he dove straight into the sea. But Savina crossed her arms. "Absolutely not. If you think I am going anywhere with the likes of—"

With one quick movement, I swept her feet off the deck and into my arms, cradling her against my chest. "Fighting with you will never get old, my little songbird."

And with that, I threw her overboard.

CHAPTER TWENTY-NINE

SAVINA

The cold water encased me, icy needles puncturing my skin. The air leached out of my lungs. I sank into darker depths, my sodden trousers like an anchor pulling me farther from the ring of sunlight on the rippling surface. My turbulent thoughts were stones on my chest, another weight dragging me down. Conleth was Prometheus, the god out to kill me to save mankind. How could that be possible? He'd kissed me, protected me. How could he have wanted me dead all along?

My hands pumped in the water, my fingers slipping through the wetness with nothing to latch onto. I tried to swim my way upward, but the ocean currents thrashed against one another, tossed in different directions by the wind and the traveling whale of a ship. My body whipped around as if caught in a storm. I lost track of the sun as a plank loomed over my head. I'd been afraid of Zeus's wrath and Prometheus's vengeance, but now I might die from drowning. I dodged the falling board and kicked harder, but I'd lost track of the surface.

A school of fish buffeted my body. Slimy scales slid across my face and I closed my eyes. *Think, Savina. You can survive. Just think.* I needed to lighten my load. But before I could even make a move, cold hands—colder than the water surrounding me—grabbed me from behind. I screamed, sending up a plume of bubbles that shot toward the lost sun. I looked down to see talons clutching my midsection. A siren.

A voice tickled my ear. "I've got you, princess. Hang on."

My back pressed against her ice-cold bosoms as her fins moved us through the ocean depth like a falcon soaring among the clouds. The water warmed as we neared the surface. We broke through and I gasped for air, my chest exploding in pain.

"You'll be okay." A hand patted my back as a sound rattled in my throat. "Cough and let it all out."

I sputtered, choking on the arctic seawater in my mouth. A guttural cough from deep in my belly allowed me to throw up the rest of the contents into the sea. A little bit of breakfast followed, but that was nothing compared to the stomach-churning realization we were bobbing in the middle of the ocean with no land in sight.

The blurry edges of my vision cleared, bringing my panic into stark focus. Sirens' heads popped up in every direction. Their hair trailed in the currents like red ribbons of blood in the aftermath of a feeding frenzy. Some collected the floundering men that jumped into the water for refuge from their burning vessel while other sea enchantresses gathered the flaming debris, swimming it deeper under the ocean's surface.

In the distance, I heard Henrik shouting. I spun toward the sound, coming face-to-face with... "Ballas?" My eyes widened, jaw hanging slack.

She smiled, her fangs indenting her plump lip. "It's lovely to see you again, Savina. We are allied with Conleth. You are safe, now."

"What?" Safe was the last thing I felt. Confusion. Anger. Betrayal. They vied for the forefront, but safe? Not even close. "How could you be working with the god who wants me dead?"

"That is not true. All will be explained. Just have faith."

I knew Ballas, Queen Yemma's general and second-in-command. Because of her relationship with my brother, I believed she would never hurt me, at least not intentionally. Which left me to deduct, either the rumor Conleth sought to slaughter me was a lie, or he'd been cunning enough to make my friends my enemies. Either way, I had no choice but to let her save me. Where else could I go?

Ballas wrapped her arms under mine and swam us around the engulfed ship. Men screamed their death howls, charging around the deck on fire, while others abandoned their comrades, jumping from the rails. I had no idea which fate had found Captain Fredrick. Was he burning with the planks, or had he jumped overboard without a care for his men like the coward he really was?

General Ballas held on to me with the grip of Atlas. Within moments, the tender Conleth had dropped into the sea appeared mere yards away. Henrik sat in the middle, arms wrapped around his waist, scowl on his face. His mahogany hair, which normally flowed and flopped on his head, clung to the sides of his face. Droplets of water congregated on his lashes.

"What in the underworld is going on?" Henrik sputtered through blue-tinged, trembling lips.

Two sirens helped Ballas lift me into the boat. I pushed up and toppled in with a thud. A groan slipped out of my mouth and I rubbed my head. "I have no idea."

"Where did all these sirens come from?" Henrik peered over the edge of the rowboat. I couldn't be sure, but there looked to be around a hundred. If Poseidon learned of this mess, Zeus would soon find out as well. Then I'd never be safe. "And why do they sound like squawking seagulls?"

Humans couldn't understand sirens unless they spoke in our native tongue, and none of the sirens cared enough to be heard by sailors or brigands. But deities like me could understand them regardless of dialect. "It's their language. It doesn't sound that way to them."

Ballas wrapped her talons around the tender's edge and lifted herself up to face me, her tail flapping behind her, the scales shimmering. She dipped her head to Henrik and then me. "Conleth instructed us to move the wreckage to the bottom of the ocean and rescue as many men as we can." She spoke so Henrik could understand. "Conleth is hoping we can avoid Poseidon's attention."

Good luck with that. Poseidon had eyes and ears everywhere. No deep-sea cave or seaweed forest escaped his notice. Nowhere to hide.

"Where are you taking the pirates?" My words garbled as I shivered. Goose pimples dimpled my limbs. My soaked clothes chilled me to the bone.

Ballas pointed her talon into the distance. "Eloqua is close enough. We are transporting them to a small landmass a few leagues from the coast where they will be rescued by Eloqua's navy."

"And what about us?" Henrik growled. He rubbed his arms. "This tender isn't for the sea. We will die out here. If not from the rough waters, from the cold alone."

"We will let nothing happen to you. Six of us will swim beneath the dinghy and get you to Anthemusa faster than any sails. Conleth will be back soon to warm you. He's meeting with his men now to apprise them of the situation." Ballas's diamond-colored eyes, the same irises as my brother, scanned my shaky body. "It won't be long."

"Anthemusa? The sirens' island?" Henrik exclaimed.

The boat bobbed with a sudden weight. "Yes, the very one," a deep voice said. "Ballas, please join the others and head in the direction of your home."

Ballas slipped back beneath the waves at the same time Henrik and I spun in the boat. It swayed, almost toppling over. The sirens below us steadied it, and I regained my balance by gripping the seat.

Conleth's godly appearance sat at the end of the tender. His charcoal hair flowed across the tops of his shoulders. Eyes like rubies blazed with orange firelight, but the flames of *The Black Hollow* lay the other way. He'd abandoned Eloqua's colors for the casual and loose clothes he'd donned on the sirens' island.

My hand struck out without thought, slapping Conleth across the face. Hard. The sound vibrated through the silence.

I sniffed, willing the pain in my chest to stay put. All that I'd shared with him—my first kiss at the top of that list—and he had deceived me. I refused to let him see me cry. But after these last few days and those I had left behind, my heart faltered. A tear I couldn't resist escaped and rolled down my cheek, warming my skin.

Conleth ignored the hit as if batted by a baby's fist rather than a demi-god. I might not be as strong as him, but I still had power behind my arm. It must have at least stung, or so I hoped.

"I understand why you feel betrayed." Conleth rubbed his palms together, then opened his hands. A ball of fire sat in the middle. With a flick of Conleth's fingers, it hovered in the air between Henrik and me. The warmth covered me like a wool blanket. "It was never my intention to hurt you with my omission."

"Omission?" I seethed, moving closer to the heated globe and farther away from Conleth. "I'd say failing to mention your real name is more than a simple oversight. Calli forgetting to tell me she borrowed my blue tunic is an omission. You neglecting to say you are the god trying to kill me is a blatant ruse."

Conleth bit back a laugh. "Does it look like I am trying to murder you? Does a killer normally warm his victim before slaying them?" His chin jutted toward the ball of fire.

Henrik nudged me in the side. "He's done nothing but save our arses. On several occasions. I believe him."

I glared at Henrik. "Coming from you, that is not comforting."

"Hey!" Henrik sat up straighter. "What's that supposed to mean?"

I sighed, realizing my words stemmed from frustration, not truth. "Nothing." I waved to the sea around us. "So, what's the plan now? If you're not going to kill me, why are you taking us to the sirens' island?"

"I am only taking you. Henrik will be placed on a ship not far from here. They've been paid handsomely for his safe return into trusted hands. Once he's onboard, then you will be brought to Anthemusa. Whatever Zeus believes you can do will not affect the inhabitants of that island. But we need Henrik safe and far away."

A sliver of fear trickled down my back. Even Conleth, God of the People, worried about the extent of my powers. If he wanted Henrik removed from my presence, he truly believed I could be a weapon of mass destruction. I just didn't want to believe it myself.

"I'm not leaving her," Henrik declared. "Calli wouldn't want me to, so I won't. I'm coming with you to the sirens' island."

Conleth eyed me as if saying, *You get him to listen to reason.*

Whether I trusted Conleth's intentions or not, I did believe on my eighteenth birthday my powers would come into their full strength and that I had been hidden for all these years for a woeful reason. No matter my fate, I wouldn't let Henrik die because of me.

I placed my hand on Henrik's arm, his drying clothes warm from the hovering hearth. "I don't know the true nature of my fully realized powers, but I can only surmise they are powerful enough to kill with a ruthlessness that excites Zeus."

"So?" Henrik ripped his arm free. "I'm not a child. I can help. It's not like you'll hurt me."

I scooted closer to Henrik. "It has nothing to do with your age or ability. You're the strongest human I know. I'd be honored to have you by my side. But you *are* human, and therefore you could get hurt. I cannot protect you from my godly powers." I dared a glance at Conleth. "And neither can he."

Henrik huffed, turning his head away from me. He coughed, trying to cover up a sniffle. "I don't have anywhere else to go. My father will kill me if he ever finds me. I can never go back to *The Black Hollow*." He laughed without mirth—a hollow sound. "Or what's left of it, should they rebuild."

"Your father will never touch a hair on your head. I won't allow it," rumbled Conleth. "And that is not true. You do have a place. Ketner awaits you in Eloqua, protected by my men. Your old friend specifically asked to take you in."

Henrik glared over his shoulder. "Ketner? How did you even speak with him?"

"I'm a god. I can pop in and out of places at will." Conleth leaned forward, propping his forearms on his thighs. "He needs you. And when I am done here, I promise to come back and find you. If you don't want to stay with Ketner and my men, you can come with me. You have my word."

My heart melted hearing Conleth's declaration to Henrik. He would truly be there for him. I could see it in the depths of his red irises. I recognized it as the same burning determination I felt in my chest when making promises to Calli.

When Henrik locked his jaw, I reached out and interlaced our hands, giving his fingers a squeeze. "It's not that I don't want you with us. I do. But what if I hurt you? What then? I would never forgive myself. After all the death you've witnessed, the loss, the pain, I refuse to be the reason you suffer more."

I pulled on his shoulder, and he willingly faced me. Unshed tears lingered on his lower lids.

He wiped one away. "Calli would be furious if I let something happen to you."

"Oh, Henrik. Calli would never be the same if I did something awful to you at Zeus's command. Don't you see? You're family to us." I let my sorrow spill out, my cheeks wet as I placed my free hand over my heart. "You live in here. The same way Calli and Rylander do. You will always be family to me, and that means I will protect you, even if it's from myself."

"But what about you?" Henrik argued.

"I will keep her safe," Conleth added. Both Henrik and I glanced up at the God of the People. His eyes glowed like the sun. "For the rest of my life, I vow it."

CHAPTER THIRTY

SAVINA

After we loaded Henrik onto the fisherman's ship and instructed him to bring Henrik to Eloqua to meet Ketner and Conleth's men, we left for Anthemusa. I slipped back into silence, not even permitting myself a glance at Conleth. My heart and my head had declared a stalemate until I could get answers from Queen Yemma.

The sirens guiding our boat sped us to Anthemusa's shores within four mornings, cutting our total journey in half. A reception party ushered us straight to the ivory castle. Birds chirped as the wind whipped through the trees. The summer sun warmed my face.

Crystal waterfalls crashed against the black rocks that framed the entrance. A mound of steam hissed into the air, rising around the palace like a crown and coating my skin like sweat. Amid the froth, the stacked and intricately carved human bones created a two-level citadel with sweeping curves and layers of buttresses. I had longed for its beauty ever since my last visit.

Ballas greeted us at the entrance and led us through the hallways to the gilded grand doors at the back of the castle. A mural of the battle between the original three siren sisters was carved into the wood, then finished in gold paint. I hadn't been around at the time of the two benevolent sisters' fall to Queen Lorelei's cruel rule, but I knew my brother was the reason the war of the sea ended and Lorelei no longer drew breath. He'd helped Queen Yemma, a peaceful ruler, usurp the throne and command the clan under new laws, as protectors of humankind. Oddly enough, the sirens now boasted a similar role to the one Prometheus had long held.

Conleth pulled on the gold handle and the door opened, a feat only achieved by the strength of a deity or siren. Despite my anger, I found myself sidling closer to him. The heat of his body comforted me more than I'd ever admit. After Fretta's death, being auctioned to lecherous pirates, and almost drowning, my nerves had frayed worse than old, rotted rope. Conleth grounded me.

My eyes darted all around the throne room. Until now, only my brother had been permitted inside on our visits. One more way my family had sheltered me.

Hundreds of sirens reclined in an otherworldly grotto, their sanctuary adorned with chaise lounges, colorful tapestries, and jagged onyx boulders that clawed their way from the depths to touch the cavern's celestial dome overhead. Some sirens stretched out in their human form, while others lounged and fanned themselves with their iridescent, opalescent tails. A mesmerizing symphony of voices—some husky and sultry, others reminiscent of crystalline bells—wove together in an ethereal tapestry of sound like a lullaby spun by angels and demons alike. The hypnotic music rendered mortal men powerless, surrendering willingly to the sirens' commands.

"It's so majestic." I wondered if anyone even heard my low whisper.

As my eyes focused in the ambient glow, it all came together: the reason why I'd been banned from this room.

Nestled in the shadows, skeletal remains of innumerable vessels littered the rocky enclave and the adjacent sandbar, resembling the bleached bones of long-forgotten behemoths left to disintegrate under an uncaring sun. I could tell these souls had died long ago. So strange they were never removed. Maybe it was a reminder of the sirens' past, or it just didn't bother them. But up until a short time ago, a sight like this would have sent me running.

Through the debris and shattered rigging lay a sight even more bewitching: a sea of affluence that glimmered with an incandescent allure. Hills of gold gleamed like a sky full of earthbound stars, their sparkle animated by the cave's unnatural light. A labyrinthine trove of opulent riches—exquisite jewelry, ornate candle holders, gilded picture frames, and myriad gemstones—cluttered the walls and formed disheveled mountain ranges of splendor.

My gaze wandered to the pool. Queen Yemma reigned on a throne sculpted from an unmoving wave, ensconced by a cascading curtain of crystalline water that glittered like liquid diamonds. Her corset, woven from strands of dark-green seaweed, appeared almost inked onto her skin. Its slick fronds ascended to caress her neck like tendrils of affectionate shadow. She peered up and smiled.

"It's lovely to see you again, Prometheus, Savina." She twirled the ends of her sanguine tresses, a crimson hue so deep it bordered on obsidian, wrapped in an intricate braid that cascaded down to her unadorned midriff.

"The pleasure is mine, Queen Yemma." Conleth bowed.

I crossed my arms at my chest. "Normally I'd say the same, but currently I'm a little too miffed for court pleasantries."

Queen Yemma chuckled. "I imagined you would be." She batted her almond-shaped eyes, like enigmatic mirrors of crystal. "You must have a couple questions."

"Yes. A few." I didn't dare look at Conleth, but I could feel his fiery heat on my skin. He was never far away.

"I'd be happy to answer anything I can." With a flick of her immense emerald tailfin, iridescent scales cast splatters of aquatic mist that fell in a shimmering rain across the floor.

"Thank you."

She waved her hands, and the chair metamorphosed into a sinuous wave that seamlessly carried her to the pool's brink and nudged her high enough to meet my eye. A diadem of bleached coral crowned her head, so meticulously polished that its labyrinthine contours gleamed as if the sun forever shone directly upon it.

"Come, let's sit." Her tail sundered itself, morphing into humanoid legs of sculptural grace—long, lithe, and impossibly flawless. Her emerald scales elongated and fused, evolving into a floor-sweeping skirt slit at the sides, through which her alabaster feet emerged as she descended the aqueous stairway to a ground paved with polished bone. Her hair, as if imbued with ethereal life, soared skyward like a splash of red wine released from its goblet, unraveling itself into elegant, pillowy curls that draped over her shoulders.

My mouth dropped. I'd never seen the transition from one form to the next.

"Where shall we start?" She walked over to a cluster of obsidian rocks and gestured for Conleth and me to take a seat across from her.

I tried perching on the uneven boulder, but after losing my balance twice, I leaned against its side. "Is Conleth…I mean Prometheus going to kill me?"

"Savina." Conleth's voice wavered. "I told you—"

Queen Yemma held up her hand to silence him. "Let me answer her. I think it will mean more coming from me."

Conleth pressed his lips into a tight line. The closest I'd seen him come to a pout.

"On your eleventh birthday, Pythia found Prometheus and told him to kill you. She believes, as does Zeus, that on your eighteenth birthday, your powers will completely mature and destroy humankind."

"But how can it come to be? How can a demi-god's abilities grow so powerful and reach so far when I don't wish for them to?" I leaned forward, resting my elbows on the rock table in front of us.

"No one knows. Not even your father." Yemma shrugged.

I swallowed. Apollo saw the future, but he always saw many paths, making it hard for him to pinpoint which was real. Even if he did see how I would end the world, he'd have a half dozen more visions that could counter the real outcome, which was why he never shared his premonitions, only snippets of what he believed were the most probable truths.

"Prometheus refused Pythia's instruction to take your life. Instead, he asked her for time—time to find another way."

I dared a glance at Conleth, but he looked into the distance as if reliving the story as Queen Yemma spoke it.

"She gave him seven years. It wasn't until a short time ago that Prometheus entrusted me with this story. He came to me for your protection. He asked nothing for himself in return. We took a blood oath." Queen Yemma held up her hand, and the faint raised scar stared back at me.

I gulped. I had heard of blood oaths before, but I had never witnessed one. They were breakable only by death.

"What did the blood oath promise?"

"In return for our protection of you for the rest of your life, he made us legs to walk on the lands outside of our own island."

I gasped, hands flying to my mouth. The air I sucked in stuck in my throat. The clay I saw on his trousers the day we met came into focus. I'd been here when it happened.

"If we were to break that oath, we would not only be sent to Hades's kingdom, but our future brethren would never bear legs, not even on our own soil. As you can imagine, we take this pledge of loyalty seriously, especially since the woman we are protecting is also our friend." She smiled, inclining her head. "We did promise Prometheus we would be discreet when taking trips on our new legs. No human will recognize our true nature." She shrugged one shoulder. "At least, not on purpose. We do tend to stand out."

I spun toward Conleth. "Zeus will kill you," I breathed. This would be considered blasphemy.

He chuckled. "I believe that is the lowest reason on Zeus's long list of reasons for wanting me dead. But thank you for your words of worry, princess."

Conleth had made a blood oath for my safety. It didn't make sense. He hadn't even known me. Only one question burned in my throat now. "Why?"

Conleth stood, closing the distance between us, and cupped my face. "I didn't have to meet you to know one life is worth saving, especially if they are innocent." His thumb brushed against my cheek. My hand covered his as I leaned into his embrace. "But now that I do know you, I'll never let you go. I'll do everything in my power to keep you safe, even if I have to sacrifice my own life for yours. You are all that matters now."

CHAPTER THIRTY-ONE

SAVINA

In the wake of Queen Yemma's and Conleth's confessions, I found my way back to my guest room on shaky legs. I slipped under the covers and laid my head against the pillow staring at the bone-made ceiling. Intricate lines splintered throughout the room where the human remains had been melded together. I followed their ragged edges with my eyes all the way to the windowsill. How fast my world had completely unraveled.

I sifted through my thoughts, pulling at the threads of deceit starting with my childhood. For as long as I could remember, Apollo had always sheltered me from Zeus. It wasn't until the trip to Jacar—the first voyage my father couldn't join—that I had seen Grandfather's wrath, and he, in turn, had witnessed my vulnerability.

My drifting mind landed mere moments after he'd taken Galen's life. The light flickered around us, and the roadside marigolds turned the color of cloud storms. Zeus's lips peeled into a grin so wicked, my skin puckered with goose bumps. He picked a flower that no longer held any color and sniffed it tossing it back into the road and then crushing it under his heel.

The memory faded.

Zeus hadn't shown any interest in me until that trip. What had happened on that excursion that caused him to take notice of me? Was it because he'd witnessed my powers? Had he not known about my abilities until then? I remembered playing with the candle lights onboard Rylander's ship and Zeus asking me how I turned them on and off. But he seemed casual, almost unimpressed when I answered him. Was it my emotions for a human that had angered him? I knew he regarded them as pests, frequently referring to them as fire ants. Or perhaps it all came down to timing? Zeus had been trying to find a way to bring the newly escaped Prometheus out of hiding. Was he looking for a power to bend to his will for just that reason? Then again, maybe a little of everything was at play. I wasn't even sure the heavens knew the answer.

No matter the explanation. I believed Queen Yemma's intentions, but more surprisingly, I believed Conleth's as well. He had been imprisoned by Zeus and tortured in ways I couldn't even comprehend, and instead of choosing to kill me—the easiest solution to his pending problem—he chose mercy over vengeance, compassion over retribution. He boldly ventured into a blood oath to shield a soul he hadn't even known. That told me more about his character, then the lies he had said to get us where we were today.

I had a choice. I could veil my heart in a cloak of denial. Or I could allow the tendrils of gratitude, trust, and burgeoning affection for Conleth to blossom. As realization seeped through the chambers of my heart, it stirred me. A sharp gasp escaped my lips, ricocheting off the walls of my sanctuary as I jolted upward. The truth about Conleth hit me like Zeus's thunderbolts.

I love him.

A knock sounded at the door. "Savina." Conleth's voice sent shivers over my skin. He knocked again. "Can I come in?"

I pulled the covers up to my midsection. "Yes," I croaked.

The door opened, drawing my gaze to his high, sharp cheekbones and plump lips. My face heated. I looked away for a moment to cool my reaction. When I gazed back, he leaned his shoulder against the frame and stared at me. "Are you still angry with me?" A smile appeared, but the force behind it expelled the usual light in his eyes. Instead, the skin around them creased.

"Not as much as I thought I'd be." I folded my hands in my lap. "But I'd still favor a sherron attack over you...for now."

Conleth chuckled, and this time the smile did warm his eyes. I felt my own lips pull upward.

"Yes, well, that could be arranged. I could open a window and you could sing. I'm sure the birds would come willingly to your bedside."

I took the pillow behind me and threw it at his head. I would never live that moment down. But since it led me to Conleth, I wasn't sure I even wanted to.

Conleth caught it without even blinking and held it to his chest. "Why don't you get some rest?"

I nodded.

Conleth placed the pillow on the table next to him and turned to leave.

"Conleth?" I sat straighter as he looked over his shoulder with a raised brow. "Promise me something?"

"Anything." He faced me, his eyes wide and hopeful.

"Never lie to me again. Promise me."

He bowed his head. "I promise."

The way his eyes bore into mine confirmed he meant what he said in this moment. Now if I could only believe it would always hold true.

As the days passed, Conleth and I sought solace in the tranquil scenery of the island. We dined with the sirens, explored the untouched stretches, and amidst the constant vigilance of Queen Yemma's guards, found a rhythm that echoed normalcy amidst the pending chaos. The runes etched around the isle acted as a barrier against the gods, yet the caution never ceased. I rarely left the castle grounds without a siren escort or Conleth. We didn't possess much, but in each other's quiet company, I found more than what grandeur could offer—a genuine care, an unspoken bond that resonated deeper than the vast ocean surrounding us.

When my birthday arrived, I woke expecting everything from dying plants to the gates of the underworld opening. Instead, nothing happened. Every hour I looked down at my hands wondering when they would become weapons. Would I change colors, grow a third limb, get ill? No one knew. I waited for a shift in my mind, body, or demeanor, but after the morning came and went with no sign of the end of the lands, I grew frustrated.

After lunch, I wondered to the shoreline where I found Conleth seated at the very spot where destiny had entwined our paths months ago. He studied the boundless water, perhaps seeking answers in its depth or reminiscing the turbulent voyage that led us to this moment.

"What are you doing?"

Conleth turned toward me and flashed his crooked, self-assured grin. "Remembering."

I laughed. "Oh, really? And what, pray tell, are you re-membering that has you so smitten with yourself?"

I crouched beside him and sank into the sand. My toes wiggled down into the cooler grains beneath. I swallowed the anxious knots lodged in my chest. We only had hours, maybe minutes, and I still had no idea what that would mean for me, for Conleth, the sirens, Zeus, or even the people of the land.

Conleth wrapped his arm around me and pulled me close to his side. I laid my head on his shoulder.

"I remember hearing a swarm of angry sherrons, then seeing the most beautiful girl in the world flailing around like a madwoman trying to escape pecking beaks. I truly wondered whether they would eat you."

I playfully slapped his chest. "Thanks for that horrific thought."

He gripped my hand, keeping it over his heart. "Then I landed on top of you and realized you had the power to change my life. That even if you became only a memory, you would always live in my heart." He chuckled, mindless-ly playing with my fingers in his embrace. "And wouldn't you know, soon after, the Fates surprised me. There you were in Cava, right before my eyes, my little songbird. My betrothed, barreling through a tavern midday with the same twisted cute pout on those pretty pink lips that I remembered from our first meeting. I knew right then and there it was no coincidence that I'd refused Pythia's plea. We were meant for each other."

My cheeks heated. "Your gilded tongue waggles again, Your Grace."

"My tongue only seems to waggle in your presence, princess." He dropped my hand and kissed my cheek.

"And now?"

"And now, what?" He tilted his head.

"Now that your fake betrothed is supposed to end humanity. What will you do?" I leaned back on my forearms, and Conleth joined me. "What is supposed to happen today and why hasn't it happened yet?"

Conleth stared out into the distance. Moments passed before he answered. "I do not know."

"But you believe that me staying on Anthemusa safeguards all the lands? That I pose no threat to the sirens or to you?"

Over the past few days, Conleth's reassurances were a melody that almost quelled the tempest in my mind. Yet, I struggled to sway to its rhythm. Zeus saw me as a coveted jewel in his divine crown, and his silence was foreboding rather than a respite. He didn't value anything that couldn't augment his might, and the lack of an oncoming army was a quiet that tolled like alarm bells. Whenever I dared relax, I felt like a hare twitching its nose in the eerie stillness before a predator pounced.

Conleth shifted to his side and, with a gentle touch, tucked away the rogue strands of my hair that fluttered in the saline breeze. His eyes, a burning forge, bore into mine as he spoke.

"I believe with my whole heart that you are safe here, and that is all I care about. I may be God of the People, but right now, I am just the god of you." His fingers drew a warm trail down the contours of my face, leaving behind a stream of heat that conflicted the cold dread within me. "I won't let Zeus hurt you. I won't let him take you away from me either." He gripped the back of my neck and drew our foreheads together.

What if, by day's end, I became a harbinger of death to humankind? The pangs of guilt bit at the corners of my conscience as faces of loved ones sketched themselves before my eyes: Henrik, Ketner, Krinny. Each smile a plea, each glance a hope of survival against the looming doom. Pythia's petition to Conleth, although a grim notion, made sense. It was a morbid realization that my sacrificial demise appeared like a logical solution. Yet here I was, amidst the veils of affection and promises of protection, grappling with the unknown.

"I should have never doubted you. I'm sorry I accused you of wanting to kill me. It's not what I felt in my heart," I confessed with shallow breaths. "It never crossed my mind a god as powerful as Zeus could be merciful." I looked away. All my life, I had only witnessed destruction by my grandfather's hand, and even if Hermes and my father didn't agree with him, they bent to his fury. I'd never known anyone like Conleth, a deity who stood up to the God of the Sky.

Conleth held on to my chin and guided my gaze back to his. "I know how your heart felt." He kissed the tip of my nose. "How it feels."

A knot in my throat began to take root, drawing out tears. "I'm scared." My nose tingled, holding in a sniffle. "What if there's no future for us? What if my powers..."

Conleth placed his finger on my lips. "You're getting ahead of yourself, my little songbird. We don't know anything yet. But no matter what happens...we will face it together."

I stared into the liquid fire of his irises. "When I am with you, I forget I am a princess without sovereignty, an aunt without a best friend, a sister without a hero, and a demi-god without purpose." My voice trembled. "I am just a woman looking at a man like he hung the sun, the moon, and the stars to brighten her darkest hours."

Conleth cupped my face. "And when I am with you, I forget I am a god who was tortured by an old friend, discarded by his peers, and mutilated by a divine animal for most of his life. I am just a man looking at a woman like she is the air in his lungs, the beat of his heart, and the blood in his veins."

I used to think of Conleth's betrothal as a death sentence. That he would be my prison. But sitting here, staring at the one person who had never given up on my life, who fought for me, with me, I knew he was my liberation.

I climbed onto his lap and sat astride him, our faces an inch apart. "This may be the end..." Conleth went to speak, but I pressed my finger to his lips, as he'd done to me. "Whatever the next moments bring, I know I am exactly where I am meant to be."

Conleth lifted a brow. "Straddling me?"

I attempted to whack him for his teasing, but Conleth captured my hand and, with swift maneuvering, had me on my back. Before I could protest, his lips sealed against mine. A curling sensation pooled in my lower stomach—warm and tingling like my first sip of brandy. The kiss started off gentle and slow. My heart beat so fast, my head spun. He pulled away, our noses touching, and his breath grazed my lips.

"I told you I'd kiss you again when you knew everything." His head slanted and then his mouth met mine. There was nothing sweet or soft this time. This kiss was wild and passionate, claiming, and when I sucked in a sharp breath, he took advantage and deepened the kiss. My mouth obeyed his command and opened for him. The breeze blew cold against my skin as he started to unbutton my blouse, never breaking our kiss. His touch slid down my waist as he pulled the shirt tails out of my pants and laid my body bare beneath him. I felt every part of me come awake, alive, unconcerned with covering myself out in the open. I reached for him, wanting him closer.

When he pulled back, I groaned in protest.

"Marry me?"

My eyes widened. "What?"

"Not because you have to, but because you want to, because we love each other. We will thwart Zeus's war—win it if it comes to that. I know we can do it together. Marry me and let us go back to rule your kingdom as king and queen for the rest of our days. Then when you die, I shall go with you to Elysian Fields." Conleth's hands trailed down my stomach, reaching the button of my trousers. "Say yes?" He undid the button and gripped the waistband, pushing them to my hip bone and stalling, waiting.

"Yes." I couldn't be sure what my yes was for, him proceeding with my trousers, our future together, or maybe both. But the word left my mouth before I dared care which.

Conleth's lips crashed down on mine. I memorized the swell of his mouth, the salt on the skin of his throat as I trailed kisses down. I realized in this moment, I wanted him. Now. Forever. Even after death. He'd asked me to marry him, but he didn't have to; I was already irrevocably his in sickness and health, until and after death do us part.

We broke apart long enough for Conleth to remove his tunic and for me to shimmy out of my trousers. My eyes roamed over his body, starting with his muscular shoulders, down to his broad chest, landing on the scars left by my grandfather's eagle. My heart swelled, clogging my throat. How strong Conleth had been to survive such agony. Zeus's brutal vengeance knew no bounds.

As my fingertips gingerly read the raised tale of scars, a soft veil of tears misted my eyes, blurring the harsh lines of the past engraved on him. The touch was a whisper, attempting to soothe the ghost of agony that lurked within those marks.

"It doesn't hurt, my little songbird. Not anymore." His voice was a gentle caress that allayed the gale brewing in my heart. Grasping my hand tenderly, he pressed a soft kiss on the inside of my palm, his eyes locking onto mine, exposing a realm of unspoken devotion. "I would traverse that hellfire a thousand times over if it charted the path to you."

I looked into his flame-red irises and saw my reflection staring back at me, a combination of want and desire. I trusted Conleth, down to my bones, with my life and with the world. My fingers traced the bare skin along his trousers, but my eyes stayed in place, latching onto his.

Conleth moaned and tilted his head back, looking at the bright sky. His skin pimpled with goose bumps as I continued my pursuit. I marveled at the coal-colored lashes fanned out along his cheeks, the way his mouth parted with each pleasure-ridden groan. *I* made him feel that way. *I* stoked his desire. I didn't worry about my inexperience. It didn't matter I wasn't his first because it would be our first time together.

He lowered himself back down, capturing my lips in his again. Our centers pressed into each other, and we both moaned. Never breaking our kiss, Conleth started to remove the last bits of clothing between us when a blast of light ripped through the sky.

As Conleth's lips retreated from mine, a gasp escaped me. "What was that?" The sky had suddenly thrown a glaring javelin of light, shattering the warm bubble of intimacy in which we'd encased ourselves.

Conleth sprang off me, handing over my shirt and pants while scrambling to retrieve his. Our eyes, now untangled, darted upward to the heavens. Another dazzling spear of light slashed across the sun, bisecting it—a force so strong it severed the glowing orb that had watched over the Earth since Gaia and Uranus's first joining.

Fragments of the sun, now an ethereal ember, rained down, spiraling in a dance as they plummeted toward the ocean's embrace. Their fiery caress turned the water into steam, spinning clouds of vapor that hovered above the turbulent waves. I blinked, my mind struggling to stitch reality into the horror unraveling before us. It had started. My powers were killing the light, the earth's warmth. This was my doing.

A lump formed in my throat. We had run out of time. Death and destruction to the land was happening and there was nothing I could do to stop it. All those moments, from my father hiding me from the world's assessing eyes, to Zeus killing Galen and all the townspeople, to Conleth arriving as my fake fiancé, to our voyage here to the siren's island, none of it mattered. Fate had other plans, and nothing but my death would have prevented *this*.

The full horror of the situation emerged in the creases around Conleth's turned down lips. "We have to go." His voice trembled against the thundering sky as his fingers reached for mine. Yet before our flesh could weave the familiar warmth, the heavens unleashed a ferocious volley of light, each bolt hungrily devouring what remained of the celestial sphere until nothing remained. As the last whispers of sunlight were swallowed by the ravenous abyss, a dense silence blanketed the land.

Silence...and infinite dark.

CHAPTER THIRTY-TWO

CONLETH

In the siren queen's throne room, I paced barefoot like a restless spirit. I didn't even have time to grab my shoes when we ran from the shoreline. At first, I'd had no idea what we were watching. Then realization struck with the ferocity of a lightning bolt from Zeus's arsenal. Savina. It was her dominion over light and dark. She wasn't the harbinger of ruin through pestilence or plague, but through cold and abyssal darkness. Her actualized power had extinguished the life-sustaining sun, aligning precisely with Zeus's sinister desires. Pythia's foresight had muddled some important details but gotten the worst part right; the sole route to averting this cosmic calamity lay in ending Savina's existence. Yet, even if her death at this very moment would resurrect the sun, I'd never do it.

A dialogue between Queen Yemma, her guards and Savina unfolded around me. They hurried to light the island up with torches just as we had done to the throne room. But I paid them little attention as one question needled the fringes of my mind again and again: how long could the lands endure a world abandoned by the sun?

"Conleth." General Ballas's voice severed the chain of my brooding, and I looked up. "Apollo has arrived. He seeks audience with you."

"Papa?" Hope warred with disbelief in Savina's voice as she moved to stand beside me, her hand finding solace in mine, her gaze unwavering from Ballas. "He's here? How?"

"He's wading in the shallows offshore." General Ballas dipped her head. "One of our guards found him during her patrol. But I'm sorry, princess, he specifically asked for Prometheus to come alone."

The island was veiled in a rune barrier that permitted only my presence, a sanctuary from divine retribution. Others of godly descent could only linger at the periphery, where the tides kissed the sands.

Savina's brows furrowed, a flicker of hurt in her yearning eyes. "No. That can't be true. He'd want to see me as well." Her gaze sought validation from me.

I kissed her forehead. "Let me go talk to him, and if it is safe, I will come retrieve you."

Her eyes, like twin oceans, searched mine, myriad questions shimmering in their depths.

"Trust me."

With a soft exhale, she nodded. "Okay."

I kissed her tenderly, then disintegrated from the spot, only to rematerialize amidst the granules of sand where Apollo awaited. The moon was bereft of her brother, leaving the stars to cast a ghostly pallor upon the land. Between their twinkle and the fire atop the torches, a soft aura lit the figure before me.

Apollo stood draped in the attire of the gods, unaltered by the tides of time. Sun-kissed locks of gold rested upon his shoulders, their luster reminiscent of forgone days on Mount Olympus. His skin, a canvas of pure porcelain, emanated a subtle glow from the divine power coursing beneath. Adorned in a short cream tunic and gilded sandals, he was every bit the deity I'd known. Yet, as a smile curled the edges of his lips, a fleeting shade of Arlo, the mortal guise he wore on Cava, emerged. The soft arch of his smile bore the tender familiarity of the man I'd encountered in the castle.

"Prometheus." He folded his arms across his chest with somber gravitas. "Under other stars, a reunion would have called for pleasantries. Yet, as we stand on the precipice of an apocalypse, niceties feel a tad misplaced, don't you think?"

The bitter truth struck a chord. "Always so profound." Mirroring his stance, I folded my arms. "How long does the land have?"

The rhythmic ebb and flow of the ocean tides punctuated the silence that followed, as though even the waves murmured prayers for the uncertain morrow.

Apollo looked to the sunless sky, then back at me with sad eyes that matched his daughter's. "The earth will stay comparatively warm to the chill of the universe for a few million years. But the humans will feel the cooling much sooner." He shook his head. "They've already suffered losses. Within a week, all will be dead."

A week?

"How do the others feel about this?" The gods must believe Zeus had gone too far this time. I couldn't imagine them wishing the world to end, especially when they were so entertained by their human playthings. If nothing else, wouldn't they miss puppeteering the lands? They had little other purpose.

Apollo leaned down and skimmed the shallow water with his fingertips. "Like you'd imagine, some are unhappy with Zeus but staying quiet. Others blame me, as Savina is my offspring. Yet there are still others who find entertainment in Zeus's misdeeds. None of the gods will suffer from this."

My jaw clenched, my teeth near snapping. I pointed to the ocean. "How is Poseidon not mad? This affects his underwater kingdom, does it not?"

Apollo wiped his hand dry on his tunic. "The top layers of the oceans will take a year to freeze over, but that ice will only insulate the deep water below and prevent the oceans from freezing solid for hundreds of thousands of years. Zeus will have created a new world by then. Poseidon's creations will be unaffected."

"And Hades?"

"He welcomes more to his kingdom, which by week's end will be overrun with humans."

I shook my head. How had I allowed this to happen? How had I missed this as a possibility? But even if I'd guessed... "It didn't matter that I saved her and brought her here. The danger was never in her hands. It was never illness or the plague, but the power she wields over the light and darkness."

"Yes. It was."

I stepped forward. The sand squished between my toes. "And you knew that."

"It was one of many possibilities I foresaw, yes."

Fire tingled at my fingertips, pleading to be released. "You fooled me. You sent Pythia to tell me believable nonsense, so what? I would fall in love with Savina rather than kill her, but in doing so slaughter every other human that walks this land?" I stepped closer, my feet submerged to the ankles. "How could you?"

Apollo shrugged a shoulder. "I gave you the chance to kill her with the information you received, did I not?"

My eyes widened. "You call that a chance?" My fists clenched and unclenched. If I could only strangle him in this moment, my anger would have an outlet. But instead, it pulsed inside me. The veins in my forearms popped as a result. How could he bear witness to this destruction? I might not have liked Apollo, but I'd never pegged him for malice.

Apollo reached out and cupped my face with useless warmth. I flinched, but curiosity stayed my hand from smacking his away.

"Would you have killed her, my dear boy?" The reflection of flames from the torches danced in his blue eyes as they held mine. He didn't know with certainty. I could feel it in his touch.

I looked away, breaking his hold. "I don't know."

Apollo chuckled. "Yes, you do."

I shook my head, hot tears rolling down my cheeks. My actions had single-handedly doomed the fate of the people I had sworn to protect. But Apollo was right. I would have never killed Savina, and now that I'd fallen madly in love with her, I'd never let another have the chance either.

"If I die now, will the sun reappear?" Savina's voice broke through the silence. I spun to face her. Tears clung to her lashes, framing red, swollen eyes.

"No," Apollo answered without missing a beat, seeing his daughter and the pain of what she'd done etched in her features. The darkness under her eyes matched the black of the sky.

Her voice hitched. "How can I use my powers to fix this? Can I create another light, something to protect the humans? Can I retrieve the sun that fell? Tell me."

"I've seen many an outcome. But as you know, I cannot advise you." The torches around us flickered, the flames hissed as if equally angered by Apollo's response.

I moved to Savina's side and pulled her into me. She came without protest, wrapping her trembling arm around my waist. Her fingers dug into my hipbone, holding on for dear life. The fact that the land would crumble beneath her very feet—and by her doing—was killing her slowly and painfully.

"I can, however, provide you with some aid in the matter." Apollo snapped his fingers, and a gold quiver outlined with red velvet trim appeared. He extended it to Savina. She left the warmth of my embrace to retrieve it.

"What is this?" She held the quiver in her hand, inspecting the fine detailing on the sides. "It looks like the carvings on my bedpost. The tale of the man who fell in love..." She gasped, covering her mouth with her petite hand. Her eyes bounced between her father and me. "Conleth is the fairy tale you told me at bedtime. The one you carved on my headboard."

"Yes, he is." Apollo walked closer to his daughter. The protector in me seized up, but the man in me knew this moment was between parent and child. Apollo would never hurt her. "And you are the princess, the warrior, the fighter, in the story. The people's salvation." He cupped her cheek and chin. "Do you remember what I told you that day in the gardens when you first realized you could kill the flowers?"

Savina nodded, tears streaming down her face. "You said all I had to do was use my powers to reverse it." Apollo wiped away the droplets glistening under her eyes, but it seemed to make her cry harder. "'For every disease there is a cure. Sometimes we don't see it right away. But your magic possesses the abilities of both life and death. In your darkest hours, your gift has the power to give back the light you've taken.'"

He snapped again, and a gilded bow appeared in the sand.

She breathed a sob, and even my heart stopped. "You never meant my ability to heal or deliver illness. You meant my ability to tear the sun from the sky. But how will I put it back?"

Apollo dropped his hand. "You can't. That sun is forever gone. But you might have the power to create a new one." He clapped, and the quiver filled with three arrows pulsing with a fire-orange glow. "You'll get three attempts. That was all I could get the gods to agree on."

The skin pinched between my brows. "Even Zeus? He knows about this?" My voice crackled like blossoming flames speaking our tormentor's name.

"Yes, even my father agreed. In fact, he found the proposition very entertaining. He doesn't care about the land." He looked over Savina's head and into my eyes. "He wants your misery. Not only will Savina need to figure out how to save the world, but you will then have to surrender and go back to the mountain. I'll need your word. That was the cost of these arrows."

"No!" Savina shouted.

I released a steadying breath. "I understand." In truth, I'd always known my life would be our one bargaining chip with Zeus. I had just hoped it might not come to fruition. "You have my word."

Savina gasped. "I won't let it happen." She glared at me. "How could you?"

"This was inevitable, my love. My escape set all this in motion."

In two quick strides, I reached her side and grabbed her face in my hands. "He will never take you from my heart." I kissed her, and when I pulled back, my lips were wet from our joint tears. "All he wanted was me. This way, you and the rest of the world will live, and I will fight another day. I escaped once. I will again."

"No!" Savina trembled. I wiped her cheeks, but I couldn't staunch the onslaught of emotions.

"We have no choice."

Savina ripped herself from my embrace, dropping the quiver, and ran to her father. Her feet kicked up water. She grabbed his hands and brought them close to her heart. "There's always a way. Tell us. I know you've seen it. Tell me."

Apollo peered at his daughter and then me. "Maybe Prometheus has something Zeus values more than his eternal bondage?"

Savina looked over her shoulder. "Do you?"

I gritted my teeth and stared down at my swaying shadow in the sand cast by the lit torches around me. "I don't know."

By the time I looked up, Apollo was gone. And I found myself faced with a choice worth much more than eternal pain.

CHAPTER THIRTY-THREE

SAVINA

I fixed Conleth with a scorching glare. "What is wrong with you? I can't stand by and let you hand yourself over to Zeus."

Conleth cradled my face, a tender touch. "One crisis at a time. We need to return the sun to the sky."

A nipping chill blew from the blanketed sky, but warm tears carved paths down my cheeks onto Conleth's hands. These arctic temperatures were nothing compared to the freezing despair that awaited humanity. But my resolve remained firm: I would never allow Zeus to claim Conleth. Never.

"Fine. We'll restore the sun, but afterward, we flee. Promise me you won't surrender to the God of the Sky. Promise me you won't return to Mount Caucasus to face that torturous eagle. Promise me!"

Conleth's lips brushed against mine once, then twice, soft and gentle. The sweetness deepened into a kiss that curled my toes, a conveyance of love and longing that transcended words. Yet it fell short of the promise I wanted to hear. When he pulled away, my tears cascaded down my cheeks in streams.

"I love you."

He smiled. "I love you, too."

His confession imprinted on my heart, a truth that Zeus could never grasp, much less take from us. My grandfather only loved himself and whatever served his agenda. He'd never understand unconditional love for another, and for that I pitied him, even if he was a horse's arse trying to end my people.

A peaceful silence enveloped us as we lost ourselves in each other's eyes. Conleth's molten gaze spoke promises, his arms encircling my waist, holding tightly as though he wished to meld our souls. My pulse danced to the rhythm of his heart, and amidst the looming catastrophe, I found a happiness I never dreamed possible. The fabled love I had sought when writing my tale as a child had come to life, even if a shadow of loss loomed, threatening to snatch it away.

Conleth wrapped a loose strand of hair behind my ear and trailed his fingers down my neck. "I'll always find my way back to you. Even if the Fates demand a parting, I will seek you out," he pledged. "That I promise you."

A shiver coursed through me, born not of the cold but of my fear of losing Conleth. His arms retreated, and my heart plummeted with them.

He lifted my chin with two fingers, tilting my gaze to his. "Now, let's go save the world."

With a soft kiss upon my nose, he stepped back, stooping to pick up the bow and quiver bequeathed by my father and offer them to me. "I'll forge a miniature sun with my powers that your arrow can carry to the skies."

My brow furrowed. "But how will it grow big enough to heat the earth?"

"That, my love, is your magic to wield. Much like kindling a flame upon a wick, only on a celestial scale."

His words danced in my thoughts. I had fueled flames before, but nothing of such magnitude. Three chances, that was all I had. I swallowed. "I'll do my best."

The golden bow shimmered with a latent vigor vastly different from the earthly bows I had mastered. Each fiber hummed. Drawing back took all my strength. The bow's unfamiliar pulse disrupted my focus and started a tremor in my elbow. How was I to shoot a flaming sphere into the heavens with a bow that felt like a figment of dreams?

"Stop overthinking it," Conleth chided.

I threw my head back, sighing up at the sunless sky. "I'm not. It's just...different. It feels different in my hands." I shook the bow for emphasis.

"I'd imagine so." Conleth's lips tipped into a teasing curve. "It's destined to rekindle the sun, after all."

"Maybe it is you who should join Cava's theater troupe." I shot back. The world hung in the balance for gods' sakes. This was no time for humor.

With a few strides, Conleth stood beside me, his hands firm on my shoulders. "This is no jest. I believe in you, wholly. You can do this."

His faith was a slim beacon amidst the ruins of doubt, guiding me to hope.

"Are you ready?"

"As ready as I will ever be."

Conleth nodded, then turned to face the eastern horizon where the sun should have been rising. His brow furrowed, eyes squinting. My own heart stopped as I watched his hands make fluid, deliberate motions, summoning a sphere of fire between them. It crackled and danced, growing steadily until it was the width of a ship's wheel, its glow casting flickering shadows over the dim, desolate landscape around us. He tossed it into the sky as if it weighed as much as a loaf of bread. It hovered there, casting a circular glow onto the sand.

I put some distance between us. With a deep breath, I nocked an arrow, aiming for the fiery sphere. If it was only this easy. Think positive thoughts, I reminded myself, forcing a smile as if that small act would help my cause. My fingers released the string. The arrow, twice the size of any arrow I've ever seen, whisked through the air and pierced the sphere, trapping it between tip and fletching. It ascended, the winds carrying it aloft. My heart caught in my throat as the glowing orb soared higher and higher. It was almost there. It just needed to...

In the next breath, the fire fizzled, unable to reach its destination, and plummeted back to the earth in a shower of embers. The sparks fizzled upon the ocean, hissing like a serpent's tongue.

My heart sank into my chest. "What happened?" I spun to face Conleth. His eyes narrowed on the steaming sea. "Now what?"

He closed his lids and rubbed at his temples. Silence hung between us. We were the world's last hope, and we only had two chances left.

"I have an idea." He glanced up and waved for me to grab the second arrow. "I'll craft a smaller, hotter one. Once it's in the sky, channel your power to expand it. Maybe that'll give it a better chance at reaching its destination." His gaze locked onto mine. "What do you think?"

"Okay." At this point, I'd try anything. Conleth conjured a hovering flame ball the size of a squash.

With trembling fingers, I nocked the second arrow. A sound like a passing hummingbird deafened my right ear.

My heart pounded against my rib cage. The string quivered under the strain, yearning to set the arrow free. Two arrows left, two chances and if I failed, all my human friends and family would die because of me. My breath caught, thinking about the last one they would all take if I didn't succeed.

Conleth swallowed as he looked at me, his eyes filled with unspoken words.

As I released the fletching, time seemed to stretch between my heartbeats. The arrow sliced through the eerie calm, cradling the fire sphere as it surged upward.

The globe ascended, a flicker of warmth coursing through the veins of the world as it climbed higher into the sky. It surpassed the dark clouds and joined the stars, reaching its rightful home. My lips peeled upward. It was working.

With my hands in prayer, I covered my mouth. Silently I urged it to expand, to unfurl its fiery wings and embrace the world with the heat it so desperately needed. But as the sphere reached its apex in the icy canopy, the flames gave a hesitant flicker.

My mouth turned downward.

"No..." My voice was but a whisper, yet it screamed to the desperation eating away at my insides. The fire sphere trembled, struggling against the cold before shattering into a rain of cinders that descended upon us like a cascade of fallen stars.

I stood amidst the failing light, a cry lodged in my throat. My breath shallowed. I wanted to see Calli again to scold her for always causing trouble. I wanted to save Henrik's arse with the help of Ketner and his snake venom. I wanted to fold myself inside my brother's arms and tell him I loved him. Gods, I wanted to marry Conleth with my friends and family there to pay witness. But I only had one more chance.

Conleth moved to face me. "It's not over yet."

"Only one chance left." My words caught in my throat. The last arrow rattled in my quiver, the final sentinel of hope, while Conleth and I shared a quiet gaze. My eyes squeezed shut as I replayed everything from my father conjuring up this celestial bow and arrow to Conleth's words of encouragement. And then I remembered...

My eyes snapped open. It couldn't be that simple, could it? "My powers."

Conleth tilted his head. "What about your powers?"

"My father always uses his words carefully. He always has." My smile pulled to my ears. "He said 'In your darkest hours, your gift has the power to give back the light you've taken.' He was specific when he said 'your gift.' I think he meant for me to do this on my own. The fire, the sun...it's my light. We've been going about this the wrong way."

I bounced on my feet. "If I were to create light like I did on *The Black Hollow* or at Ketner's, I wouldn't ask you to create the flame," I shook my head feeling foolish to have missed the obvious, "I would just have conjured it on my own. That's why this isn't working."

My chest tightened as if gnarly fingers coiled around my heart. I'd been hidden for so long, told to moderate my powers, I never thought I had it in me to do it alone, but it had always been me. How could I have missed that?

Conleth wrapped his arm around me, his smile so bright it was blinding. "I think you are right, my little songbird. This is your moment to give mankind light." He released me and plucked out the third and final arrow.

I gripped the gold shaft below his curled fingers.

"You can do this." Conleth released the arrow and stepped back.

The pad of my finger grazed the tip, lighting a spark at the end, just like I would a wick. The modest flame came to life and danced in the breeze like a woman seducing a man with her hips. I pinched the hard center in the feathered fletching, its cold metal familiar against my skin. Each quiver that ran down the arrow's length as I notched it seemed to echo my nervous energy.

With a slow exhale, I drew the bowstring back, my fingers trembling against the strain. As I released the arrow, the world seemed to hold its breath, including myself. I started to shake. I didn't want to feel the fear creeping up my spine. Earlier today when I laid with Conleth on the sand, willing to give him another one of my firsts, I felt brave. I yearned for that feeling again. I wanted to be the one who faced peril with my head held high, but I was scared. Terrified. I knew this was it.

The arrow's feather's nicked my cheek in a stinging farewell kiss. It surged through the veil of darkness with the small ember leading the charge on the tip, its light shrinking to a speck.

My eyes followed the traveling flame, my lower lip quivering. "The light is too small. It's going to burn out."

"Have faith." Conleth's eyes stayed glued to the sky.

I wanted to close mine, to squeeze them shut until the inevitable happened and the Earth breathed its last dying breath. But if Conleth could look, so could I.

"Expand it. Now," Conleth commanded.

Just when the last glint of hope appeared extinguished, a ripple surged through the fabric of reality. I summoned my ability from every corner of my existence, digging outward instead of down. As if my veins ignited, a surge of power opened my eyes. The ember shivered. It began to pulsate, in conjunction with the beat of my heart. Slowly, almost joyfully, the sphere unfurled its flames, each tendril of fire a defiant cry against the dark background.

The fire roared and spun as it expanded and soared, each rotation thrashing out a new limb of warmth to break the icy chains that had bound the world in a deathly grip. It bloomed and blossomed into a magnificent sun, its radiant arms stretching across the sky, bathing the world in a golden embrace.

As the first rays of sunlight kissed the frozen land, the world awakened from its slumber, each blade of grass, each leaf seemed to rise in a hymn of gratitude. Every creature rejoiced as one with their unique voices. We'd done it. We'd saved the land.

I turned and looked at Conleth, but he wore a frown, a reminder our battle wasn't over. Humankind might have been spared but now we had to deal with the price Zeus had demanded. Conleth's imprisonment.

CHAPTER THIRTY-FOUR

CONLETH

The shining sun awoke the horizon, the warmth cradling my shoulders like a blanket fresh from the hearth. Savina had done it. She saved mankind, just like I knew she could.

The sky transformed, the darkness peeling away to reveal a blue as clear as Savina's eyes. Birds descended in graceful circles, gliding through the puffy white clouds while distant trees swayed in soft rhythm. Waves, in their joyful cadence, danced toward the shores, their white crests shimmering like diamonds as they caught the sun's caress.

Before I could enjoy our success, the gossamer light ebbed into a shadow that spewed the forms of Zeus, Hermes, and Apollo. They waded in a line in shallow water, eyes fixed upon me. Their divine contours cast an arresting glow under the gentle veil of sunlight.

Adorned in draped folds of linen, they seemed to have stepped straight out of Mount Olympus. The twitch of Zeus's jaw was discernible even at a distance, his visage sculpted into sharp features far distinctive from his squared-off earthly guise as Zenith. His hair, now a cascade of white, fluttered in the soft breeze as he advanced ahead of his offspring.

Savina's shoulder grazed mine, her fingers finding and entwining with my own—our united front. I dared not meet her gaze, the lump in my throat swelling. The inevitability of parting from her loomed, a cruel knife twisting in the heart of our victory.

"I must say, I'm impressed." Zeus jerked his chin toward the sky. His deep voice, devoid of the fury I had braced for, echoed across the serene landscape with a light, airy essence almost like genuine admiration.

"Grandfather," Savina acknowledged first. "Father, Uncle."

My eyes flitted between Apollo and Hermes, their faces sculpted into stoic neutrality.

"I'm pleased you've preserved the lands." Zeus inspected his nails with a flick of each finger. "Repopulating would have been an irksome endeavor. I rather relish the antics of my current playthings."

I fought the urge to roll my eyes. Trust Zeus to twist the narrative in his favor. The God of the Sky, whose ego seemed to stretch beyond the heavens, always found a way to perch himself atop a pedestal of superiority.

His gaze lifted to mine. "And now there's a homecoming to celebrate." He beckoned me with his hand. "It's so lovely to see you again, Prometheus. Imagine my distress over your sudden disappearance. And to think you hid alongside us as my darling granddaughter's betrothed," he all but growled, despite still amusing himself with the concerned friend charade. "It'll be wonderful to have you back with my beloved bird. You've been sorely missed."

His triumphant smile leered across the beach. The fire I possessed tingled at my fingertips. Zeus had gotten exactly what he wanted: my recapture. Whether humans lived or died, he couldn't care less. He yearned only for the restoration of my punishment and the sick sense of balance and power he gleaned from knowing a rebel's liver was being gorged on each day by his maddened eagle.

"No." Savina positioned herself between me and her grandfather. "Take me instead."

"What!" My exclamation mingled with Apollo's resounding, "No!"

Zeus's brows knitted together, a hint of surprise momentarily altering his demeanor. "That is not possible."

"Yes, it is. Anything is possible for the God of the Sky. Is it not?" Savina took a bold forward step that Apollo mirrored. But Zeus stretched out his arm, stopping his son's advance. "My life for his. Take me to the mountain to endure this punishment, for it was I who saved humankind this time, not him. It is now my penance to serve."

"Absolutely not." I seized her forearm and pulled her back to my side. Facing Zeus, I countered, "I am willing to serve you and return to the mountain. There will be no fighting. I gave Apollo my word and I intend to keep it."

Savina pushed my shoulder, and my eyes widened. "Be silent." She stormed once again into the no man's land between our parties. "If he goes, I go. You'd best find two eagles, Grandfather, because I will be joining him." Her voice resonated with unwavering resolve, the same courage that had bound us together in the face of peril, again and again. But her actions were reckless and foolish, even if they swelled my heart with love.

Zeus's eyes narrowed, scanning the defiant stance of his granddaughter before drifting to the firm resolve in my eyes. He stretched out a moment of a silence before he finally spoke, his voice a controlled storm. "Bold words, Granddaughter." He emphasized her title just as she had his. "It appears the mortal realm has cultivated a certain...aud acity in you." His eyebrow jumped, almost amused. But beneath, his gaze hardened. "Though you must understand, the whims of mortal heroics can't tip the scales of cosmic justice. Your mother makes you of no use to my mountain or my precious pet. You would die in one day."

"How dare you speak of justice?" Savina gripped her waist. "Death by Prometheus's side is a more tempting offer than a life lived without him."

"I won't have it," I tried to thunder, but it came out a raw rasp. "Savina, go back to Queen Yemma and wait for your brother and his ship."

Savina looked over her shoulder. "I didn't ask you for your blessing or your commands. I am the rightful leader of Cava and with that comes the right to make my own decisions. So stand down."

A growl lodged low in my throat, but I held my tongue. With my powers itching to defend her and myself, I briefly considered trying to reduce Zeus to ash, but I'd never win, not with his offspring by his side. And then there was Savina. I wouldn't chance her getting hurt.

"What about a mercy kill, for your sake, precious one? Instead of torture, I'd be willing to smite him right now. Would that suit you?"

Savina's head snapped back as if Zeus had just slapped her. "A mercy kill? Are you mad?"

She charged like a bull, but I shot forward and hauled her back with an arm around her waist. "I will go with you," I said to Zeus, then whispered in Savina's ear, "Stop this. I will find you again. I promise. Let me go."

She inclined her head to the side, and several strands of bright red hair blew across her nose. "I will not."

"Hmmm." Zeus touched two fingers to his lips. "This is interesting. You love each other with a fierceness I hadn't accounted for." He kicked his sandaled feet as he walked through the water. "All this time, I've been looking at this the wrong way."

"Father." Hermes broke rank and spoke for the first time, sloshing behind Zeus. "What if we just let—"

"Hush." Zeus held up his hand. "What punishments are death and torture for a god who has something, or rather someone, to live for?" He tsked. "That cannot be."

"No." Apollo lunged, spraying water, but Zeus already had his hand in the air. A jagged bolt of pure ethereal energy shot from his palm straight into Savina's center. A sharp cry escaped her lips as she crumbled, and I with her.

Time seemed to stretch. Blood covered my midsection, sticking my clothes to me. The full horror dragged my heart down like a boulder at sea when I stared into her lifeless eyes.

Zeus killed Savina.

I fought for breath through a tightening throat. The only sound was the anguished sob that tore from my chest.

"Now that is a torture I can live with." Zeus smiled down at the lifeless body in my arms. "This is a depth of pain no eagle could ever inflict. Every breath you take will be a reminder of this moment."

I started to shake. Uncontrollable tears cascaded down my cheeks. "You sick, twisted—"

"Be careful, Prometheus," he snapped like a dog protecting a carcass, "or I'll send her to Hades's realm instead of the Elysian Fields."

Apollo shared a look with Hermes, who then popped out of existence. He dropped to his knees and extended his hands, reaching out for his daughter. I pulled her away, tucking her closer to my chest. "Don't touch her. You had the power to save her, and you didn't. You are no better than your father."

"I..." He looked over his shoulder at Zeus. "There were so many outcomes, and this is the one you choose?"

Zeus dismissed his son with a flick of his hand. "Don't be dramatic. It's not as if she's suffering." He pointed to me. "But he will. For the rest of his days."

CHAPTER THIRTY-FIVE

SAVINA

My eyes blinked open. All around me were radiant, white clouds pillowing my body. I looked down. No ground below me. I looked up. No sky above me. My gaze darted around the bright abyss. Nothing but miles of dazzling haze. What happened? Where was I?

I rubbed my temples. The last thing I remembered…

Zeus killed me.

My hands gripped my stomach where the thunderbolt had hit. No blood or ripped clothes. My tunic was intact, tucked into my trousers. Apparently when you die, you didn't take the injuries or torn threads with you.

I spun, searching for a hint of understanding. But all I saw were miles of glistening clouds. My mind raced, landing on one thought…

Conleth.

The inside of my throat thickened, and I squeezed my eyes shut. How could that be our end? How could that have been the last time we were together? I willed my eyes not to cry but it was pointless. Tears streamed down my cheeks, a warm wetness I didn't dare wipe away. With each passing second, the sadness grew. We might have saved the land, but we'd never get to enjoy it together.

"I never got to say goodbye," I whispered.

"Most death is like that." Uncle Hermes popped into existence from nowhere.

I twisted my head and stared at my uncle with wide eyes. "How are you here?" My gaze darted around. "Actually, where are we?"

Hermes tilted his head. "This is the in between."

I cringed. That did not sound promising. "Why am I here? Why did grandfather do this?"

Hermes plopped down on a cloud, his legs dangled below the white puff. "You exposed Prometheus's weakness and provided Zeus with a too perfect punishment, far worse a fate than death."

"Love is not a weakness." But even as I said the words, I knew I had made a fatal error. All my life, my father and uncle had warned me not to show emotions to my grandfather and in the most important moment of my life, I had forgotten. My stomach twisted. Death meant never seeing Conleth again, never sharing another moment together, never saying goodbye.

"So, this is it?" I waved my hand around me. "I live on a cloud for the rest of my days in the in between?"

Uncle Hermes folded his arms, the caduceus tattoo on his forearm danced with his flexed muscles. "You have a choice." He pointed his finger to a golden gate made of pure, solid sunlight emerging before my eyes. "You can walk through there and live your days in incomparable bliss."

I scoffed. Bliss without Conleth might as well be despair.

Hermes's eyes narrowed. "It is not all that bad. The moment you cross to the other side, it will become a paradise of your choosing, where you can have adventures roaming endless lands with your friend Galen by your side, sit at a hearth with your mother, or sail a golden sea with Krinny. They're all waiting there for you."

I stared at him, mouth hanging open. "Krinny is dead?" I staggered, choking on the words.

A somber nod answered. "Zeus killed her for failing to keep you in the castle."

I covered my mouth to hold in a whimper. Powerful, fierce, but full of love Krinny, reduced to the keeper of Zeus's favorite pet and slain for not tightening the choking leash. Had he thrown her aside like rubbish, as he had Galen, as he had me?

Gods, what I would give to tell Krinny how sorry I was. To hug her broad, sturdy frame until my arms ached and tell her how much her care had meant. That no matter my frustrations, with her nearby, I'd always felt safe. She'd deserved so much more.

"You could be with her again," murmured Hermes. "You could be with all your loved ones. I would make certain of that."

I could run to her, apologize for the lie that had broken our bond, tell her I should have done it differently. But how many more would walk through those gates after me? How many more of my loved ones left behind would incur Zeus's wrath? So many people were already dead because of my grandfather, and who knew how many more had died in the last several hours? There might be hundreds or thousands of new lost and confused souls wandering the underworld or Elysian Fields because of his need to punish Conleth.

"Not all my loved ones." A pang stabbed through my heart at the thought of Lou, Adelphi, Calli, Rylander, Ketner, Henrik,...Conleth. I'd found my fairy-tale king, and yet I'd never sit on the throne as Cava's queen. But that didn't ensure that Zeus would leave my people alone. He would keep toying. Keep lashing out like a child at every conceived slight. Keep preying on young women and torturing young men for sport, as he'd done since he first slew his father, Kronos.

"Every choice has a companion."

"So?" I scrunched my face. "What's my other option?" Typical god, drawing out the possibilities.

"Or you can sit with me a while, watch what is happening on Anthemusa, and take a gamble in the in between. If it doesn't go favorably, you will be stuck in this white cloud for many years to come. It will be harder to get you across the gate, maybe even impossible. Demi-gods are not meant to come and go as they please. You could become stuck in this void forever."

My palms itched, and fury heated my cheeks. Stuck in a white wonderland, empty of life. No one to talk to, dead or alive. What kind of choice was that?

The gates sparkled, casting sunbeams across the cloud fluff at my feet, beckoning me to a guaranteed paradise. Eternity with loved ones. Second chances: To make up with Krinny. To have that river ride with Galen, let her know how I so admired her spirit and convey the joy she'd brought a little girl who'd never had a friend. To tell my mother that she never had to be perfect for me to love her.

The rest of my family would join me eventually. I could wait.

But Conleth?

I closed my eyes, squeezing tears from my lashes, and thought about the siren island. The rolling waves, the sand heated by the sun I created, my body pressed up against

Conleth's. In my head, I heard the sherrons' squall, the trees whipping in the wind at the moment I promised Conleth forever. Gods, what we could've accomplished together—the firebringer and the harbinger of light and death who'd both dared deny Zeus his unearned and oversized share of the world. Cava could have flourished along with our love. Cava...where I'd shared countless moments of laughter with my niece in the shelter of my room. A room I'd snuck in and out of to frequent the town and tavern to make memories with Henrik, Ketner, and Calli. A place where I'd never been too far from the hugs and warmth of my brother's arms. Never as far as I stood now, at least.

My life, my family, and so many loved ones were all below me. Those waiting through the gate would still be there in the future. I wanted to return home, and I'd take any chance to see it again, even if that meant an eternal life on a cloud. At least I could whisper a goodbye to Conleth before this pretty but insubstantial world closed back up with me inside.

Opening my eyes, I sighed. "Let me see Anthemusa."

His eyes softened. "As you wish."

A hole parted in the clouds before us, and I crouched on the cottony edge, looking down on Conleth rocking my lifeless body. His swollen eyes matched his reddened cheeks as his body shook. The creases around his mouth twisted with his shortness of breath.

My chest ached as if someone had ripped it wide open. I did that to him. I gave Zeus the opening he desired to tear Conleth's heart from his chest. How could I have been so foolish, so naive? Tears welled up and spilled down my face. I wiped at them furiously knowing this could be the last time I laid eyes on my love and wanting to soak it all in without my vision blurred by emotions...even if it broke me.

"I'll do anything. Anything you want," Conleth cried, grief fraying the edges of his voice, his vulnerabilities laid bare on his anguished, blotchy face.

My grandfather laughed. "But I have what I want." He drank in the sight of Conleth's tears falling on my limp body. "Your pain."

Zeus was never going to give Conleth and I our chance at a happily ever after. I could tell by the curve of his lips and the satisfied twinkle in his blue eyes. He had gotten exactly what he aimed for: Conleth's agony.

My love glared up at Zeus, probably seeing the same thing I saw. "You may have my pain but without your precious bird, you are nothing but my equal." He laid my body down, kissing my forehead as if saying farewell. He jumped to his feet, grains of sand clung to his blood-covered trousers. "I think it's time you joined your brother, Hades, in the underworld, and stayed there for good."

Zeus growled. "How dare you threaten me?" He threw his hand out. White light pulsed from his palm, arcing straight for Conleth.

I gasped, my hands covering my mouth. My love moved quicker than I'd ever seen, avoiding the bolt. But I wobbled as if I had been hit. My feet couldn't find purchase. The same sensation washed over me as when I had been sent to the in between. I released a strangled cry.

Uncle Hermes let out a harsh curse, reaching for me, but it was too late. I slipped through his grasp and the glittering clouds, the world ending for me on the heels of a burst of red blinding light.

CHAPTER THIRTY-SIX

CONLETH

A pollo moved out of the way as I swung at Zeus, connecting my fist with his jaw. He stumbled, sloshing water at his sandaled feet. His hands clenched into fists at his side as he steadied himself. "You thought it was bad before." He released a harsh chuckle, tossing his head back. "I *had* sent her to the gates of Elysian Fields but now she'll rot in the underworld."

"No!" Panic ignited in me like earth cracking under my feet. How could he subject his own offspring to a life in a desolate, dark nightmare?

Zeus raised his hand again, a burst of light sizzling against his skin. I dove out of the way into an oncoming wave. The lightning bolt missed my head by millimeters, stabbing the sandy earth instead. Fish scattered. Like crystals, they glittered as they flicked back and forth in the sunlight. The same sun Savina had hung in the sky.

Savina.

My purpose.

My world.

My love.

Fire ignited in my palms, a renewed strength burned inside of me. Zeus sent Savina to the underworld. I'd never rest until I found a way to get her back.

I sprang up. My soaked clothes dripped off me, weighing my body down. But they couldn't stop me. My fury fueled my movements. Savina shouldn't have died to save my soul. Zeus made a mistake the second he laid a hand on her. I held up my palms and spit fire at the God of the Sky. Zeus ducked each and every one. Only his long curls suffered when a flame sizzled the ends. The smell of burnt hair filled my nostrils.

"Are you going to do something?" Zeus chided his son in between short breaths.

Apollo held up his hands. "I believe this is between Prometheus and you."

Zeus growled at his offspring, then charged me. His legs kicked up water as he ran in the shallow end. I threw my body into his, taking him down under a wave. He struggled against me as we tumbled through the current, but the tides offered him solace as he slipped out of my grasp. Before I knew it, hands plunged through the ocean surface and wrapped around my throat, squeezing the life out of me. He lifted me from the depths. His face contorted, teeth bared.

Blue angry eyes met mine. "You think you have the power to stop me. The God of the Sky." He gripped harder, making it hard to breathe. "You are nothing." He forced my head back under the water.

Bubbles erupted around me as I thrashed beneath his weight. If I could just put space between us, I could break out of his hold. The sand and seashells shifted under me as he pressed me farther into the sandy floor. Their movement gave me exactly what I needed. I managed to shimmy my knee between us and kicked him.

Zeus released me and stumbled backward. I clutched my bruised neck and tried to sit up. But before I could even suck in a breath, his hand, a blurry outline above the surface, rose. I tried to roll but didn't get far enough. Like a sword sinking into human bone and tissue, his thunderbolt ripped through my shoulder blade. Black spots exploded in my vision as my lungs wheezed. I ignored the blooming pain in my side and pressed off the ocean floor. I sat in the sand staring up at Zeus, my body half submerged as I gasped for air. My hand gripped my injured shoulder. Blood pooled through my fingers.

Zeus smiled. "I will kill you just as I did your precious love, but I will make sure you never find in each other in the underworld and that you suffer a thousand deaths by Hades's hands."

Not this time. I lifted my uninjured arm and flipped my palm upward. Each finger released a flame in the shape of blades shooting right into Zeus's chin and neck. Ichor seeped through his pale iridescent skin as each blaze left their mark.

Zeus's expanded eyes met mine. His lips parted. His face twisted in disbelief as he fell back down into the ocean's floor, right beside me. The water turned red around us.

I remembered the moment Zeus trapped me on his mountain, the beak of his beloved pet ripping through my flesh and feasting on my liver, and his laugh carried on by the wind, echoing around in my mind for years. This moment felt like retribution for the past *and* the present. This was his time to die. I held up my hand to deliver the final blow, but Apollo stepped between us, blocking my target.

Apollo's face tightened, a sobering look in comparison to the indifference he wore moments ago. "Enough."

He leaned down and helped his father sit upright. The ends of Zeus's white hair were stained red, sticking to his slashed throat. He coughed and sputtered up a mixture of water and ichor. His son held onto his back with one hand and gripped his injuries with the other, healing them with his godly touch. Zeus's skin sewed back together, the holes in his chin and throat closed before my very eyes.

I ground my teeth. Apollo stole the one chance I had at vengeance. I would never stop until...

"This feud needs to end." Apollo sighed. "How about an exchange?"

My lips pressed together. I had nothing to say. I wouldn't sit here and believe Zeus to do right by his son or myself no matter what Apollo proposed.

"What exchange?" Zeus growled, smoothing out the ends of his wet hair into a ponytail.

Apollo reached his hand out to his father and helped him stand. "Conleth has information that could be valuable to you, maybe worth my Savina's life." He reached out for me this time, but I waved him off. I would not accept his help. Not now, not ever.

Zeus's gaze volleyed between Apollo and me. "What could this worthless being know that would be of any merit to me? All I want from him is his suffering."

"He might have information that would secure your future." Apollo raised a brow.

Zeus spun toward Apollo, teeth bared. "If you know, why do I need him? You can just tell me."

Apollo grinned. "I see thousands of futures, Father. But Conleth's foresight allows him alone to know which one is true. In this case, you will want to make sure you have certainty."

I had no clue what Apollo was wagering but I paid no mind to it and let him work his magic. Getting Savina back was my only concern. If he could wager a deal to do so, then I would swallow my pride and gladly hand over information to save her.

Apollo turned to me. "If Zeus allows you to retrieve Savina from the underworld, would you be willing to tell him what you know about Thetis."

My eyes widened, my mouth opened in the shape of an olive. The name was but a whisper, but it carried its weight tenfold. How could I have forgotten? Zeus has been fawning over Thetis for years, always fighting with Poseidon for her affection. Thetis was the answer to saving Savina and reclaiming our future together.

Zeus's jaw ticked. "What about her?" His voice boomed, quaking the ground below me.

"Not until you swear a blood oath that you will permit Prometheus to retrieve Savina from the underworld and allow them to live as husband and wife and reign over Cava as King and Queen without worry you'll come for Prometheus again. You will also allow him into Elysian's Field when it is time for Savina to die a normal human death." Apollo chose his words carefully.

With a grunt, Zeus dipped his chin.

A dagger materialized, hanging in the air between us. The emerald jewels glinted off the sun, the blade reflecting the rays. Zeus reached out and grabbed it, slicing it over his palm. Glittering red blood dripped from its edge. Then he threw it at me, refusing to look me in the eyes. I cut my own hand and reached out for his. Apollo sealed our hands together in a blood oath as Zeus and I both swore our vow at the same time.

Zeus ripped his hand from mine. "Get on with it. Tell me what you know about Thetis."

I ran my fingers through my wet strands, slicking my hair back. The sooner I revealed the truth about Zeus's future, the sooner I could get to Savina, but I couldn't deny the satisfying taste of retribution in my enemy's surrender.

"Beautiful as the nereid Thetis may be, she will also be your downfall should you give yourself over to her temptation. The son she births will one day rule over his father." Zeus would fall from his throne and Thetis's son would rule. It had been a fate I wished on him since I found out about the prophecy.

"If Thetis births a god's child, her son will be greater than all the gods, including you, but should her son be born to a human father, he will only be a great and mighty man." I looked out to the ocean. Zeus wasn't the only god that could doom the Olympians. "If I were you, I'd speak to Poseidon since he, too, lusts for Thetis. Her son will overthrow his father; that is a fate even you cannot change. But maybe if you intercede now, you can at least make certain that father is human and save the deities' future." I sucked in a breath, waiting to see how Zeus would react.

Zeus's cheeks inflamed, red splotched dotted up his now healed neck. "And so it will be done." Zeus clapped, and the air I had been holding escaped. I slipped through the earth and gasped for air as I clutched my throat. My eyes squeezed shut, and when I reopened them, I stood on cold, brittle black sand in front a blood-red sea, my body completely healed and dried.

Savina sat with her back to me, her shoulders vibrated in rhythm with her sobs. Her vibrant red hair fluttered in the wind, reminding me of the ball of fire she created and hung in the sky. How strong and resilient she was, so fierce and clever. So irrevocably mine!

I smiled. We might have been in the underworld but to me Savina would always be my paradise.

CHAPTER THIRTY-SEVEN

SAVINA

I stood sentry above the flamed colored sea that mirrored the blue one on Anthemusa. Somehow I ended up in the underworld. Alone. No teasing uncle. No white iridescent clouds. No human, spirit or deity to explain why. The ocean only went so far and then nothing, just a dark, black void. Behind me, dying plants and other organisms littered the black and brown sand. To my right and left, exactly the same, then nothing but darkness. The only reason I even knew this was Hades's kingdom was from my Greek education. We were taught a soul sent to the underworld would end up in a place that appeared familiar, but as a dim, gloomy version outlined in a void of darkness.

Time moved differently here. I had no reference to whether I had been here for minutes, hours or days, only that this nightmare would be for eternity and me its prisoner.

Exhaling harshly, I watched the thunderous red waves. Their commanding clash with the bristle brown shore muffled my cries. No one ever paid attention to the waves that rolled away from the beach—those less forceful currents were always harder to see. Yet they were there all the same and just as vital to the tides. I always believe my fairy-tale prince would ride in on his thundering golden chariot or white horse—unignorable and undeniable. But true heroics hid in subtlety. The real prince charmings didn't boast their victories or strengths. It was the waves that drew you in that deserved your love, not the ones that crashed upon you, demanding your fealty.

Conleth was one such man, the one of my dreams, the one of my ambitions and I lost him. Zeus had sent me to the underworld and the gods knew what he was doing to Conleth right now. Even if he ended his life, he'd never let us share our nightmare together.

I wandered back to the brown and black beach, sitting where the damp sand met the foamy red sea. With legs stretched out and trousers rolled up to my knees, I submitted my bare feet to the cool embrace of the lapping shallows. As the wind whispered against my skin, a fresh batch of tears cascaded down my cheeks. My shoulders juddered with my cries. A maelstrom of emotions sank into my heart, and the song Fretta had hummed aboard *The Black Hollow* revisited my mind. The melody filled my chest until the tune slipped from my mouth.

"Are you no longer afraid of your flock, my little songbird?"

My heart stopped.

That voice.

Conleth.

The underworld was truly cruel. Would the rest of my days be filled with tortuous moments of his memory? Would I always think I heard him speak only to be met with disappointment? How I longed for the in between where I was met with silence.

"Or maybe it is that you believe your pitch has improved since being in the underworld?"

I squeezed my eyes shut. *He's not here. He's not here. He's not here.* Maybe if I repeated it enough times, I'd believe it.

"Or maybe you worry this is not real and I am all but an illusion created by madness?" The voice sounded as if it were closer than before. "But I am very real, as real as the love I have for you, as real as the truth I've come to take you home."

I pressed myself up to stand, then turned, ready to yell at the empty abyss for messing with my mind. But my gaze stopped when a familiar man's form appeared. Shadows cast across his face from the reddish-brown sky outlined in charcoal.

Air froze in my lungs. I couldn't speak. I was afraid if I did, I'd sever this moment and the mirage standing before me would disappear.

Conleth flipped his palm and fire blazed. He tossed the flaming sphere into the air and smiled, tipping his lips up at the corner. His coal-colored hair blew in the breeze while his flamed-colored eyes dark with longing and love focused on my mouth. He wore the same outfit from when we first met, a loose white tunic rolled up to his elbows and grey trousers. He stepped closer and I stepped back, terrified to believe in this moment.

"It's me, Savina."

My hands flew to my cheeks. "Is this real? Are *you* real?" I didn't dare blink, for fear he would disappear. Even if this was Hades torturing me, I'd take it because seeing Conleth again wasn't a nightmare at all, it was a dream.

Conleth chuckled. "It's real, my little songbird." He flicked the ball of fire and it sizzled into ashes. "I'm here and I've come to take you home."

Home. He said home. Before I could let doubt seep in, I took off, running to him. He moved, meeting me halfway. I flung myself into his arms and wrapped my legs around his waist, my hands clasped behind his neck. The feel of him, warm and solid, against my body sent a rush so powerful I shuddered.

"How?" I breathed. "How is this possible?"

Conleth's hand slipped up my neck and gripped my cheek, then he closed the distance and pressed his lips against mine. Tears fell from my eyes, but I never broke our kiss. Instead, I melted into him, savoring this moment. I didn't believe I'd ever get this chance again and now that I had, I wouldn't stop. I could taste the salt of my tears and the sea on our lips. Our kiss became more desperate, more wild. As if Conleth knew I'd never break away, he slowed the moment and teased my lower lip with quick nips. We were both breathless as we pulled apart, staring into each other's eyes.

Conleth lowered me to the ground and planted a chaste kiss to my forehead.

"Did Zeus kill you? Is that how you got here?" I clutched the front of his tunic afraid if I didn't hold on, he could disappear.

"No." He cupped the side of my cheek and rubbed the pad of his thumb over the wetness on my skin. "This was your father's doing. He knew I had information that your grandfather would want. He leveraged it in a deal between Zeus and me."

"What deal?" I tilted my head, leaning into his embrace, soaking up as much warmth from his body as I could get.

"I knew of a goddess Zeus was pursuing and of the powers her son would have over his father. If Zeus or any other god bed Thetis, her offspring would overthrow them. Now Zeus will make her bed a human and the gods will be safe from Thetis's child."

I gripped harder, my nails digging into his shirt. "How does sharing that information keep you safe or bring me home?"

Conleth smiled, the same one that always melted my heart. "We entered a blood oath. For that information, he had to let me into Hades's kingdom to retrieve you and bring you back to Anthemusa."

"What about you? He can't take you away from me. I won't go back without you." I stepped out of his hold, immediately feeling chilled to the bones. I wouldn't lose Conleth again. My heart couldn't take it. "I'd rather live the rest of my days here, in this," I waved at our bare, desolate surroundings, "nightmare, than ever live a day deprived of our love."

Conleth wrapped his arm around me and pulled me back into his embrace. He kissed my forehead. "If you will let me finish, you'll hear that the blood oath included me."

My mouth gaped and Conleth chuckled.

"You and I will be free to marry, to lead Cava as King and Queen, and when you die, I will go with you to Elysian Fields. We will never be apart again." Conleth's arm tightened.

My eyes widened. Words escaped me. My father—his methods forever a mystery, and perhaps always will be—but this gift, it was a gesture that would bind me in eternal gratitude to him.

My heart pumped so hard I barely heard myself speak. "Then we can go, together?"

Conleth's hand slipped down my arm and threaded his fingers through mine. "Yes, we can go home. Together." He lowered his head, brushing his lips over mine. My mouth immediately opened to his. My eyes closed and I sank into his embrace.

The squall of birds sounded around us, the crash of waves, the sweet smell of blooms.... My eyes snapped open, and I spun in Conleth's arms.

Anthemusa.

My lips peeled into a grin so wide, my cheeks hurt. It wasn't too long ago that we'd sat on the same beach making promises of commitment. But this time, there'd be no darkness to interrupt us, no villain to staunch our lovemaking. We were free of the prison forced upon us, and I wanted nothing more than to act on that liberty.

Conleth ran his hands along my spine, spreading shudders of near-painful desire through my torso. He leaned in, and our lips met. When we kissed, I saw our future, the kingdom we would lead, the children we would have, the country we would love. I pulled him tighter, memorizing the beat of his heart against mine.

"Thank you for saving me."

"We saved each other." He kissed the line of my jaw, trailing down my neck and chest. "To think I almost lost..." His voice strained as he ran his palm down the thin fabric of my tunic, fisting the hem in his hands. He lifted it up and over my head, tossing it to the side and leaving me bare to the hips. The cool wind caressed my skin, causing me to shudder.

"I love you." The ardor in his voice broke open my heart. I threaded my hands in his hair and kissed him with the passion of a thousand nymphs desperate for his touch.

We kissed for so long, my lips went numb. Warmth melted along my skin as I guided his hands along my bare body. He sucked in a breath and trembled.

"Gods, I love you." He repeated, then pulled off his own shirt and laid me down on the white glistening sand, hovering over me.

"I love you." I traced the taut muscles along his back with finger-light touches, and his skin puckered in response.

In the background, the ocean and the birds created their own symphony. The sun I made bathed us in its glory. The land was happy, and so was I.

My gaze traveled above Conleth's head to the shining orb I'd hung. "I'll never get tired of its warmth." Then back down, meeting his eyes. "Or yours."

"Nor will I, my little songbird. Nor will I."

Epilogue

Savina

I winced as the jeweled comb dug into my scalp, guided by Lou's less than gentle hand. I never thought I'd miss having lady's maids when Lou and Rye first changed things around the castle, but now I wondered if I'd walk down the aisle with a bird's nest for hair and a trickle of blood from brush tine marks on my forehead.

"Good thing you can make anything beautiful," huffed Lou. Even her compliments often came out as growls. Part of her charm, in my opinion. She stepped around my front, backpedaling to appraise her work. The sun I hung shone through the window, catching the gold in her blonde hair and fuzzing the whiter strands so her whole head glowed.

In the emerald silk gown I'd commissioned for her, with its brocaded bodice and flowing, floor-length skirt that hid her wide-legged, masculine stance, some poor fool might mistake her for delicate. But even as I thought it, she tugged on the bodice, shimmying in it and scowling as if it were a vice around her breasts.

Calli drew up beside her, walking sideways and lifting her green dress up to her shins as though she suspected the garment might trip her out of spite. I'd had the fabric bustled at the hips so that the skirt only brushed her ankles, knowing how she valued mobility, but apparently, I hadn't accounted for it enough.

Of course, I wasn't fairing much better. Besides my somersaulting stomach, I had grown accustomed to lighter dresses and trousers after my mother died. I hadn't been in something this heavily ornamented or this plain heavy in years.

"I guess it's all right," said Calli, tilting her head far left. "*I* think it's pretty, anyway." Her smile faltered. "You know, Krinny probably could've added braids or something. She got rather good at keeping me presentable, even if it meant braiding my hair so tight I couldn't feel my scalp." She massaged her head, caught in a memory.

"Every day I think of something else stolen from us by her death," seethed Lou, her face a marble bust—severe and fearsome as Athena in her armor, dress or no dress. Although Lou might resent that sentiment; she had a renewed hatred for most of the gods, their whims, and their selfish acts guised as justice. I doubted she'd get along with Zeus's favorite child. She'd sooner put Athena's head on a spit and present it to him.

"Like her good sense not to stare at a nervous bride as though she's wearing a sherron for a hat," I tried to tease, but the melancholy in my voice staled the room.

Calli's answering smile bore little light. "Sorry. You really do look beautiful. More than usual, even." She winked, and it seemed to lift her spine along with her spirits. "Krinny would've had to use that stare of hers to ice the veins of every man at the ceremony, just to keep them from getting ideas."

I swallowed, regretting all the words left unsaid to my dear friend. "I just wish I could see her in the pews." *I wish I could look out there, see her smiling, and know she'd forgiven me.*

A knock came at the door, and I popped out of my seat. "Conleth, that had better not be you. I'm not ready!."

"No, it's a far more dashing adventurer. Oh, and Ketner." Henrik's snort at his own jest was drowned in Calli's gasp as she charged the door. I heard a rip somewhere in the folds of all her satin, but she plowed on, half falling against the handle before yanking it.

Henrik had his arms open and ready, wearing a smile full of excitement and longing that she covered in an unabashed kiss. Fingers in his hair, she wrapped herself inextricably around him, oblivious to even her mother's loud, disapproving cough. I swore Ketner's mouth twitched in a smirk, but in the dim light of the hall, it was hard to tell.

"Gods I missed you," Calli panted between frantic kisses all over his face. Then her voice dropped to a low purr that put a blush on my face as she yanked him closer by the open collar of his seafarer's shirt. "I'm never letting you out of my reach again."

"I wish to be nowhere but in your claws, little sphinx," murmured Henrik, looking rather blurry eyed and punch-drunk.

Lou leaned into my side and grumbled, "I'm going to have to excuse myself before I stain your dress with vomit or blood."

I held in a snicker. "Understood."

She shot Henrik a sour frown that really had nothing to do with him and all to do with his father as she pushed past, shoulder bumping the boy on purpose to break the pair temporarily apart. She exchanged nods with Ketner before vanishing.

Henrik detached his lips but never even saw who'd knocked him. He let his hands trail across Calli's back and hips as he took in the dress, head rearing back. "Please tell me you're really my sphinx and not a shapeshifting nymph come to strangle me with satin."

Calli threw back her head in a laugh and unraveled herself, though she kept her hands cradling the back of his neck. "Don't worry. I'm only disguised as a proper lady today."

Henrik squeezed her middle with one arm but looked to me. "Congratulations, Savina." He tossed his head toward Ketner as he added, "I'm glad we were able to make it for the big day."

"Me too. Now Calli will be smiling for the portrait." Thank the gods. She's been moping ever since Conleth and I arrived back in Cava. Speaking of.... "Have you spoken with Conleth yet?"

He shook his head. Of course, he'd come looking for Calli straight away.

"There's still time before the ceremony. Run along and find him. He's got news for you." Calli and I exchanged knowing smiles, both well aware that Conleth intended to offer Henrik a position in the royal guard's training regiment and permanent residence in our castle for as long as he wished. We probably owed him even more, but I suspected the only thanks he really wanted was permission to see Calli freely. I had already persuaded Lou, though I'd about lost my head in the process.

Henrik's gaze volleyed between us. "News? Better be good. I've had all the catastrophes I can stomach."

"Oh, I think you'll find it favorable," I teased.

With a smile, he tugged Calli's hand. "Come on, let's go find the groom."

She went eagerly, though I suspected she'd rather find a dark corner than Conleth. I'd have to have the servants watch them. Too much alone time might lead to the sort of trouble that Lou would not forgive.

Speaking of watching over them ... I looked to Ketner, who'd stepped into the room. "Thank you for coming back and for being there for Henrik. I'm so pleased you agreed to Conleth's arrangement. Henrik will need family. He will need all of us."

"Who else will save his arse." Ketner chuckled. "I will be happy to watch over the boy and guide his education. But right now, this is your day and I must say, you look ravishing. Powerful and beautiful, as always."

My smile crimped my eyes. "Thank you, Ketner." I waved him off. "Go relax, will you? I'm certain you deserve it after a voyage stuck with Henrik, Vanden, and Flick. There are refreshments in the banquet hall, and I won't tell if you have some early."

"I will wait in the sun for your grand entrance with all the rest." With that, he took his leave.

Alone in the room, I gathered my courage and rose from my seat to confront the mirror. The view came as a pleasant shock. With half my hair pulled back from my face, the dangling sapphire earrings—that had once belonged to my mother—sparked along with my eyes, enhancing their shine rather than overshadow them. The comb tucked into the loose bun at the back of my head poked up like a miniature crown. The dress brushed the ground, its entirety made up of blue satin and white lace embroidered with cobalt and silver threads in the shapes of celestial bodies, with woven pearls acting as stars. The lace sleeves covered my arms and the backs of my hands, letting the low neckline provide the only skin on display, a sapphire sun pendant resting on my chest. I took the heavy silver cloak from the back of the chair and draped it over my shoulders, then pulled the loose half of my hair forward, free of the high, elegant collar.

I look like a queen. The smile came slowly to my lips as I realized that, for the first time, I felt like one, too.

Imagining Conleth's face when he saw me, I performed a twirl for the mirror. But my grin turned bittersweet as I wondered what the loved ones I'd lost would think if they could see me now.

Staring into the mirror, I imagined my mother behind me, a hand on my shoulder, the other fussing with my hair. She would've made it a tapestry of crisscrossing braids and artistically piled curls. Krinny, though, couldn't have cared less about how I looked. I pictured her on my other side, in her best vest and trousers, hair in a tight updo, drilling me about whether I was nervous, if I needed a glass of water, if the bodice ties were too tight. "You could faint, you know. Maybe I'd better check them again." Despite her intimidating size, she could hover like any mother hen if she cared for you. I bet she would've loved Galen. And with that thought, the young girl in disguise appeared behind me in my mind's eye, lounging casually against the chair, a candied fruit treat clutched in one hand. "When ye get loose of all those frills, we'll go find some actual fun. What do ye say, wee fox?"

A real figure materialized behind me, banishing the ghosts with his golden light.

I gasped.

His blue eyes roamed over me. "You look radiant as the sun you put in the sky, Little Rose."

"Father." I tried to loosen the corners of my stiff smile and failed. I still tasted the sour betrayal of his collusion in Zeus' many heinous acts. Though he'd once warmed my heart on the coldest of days, I now hesitated to go to his arms.

Sadness lessened his godly glow and drew down his flawless brow. "One day, I will appear, and you will embrace me as you once did. I swear it. You may not understand my actions, nor support them, but my movements are made with precision to ensure your best future."

I turned, pooling tears threatening to mess up my powders. "I don't understand." I shook my head. "I may never. But thank you for saving Conleth and for giving me a chance at happiness. A life without him would have never been a life at all." I believed my father knew that and even though his methods didn't make much sense to me, I did believe he tried his best to give me my happy ending.

"I love you. You will always be my father, whether I understand you or not." I extended a hand, letting his warm palm envelop it as I gathered myself.

Apollo offered me his elbow, and I took it with a true smile blossoming across my face.

"Ready?" he asked.

"More than ever."

Conleth

This courtyard lined with rose bushes already carried a cherished memory, but I intended to fill it with many more, starting today. I waited beneath a hand-carved arch, its soft wood etched with the phases of our fairytale, from the sherron swarm to the glorious blaze of Savina's sun. After all the turmoil the gods had put her through, Savina had balked at taking our vows in any of their temples, and I had assured her I'd wed her in the belly of a sea serpent if needed, so long as she'd have me.

But the gods still had a presence here. Hermes stood beside me, waiting to bind our hands in silk and use ceremonial words to declare to the world what Savina and I already knew—that our souls were bound for eternity. I recognized Artemis by the daring slit in her silk dress and the arrow-shaped pins that held up her hair. Apollo would lead my bride down the aisle.

Zeus hadn't been expressly invited, but he hadn't been barred either. So, when he'd appeared in his cold, militaristic Zenith form and claimed a seat beside Artemis, I'd greeted him with an inclined head. For now, we stood on tentative but even ground—our bargain struck and honored. I didn't know what he intended to show or prove by coming, but I found I didn't much care...today.

The rest of the crowd brightened the already pristine day with low, chipper talk. I saw faces of friends old and new. The sirens took up two whole rows of the pews brought here from Apollo's temple, their red hair putting the roses to shame. They shifted their new, unpracticed legs, unsure whether to sit with legs crossed or side-saddle. In the first row sat Vanden and Flick, who'd whistled and laughed mercilessly when I'd first donned my extravagant black and silver coat, with its celestial embroidery and many long clasps down the front. Although, what had practically choked them were the tight, slim cut trousers and high boots. But they'd gotten themselves under control for the ceremony, although I had a sneaking suspicion they'd gotten into more celebratory rum than I'd realized. That or they were particularly hot in their own finery, which merely consisted of better-tailored vests and pants. Ketner sat between the Sottom brothers, all of them catching up with their heads together.

Commoners had flooded the palace, congregating around the gates, itching for a glimpse of the elusive queen. We'd let in as many as would fit, including Jebba and Leon, whom I'd met at the tavern on my first day in Cava. They sat stiff, eyes darting around everywhere as though they felt out of place in their wool ensembles. I offered an encouraging nod when Jebba momentarily caught my eye, and he returned something more like a clumsy bow. The townsfolk who couldn't be crammed into the courtyard were being fed a feast outside the gates, entertained by court performers in place of the nuptials. Those inside, pointed and awed over everything in sight, their excited chatter livening the air.

But when the lyre player struck up a tune and the castle door opened onto the courtyard, every head turned, and the only face that mattered was hers. My songbird. The Sun Bringer. Queen of Cava. And the most gorgeous creature I'd ever seen.

Not even Apollo shone brighter. In fact, he hardly existed next to her. She put the gods to shame, and not just in appearance. She'd raised a mirror to the ugliness that lurked inside some of their ancient hearts, and I knew she had no intention of lowering it. She'd let them come today, and as she strode down the aisle, searing her smile on my heart, she kept her shoulders strong and her head high so they might see her power. See that she was done fearing Olympus.

Pride and love swelled in my chest and then my throat. After centuries of a half-existence shrouded in loneliness and torment, I was finally about to truly start living. The realization brought about my first tears. I blinked them free, returning her smile, and when she drew close enough, I reached for both her hands before Hermes instructed. I hardly heard him address the crowd because Savina and I were locked in a silent conversation, swapping promises stronger than the generalities in Hermes' ceremony. Promises to burn for each other every day. Promises to listen in between our jests and our fights. Promises to protect Cava and the people who depended on us with our very lives. And, if the gods dared try to tear us or our land apart again, a promise to topple Olympus itself.

But for now, I would have and cherish my bride. As Hermes stopped his prattling, I took Savina in my arms, and with my lips on hers, vowed to love her like a human. For human love, though it could not stand for millennia like the mountains of earth or the stars in the sky or the thrones of immortals, it reached higher, blazed brighter, and fought harder than them all. So long as I had Savina, I knew I'd never face another night, another hardship, or another cold mountaintop alone.

ACKNOWLEDGMENTS

Oh man, this was a wild one, full of "fire." There's so many people to thank, especially to everyone who helped in the 11th hour....

But first, I'd like to start with everyone who supported me on Kickstarter. Without your backing, I would have pushed this MS off until 2024. So thank you for the encouragement, support, and enthusiasm.

Next my beta readers: Tia, Belinda, Maria, Jenna, Kylie, Ashley, Kristina, Penelope, and Leslie. What would I do without you? I am so grateful for your kind words as I worked to bring this story to life! Your feedback was pivotal. Your keen insight and attention to detail got this puppy in ship shape. Thank you for joining me on rough waters and guiding me to smooth sailing! (Anyone else loving my pirate analogies?)

My street team, Dana's Darlings, thank you so much for your continued support and encouragement! It means the world to me to know that I have such an amazing group of people in my corner. Your complimentary words and passion for literature keep me motivated and inspired to continue doing what I love. I'm so grateful for all of you. Big HUGS!

Hannah, you are my super power. Without your edits and ideas, I'd surely sink. ;)

Jennifer Eaton, you are my balance between the underworld and Elysian Fields. When I need tough love, you are always there for me and I wouldn't want it any other way. There's a reason I found you. I truly believe that. Thank you....never stop telling me to do better!

Jay Aheer, we did it again. This series is stunning and it wouldn't have been without your designs.

Jill Mac, my PA, you are not just a PA, but a hell of a friend. Thank you for your support and keeping me in line, and doing all the math at book signings.

To my father, thank you for always supporting me. I can't be easy...I'm your child after all, but I do everything with kindness, love, and compassion, just like I was raised. There are moments when I think about mommy that make my heart sever, but you always know how to make it whole again. She'd be so proud of us. I know I am.

To my mother, I wish every day you were here to see me live my dreams. Losing you, broke me. But because of your love, I will never stop daring to fly. Thank you for being the best mom a little girl could have asked for and for giving me the tools to be the best woman I can be.

To my husband, Jason. There's not another soul in the world that my heart beats for. You are the air to my lungs, the blood in my veins. One day, they will write stories about us....I can promise that!

FREE eBOOK/ SCAN NOW

The Reclaimed Kingdom

by

Author Dana Claire

Also by Dana Claire

OLYMPIAN WARS SERIES

- War of the Sea

- War of the Land

- War of the Mind (2024)

HUNTERLAND SERIES

- Hunterland

- Hunterlore (2024)

- Hunterlove (2025)

FRIDAY NIGHT GRIDIRON SERIES

- Sideliners

- The Offensive Line (2024)

- Final Kickoff (2024)

THE BLOOD-LIGHT TRILOGY

- The Connection

- The Awakening

- The Reprisal (2025)

THE RECLAIMED KINGDOM

(Standalone...for now)
To Learn More About Dana Claire, Scan Here!

About Author

Dana Claire is an award-winning author whose stories explore identity, fate and destiny in the crossroads of romance and adventure. But her writing career didn't begin when she published her first book in 2020. It started as a young girl when her mother, an elementary school teacher, inspired her to create imaginary worlds between the pages. Dana's love of romantic tension, the supernatural and non-stop action has elicited positive feedback from many readers, as their online reviews reveal her flair for spine-tingling action and unforgettable characters. But it's not just readers who love her; literary critics have also taken note, and Dana was given The Moonbeam Award for *The Connection* in 2021 and The PenCraft Award and The Moonbeam Award for *War of the Sea* in 2023.

Dana is now sharing her stories through speaking events and book signings, introducing more readers to the worlds she created. As a published author, Dana is living her dreams; seeing her name on the spine of a book, creating worlds that combine love, science fiction, the paranormal, magic and adventure, and fulfilling what her well-read, compassionate, patient and selfless mother would have dreamed of doing with her: writing books, telling stories, and changing the world, one reader at a time.

www.ingramcontent.com/pod-product-compliance
Lightning Source LLC
Chambersburg PA
CBHW030930260626
47169CB00002B/427